O JERUSALEM

R. P. HANNA

authorHOUSE

AuthorHouse™ UK
1663 Liberty Drive
Bloomington, IN 47403 USA
www.authorhouse.co.uk
Phone: UK TFN: 0800 0148641 (Toll Free inside the UK)
UK Local: (02) 0369 56322 (+44 20 3695 6322 from outside the UK)

© *2023 R. P. HANNA. All rights reserved.*

No part of this book may be reproduced, stored in a retrieval system, or transmitted by any means without the written permission of the author.

Published by AuthorHouse 07/18/2023

ISBN: 979-8-8230-8250-1 (sc)
ISBN: 979-8-8230-8251-8 (hc)
ISBN: 979-8-8230-8249-5 (e)

Print information available on the last page.

Any people depicted in stock imagery provided by Getty Images are models, and such images are being used for illustrative purposes only.
Certain stock imagery © Getty Images.

This book is printed on acid-free paper.

Because of the dynamic nature of the Internet, any web addresses or links contained in this book may have changed since publication and may no longer be valid. The views expressed in this work are solely those of the author and do not necessarily reflect the views of the publisher, and the publisher hereby disclaims any responsibility for them.

This proto-cinema is a theological melodrama, an anti-historical unromantic, techno-magical realistic science fiction satire set in an alternative reality where extremist mentalities prevail.

Expect nothing simple.
Christina helped me find a balance.

RPH

I
MEETINGS

The First Meeting: London
"I have great sorrow in my too-small heart."[1]

The Archbishop's niece stared—with some slight astonishment—at the young atheist sitting opposite her.

"Let's get serious and just finally admit something," he insisted with an intense glint in his eye, "this *God thing* is an illusion. A *delusion. A lie*. And for that they go around killing each other and the rest of us too?"

Emma said nothing and felt embarrassed. She had learned to condemn the sin but forgive the sinner. She was able to apply this principle to the present green-eyed, black-haired man. However, she found herself in various difficulties: one problem was that to be honest with him she should now identify herself as a modest believer in much Church of England doctrine. She made certain exceptions, of course; but in the main she found sufficient intellectual humility to accept the wisdom of the centuries as transmitted by her elders. This included a secular principle of moderation in most—if not perhaps all—things. This militant atheist called Jack was moderate in nothing so far as she could tell. Still further, she'd somewhere learned tolerance of other systems of belief; she was exercising her tolerance just now. She was tolerating Jack's intolerance. Had she made the right moral choice? It was unclear.

In any case she could certainly understand how, in these weeks just after the bombings of the World Trade Center and the Pentagon, that

---
[1] Williamson, Emma, *Deus Ex Machina*, (London: Confessional Press), 2040, "Introduction," p 1.

non-believers should be just as unhappy about the state of the world as believers must in all good conscience find themselves.

"Those of us who don't believe any of this nonsense are going to get killed in the cross-fire between nut cases who do believe. It's already happened. Why should we not stand up against deadly delusion?"

She felt like looking over her shoulder to see if anyone else was listening to Mr. Jack Foote's tirade. She allowed herself a quick glance around; so far as she could tell, without staring too obviously, no one in the coffee house was paying them any attention. She stirred her raspberry and vanilla tea, and chuckled to herself. She was being a little paranoid. Furthermore she really did understand that kind of theological scepticism that freed her companion to reach his extreme conclusions. She'd just let such doubt quietly languish in some grey area at the back of her brain. God was too complicated to fathom intellectually, but viscerally she knew he/she/it—the 'Great Whatever'—existed. Human ideas come and go. Useless notions vanish, but substantial truths abide—even when they are unprovable. God arrived with man, and as long as we survive, god will, she thought . . . in some form or other. And anyway, God isn't an absolute anything. God evolves *and* abides, as all existence does. That was probably some kind of heresy; but she really didn't want to get into the whole god-thing right now. Dishes clashed and a pot clanged in the kitchen behind the swinging door—accidental cymbals announcing nothing. But the man sitting opposite her obviously had God right in the front of his brain.

"This God guy is an *invention*. People made him up. It's just so obvious that it spits right in your eye."

Then came an obnoxious interruption to his obnoxious tirade: "*I am an Antichrist-a! I am an Anarchist-a! I am . . .* " It stopped when he pushed a button on his phone.

"What on earth was that?" said Emma. "It frightened the life out of me!" This was not quite true, of course: she'd been more amused than scared by the ringtone. But the caution in her soul about this handsome young man bred an ability to practice a very slight, polite, wilful deception.

"Sex Pistols. 'Anarchy in London'. I downloaded it just for today. Are you into ringtones?"

"Not really," said Emma. "I prefer discrete vibrations. And why Anarchy?"

As if to suggest that her question was somehow inappropriate, Jack raised a black eyebrow over a green eye. Emma felt herself blush. She suppressed her anger with herself.

"So," Jack continued. "The real question is why people don't say it to each other a little more often. God is a Big Lie. The biggest lie ever."

She allowed herself a long pause while she looked around again. While she was looking elsewhere, she could feel his eyes traveling over her face, inspecting her. Was he looking at her as a woman? Or as a political friend? He was waiting for some response, but she couldn't think of one.

"Ah. But you suspect that a lot of people think it, don't you? They just don't have the courage to say it; or they're too polite. That's the damnedest thing. We atheists have always been so polite to the poor, deluded believers."

"Well of course." She didn't want to hurt his feelings by telling him that his great original insight was perhaps a little more obvious than he knew. She didn't want to offend him. He interested her, despite—or perhaps because of—his intensity. He had energy and enthusiasm. He was very alive and free. That made him attractive. And his eyes, the windows to his soul, were green. She wasn't really alarmed by his radicalism, although she thought fleetingly about telling her uncle about him. Church of England people needed to know—and she knew they were willing to hear—about the existence of people like this young man, with his black hair falling across his forehead.

Emma had met Jack at an anti-WTO rally in Trafalgar Square several days before. He'd been standing off to one side of the crowd, watching the protestors—not participating himself. For some reason, she found herself watching him. She was sitting on the stone railing beside the National Portrait Gallery, and he came to sit next to her. When she tried to stand on the curved surface of the stone wall she had tottered and nearly fallen, so he had reached out to steady her—without even looking up, as if just assuming that she'd accept his courtesy. So she'd taken his hand and found this stranger's palm unusually warm. It was just a sense she'd had of temperature. Nothing more.

Somewhat bemused, she'd watched the demonstration in protest against the exploitation of the world's underclasses. Or in protest against something. It wasn't quite clear what. And for just a moment, she'd held the stranger's warm hand.

"What do you think about all this?" he'd asked when she stepped back down to his level and pulled her hand free. The way he asked the question made her think that he had formed his own sceptical opinion of the protests.

3

She hadn't been sure what to think. They'd wandered away from the noise of demonstrations and found an elegant restaurant, tucked safely away from the street. His phone rang repeatedly . . . *I am an . . . I am an . . .* and he seemed to be talking to half a dozen different people in a cryptic way, mostly saying only "yes" and "no." Listening too closely to his end of the conversations seemed rude, so she'd tried not to. But she had the odd impression—an almost subliminal sense—that he was talking to someone, or to several people, who had some knowledge of the demonstrations that they'd both just avoided. In between blasts of the Sex Pistols, they'd talked about the dire state of the world. They also agreed to meet again in a few days.

Now, a few days later, in a comfortable café in north London, she studied him. He didn't seem to be at all interested in her as a woman, which made Emma feel both relieved and a bit miffed. He appeared to be focused only on his ideas, on his one idea. But the fact that he stayed so focused on his *idée fixe* made him all the more challenging. She wondered if she couldn't distract him.

"If everything they do is done in what they call 'God's name,' then everything is done in the name of nothing real at all, in the name of some confused cloud of images invented by primitives to explain the inexplicable." On and on he droned. He said that people today followed the primitive ideas, even after they had perfectly good scientific explanations of natural phenomena. He complained that religious thinkers had elevated their inherited collective daydreams to the status of ultimate, indisputable truth. The philosophers have a word for this, he recalled: 'hypostasis.' Religious truths were vestigial. "We carry useless ideas in our heads," he argued. "Sometimes they get infected, like your appendix or your tonsils. Fanaticism is mental appendicitis. Then we have wars and crusades and pogroms."

He seemed not to be sufficiently self-aware to notice that he was just as fanatical as the worst of those he so criticised and despised. He'd been to university, she could tell. Which one, she couldn't quite work out. His accent had a slightly American twang to it. Or was it Canadian? She would ask him, when she could get a word in. She wasn't yet sure if he had a sense of humor; but there was a certain lyricism in his ranting. Underneath she sensed a poetic soul, a romantic raging against the dark. Byron and Shelley might have been like that. But he certainly wasn't English. For one thing, he spoke just a little too loudly, as if daring the other people in the room to overhear and contradict him. He didn't have the quiet, conspiratorial manner of the English at conversational play in a public place. But she had grown very tired of English men—especially those young ones who were so much more interested in each other than in women.

How old was he? Twenty-five? Thirty-five? He was a man, at least. Slightly chiselled, slightly weathered. She liked her men to look like men, not boys.

He continued banging away: "These religions may work pretty well for people in little villages scattered around the rainforests and isolated up the mountainsides. Give a set of values to live by, structure daily activities. That sort of thing. But once these damned religions begin to operate outside their own little worlds, so that they come into contact with other religions, they start having really bad consequences. Religions start to be reasons to murder other people. Religion has become *the* great evil in the modern world. It used to be fascism and totalitarianism. Now it's religion."

He appeared to run out of steam, so she asked him casually, hoping no one would hear: "Which religions do you have in mind?" Maybe it was perverse to prompt him to make a few more pretty obvious remarks, but she couldn't resist.

"Which religions? All the monotheisms, at least. Christianity. Islam. Judaism. There's some evidence that the polytheisms are a bit more tolerant of the multiplicity of truths."

The Sex Pistols on phone rang again. She wondered again who his friends were. But most of all she wondered why this young man was so angry. What had religious belief done to him to generate such outrage? It would be interesting to find out and tell Uncle Richard about it.

In a Darkroom

In a Darkroom of no clear time or place, its black walls spangled by blinking lights, a real fantasy is playing out. The room is something like the nerve center of a television network, or the control and command room for a military operation. Yet it is neither of these. On one wall, a large flat-panel television screen shows a front view, then a profile view of a gray-bearded man in long white robes, wearing reflective sunglasses, and an over-sized turban.

An androgynous, sarcastic voice intones, "Hail weird fellow on the screen, electric traveller over the whole wide world, go on about your evil ways: thrice to nine and thrice to mine, and three times three to make up nine. Your curse is all wound up."

A second voice from an invisible female chimes in, "Client wants Islamic shots—bits, pics, frags, symbols."

"Yep. Capture and ice 'em," says a third voice—male, bored.

We see only fragments of people in the dark: a chin, a cheek, a hand lit by the glow of screens. The big screen shows first a giant golden dome of a mosque, then an isolated minaret, a crescent moon, Arabic writing, a book that might be the Koran.

"So what's with the human intelligence?"

"We have taps into two, maybe three agency contacts in Istanbul. Our Istanbul brothers and sisters are on the case. Meantime, we have international broadcast collection in progress."

"Good," says the voice of an older woman. "These new bomber boys may yield really good JPEGs. Anyway, our client wants them. A real chance for obscene profit—just like the big boss wants. What Mr Commos doesn't know about certain of our activities won't hurt him," she observes wryly.

We are, actually, in the underground office of the London branch of the Commos Foundation. Mr Georg Commos, who made his billions in the business of electronic international currency exchange, is now paying something back to the world that made him so wealthy. He has subsidized the creation of Commos Foundation franchises in major cities all around the globe. He specializes in global communication; his Foundation Franchises offer young people a chance to enter the world's enormous silicone brain. His policy is to create each of his branches, and then withdraw, god-like, into some earthly heaven of the super-rich, leaving each branch to undertake entrepreneurial activity in order to survive. His only reward is access at will to information any of his branch offices has uncovered. His London Cosmos branch is obedient to his policy in this regard. They have also acquired a wealthy client from whom they hope for income.

"When the hurly burly's done," chants the nasal voice. "When the battle's lost and won."

A silence follows. Much flickering, and fading down and blazing-up of images in the dark. Disembodied hands beneath disconnected foreheads turn dials, throw switches, adjust levers and knobs.

"Who are these Istanbul bombers?"

"So far as we can tell, they're not even close to rational. But their visuals are spectacular," says the maternal voice. "Really good footage if we can get a camera up close. Word is they're planning something big, photogenic. Lots of blood. Stacks of corpses."

A door opens and a shaft of painfully white light pierces the darkness for a few moments, before the wheezing sound of a pneumatic doorstop extinguishes the brief, blinding ray.

"Who's newbie?" someone asks.

"His name is Mr Foote, Jack Foote," says the older woman.

"Movie director man?"

"The same," she confirms. "I know him rather well, in fact."

"You here to evaluate the crop? Weigh it up? Price it?"

Silence.

"Care to respond, Mr Foote?" asks the woman, like a mother speaking to a difficult but much-loved child.

"OK. I'll respond. I want to see if you're getting what I need."

"What do you need?"

"Religious symbols."

"We know that. But which ones?"

"All of them."

"See if there's anything you like tonight."

Images flow in the silence. Mosques. Imams. Minarets. Bearded men. Veiled women. Turbans on and off heads.

After a time the Client abruptly announces, "Goodbye, everybody. Keep your eyes open for anything sensational. Let's violate taboos. I need religious outrages—catastrophes of faith." The door opens; light slices the darkness then vanishes again.

"Where's he get his money?"

"He's clean," says the older woman. "Money's from a rich uncle."

"His money bought our Deus Ex Machina body armour for Trafalgar? Did someone say that?"

"That's right. Those Kevlar vests were expensive. He may even guess what he paid for." The woman's voice has a quiver of condescending, maternal affection for the rich client.

The Second Meeting: Istanbul
"I am a Turk who thinks between two worlds."[2]

"You wish know why they die?" Muhammad whispered. Ersan was sitting opposite the young man at a formica-topped table in the back corner of the shabby café. Muhammad was about 18 years old, unsmiling, serene. He sat with his hands open on the table, palms upward. It was almost a gesture of prayer: he was ready to receive what Allah might give.

Ersan shrugged, disconcerted by the young man's certainty. The terrorists who had brought down the world trade center and bombed the pentagon would have had the same certainty. He was hoping to identify and describe the sources of such utter lack of any doubt. He pulled his shirtsleeve cuff about a centimetre further out from under the sleeve of his new blue suit. He slipped his index finger under the cuff and felt his pulse. It was steady; he tried to make himself relax. This workmen's den smelled of sweat, coffee and cheap disinfectant; Ersan was out of place—a westernized Turk intruding into the world of Anatolian peasants come in from the countryside to strive and suffer in the city. He should perhaps have dressed differently for this occasion—worn old clothes, disguised himself; but on the other hand, why should he pretend to be someone he wasn't?

A waiter brought them tea on a stainless steel tray suspended from his fist by three strands of metal chain. His hairy hand put a saucer of sugar lumps down between the teacups. The customary little glasses of water followed. Ersan and the boy were silent, waiting for the waiter to go away after wiping the chipped surface with his dirty cloth. When the rag began over-elaborately to rub the bent chromium edge of the table, Ersan realized what was required and put a half-million lira note down beside the cups. The hand picked it up. Then the waiter's great fist reached up and turned the unusually small photograph of Atatürk around, so that the famous face was now facing the wall. With this, Ersan thought he noticed a slight change in the atmosphere in the room.

The young man had his back to the wall, in the corner of the café just below the required portrait of the great secular leader—who was now not supervising the proceedings. The youngster sat so he could see everyone.

---

[2] Felsefenin, Ersan. "Introduction," *The Cognitive Structure of the Terrorist Mind*, trans. R. P. Hanna (Istanbul: Bosphosphoric Press, 2007), p.1.

The television on its little platform was playing high above his head, showing a match between Galatasaray and Efes. At first the location in the room seemed like the worst place for secrecy, since all the men present had their blank-looking faces turned up toward the television four feet above the youngster's head; but in all Istanbul, this was the coffee house and this was the very table and the very chair where Muhammad had chosen to sit. Ersan let the boy feel that he was in control.

"You are not true serious Muslim, if you need to ask about reason for *jihad*."

"I asked merely for an interview. I have not asked a single question yet," Ersan replied.

"True. But I know what you have in heart. My Sheikh taught me about you when he established interview."

Ersan shrugged again. Who was he to doubt one as wise as this youngster's Sheikh? Playing humble didn't come naturally to Ersan, but it was necessary if his plan was to work. He was pretending that he was only a lowly reporter interviewing the boy for a newspaper article about Istanbul's 'New Young Conservatives'. In reality he was a renowned Professor researching material for his ground-breaking book about radical Islam. He might already have a London publisher for it. It would make his career—even earn him an appointment in a United States university, if he wanted one. He envisioned something in New York—maybe Columbia. Perhaps they would make him an offer that he would graciously decline. His book would be a real contribution to the field of comparative religion, presenting an understanding of the cognitive structure of radical Islam. He'd explain how suicide bombers thought, the logical sequence of their beliefs and understandings. He wanted to test his hypotheses out on this boy. Ersan had a vague fear that his deception would be uncovered; but he was pretty certain that Islamists didn't read academic journals and wouldn't recognize him. He was also fairly confident he could manage to publish something about this interview in at least one of the Istanbul papers. Then he would be safe behind his cover.

"Is machine recording?" the youngster asked, pointing toward Ersan's breast pocket where, in fact, he had a tape recorder.

"No."

"Why should I believe?"

Ersan took the little black plastic box out and put it on the table for Muhammad to see.

"Other machine hidden?"

The boy's mentality clearly included doubt, thought Ersan—but doubt focused only on the non-believer, never on his own kind.

"No," said Ersan. "I have no other machine."

"I could have you search, there, in toilet." Muhammad nodded across the bleak room in the direction of the half-open door to the filthy closet with a hole in the floor and two painted footprints beside it. Ersan was so Europeanized that he found squat toilets frightening. He certainly found the prospect of being searched by two of Muhammad's friends unpleasant, especially in a dank little room with the smell of excrement welling up from the hole.

The boy glanced down at Ersan's tape machine and could see that it wasn't running; perhaps he noticed, too, that the tape cassette was still at the beginning of the reel. He nodded appreciatively. "I believe, but you exist ignorant. You participate *jahiliyyah*. Ignorance. It will be eliminate. Soon infidel have no choice. Ignorance will end. You will submit."

Ersan made another gesture. He was developing a vocabulary of ambiguous hand signals. This time he spread his hands away from each other in a movement that he hoped meant something like "It is all beyond my control. My fate is in your hands."

Suddenly Muhammad closed his eyes, and whispered in Arabic, a passage that Ersan almost recognized.

Whoso chooseth this quickly passing life, quickly will we bestow therein that which we please—even on him we choose; afterwards we will appoint hell for him, in which he shall burn—disgraced, outcast:

But whoso chooseth the next life, and striveth after it as it should be striven for, being also a believer—these! their striving shall be grateful unto God.

It was probably from the "Night Journey." Ersan was certain he had heard it before:

The fifty-five-year-old intellectual, educated at the Sorbonne, able to speak French, Turkish, English, and a little Arabic, sat across the table from a youngster who was little more than a boy, who probably spoke only Turkish although he had memorized passages from the Koran in Arabic as well. Muhammad had attended a *madrassah*, which had taught him only what his namesake, Muhammad, reported that the Angel had said. Ersan understood what this present-day Muhammad believed: the voice he heard when he recited the only text he knew was Allah's own voice.

O JERUSALEM

The boy believed—without reflection on the existential status of his own mind—that his recitation was Allah speaking. His voice *was* God's own. With his primitive consciousness, Ersan realized this boy could control *him*, a university professor—a westernized, perspicacious, multicultural descendant of the ultimate Ottoman and Europeanized sophistication. Ersan kept his face frozen to hide his sense of the absurdity.

Muhammad reached across the table and pushed the "Record" button on Ersan's machine. The older man felt a little rush of adrenalin.

"If I do not like what say, we erase," Muhammad informed him, gently tapping the machine as if to confirm his familiarity with such equipment. Ersan nodded. "I also have equipment." He reached into an inner pocket of his leather jacket and produced a tape recorder of his own. He placed it next to Ersan's machine on the table. Ersan saw that Muhammad's tape recorder was already recording.

"You are surprised we have own?"

Ersan raised his head and clucked his tongue, meaning "no".

"We take what Allah permits from ignorant ones," Muhammad whispered. "This machine is fruit from the tree." He tapped the tape recorder.

Suddenly the men in the café rose in unison and raised their fists into the air, staring at the place above Muhammad's head. A collective cry of victory began in their throats: "Hu ... ." But this was followed by a great groan, as the men sank in unison back into their seats. They looked gloomy, but continued to stare at the television, where Glatasaray had almost scored a goal. Muhammad looked at the men with contempt. Marvelling at how well the boy's face expressed dismissive loathing for anything non-Islamic, Ersan turned to view the scene behind him in the café. Ironically, he actually agreed with Muhammad: it was pathetic that these men had nothing more interesting in their lives than sport. Different cognitive structures could result in the same judgment. His book should make that point.

All but two of the fifty or so faces were fixed on the television; however, at either side of the large glass window, like book-ends framing the dark street outside, two men sat unmoving, staring at him—independent of each other, but identical under their turbans, with their full, clean, very black beards. They were different. Ersan felt himself shiver.

In a Darkroom

Video display screens flicker. The hush is punctuated by the odd bored sigh. Images of a vast sky—of enormous, table-flat fields, of giant grain elevators, of farm buildings, of great beasts of harvesting machines silhouetted against the horizon—all float across the screens. The images could be still photographs except for a wave passing through the heads of the wheat standing ripe and yellow in the fields, or a car, passing peacefully down a deserted, distant road in a two-dimensional and yet infinite landscape.

"Now client wants Christian stuff?" asks one invisible, incredulous voice.

"Yep."

"What for?"

"Ours is not to reason why. Ours is but to view and sigh."

"Is he suicidal? Trying to bore himself to death?" asks a youngster.

There is a comic chorus of sighs.

"How many channels are we monitoring?"

"Four in Kansas. More in Oklahoma, Nebraska, Missouri. They're all the same. Get one you got 'em all."

"Churches. That's what he wants, now. Before he wanted mosques; now he wants churches."

"Hard not to get churches. Nothing but churches. Churches here, there, everywhere. A plague of churches."

"Get religious services."

"Every morning. On air. Radio. TV."

"Must be hell to live in Kansas."

"Kansans don't think so."

"Are you sure the client wants this stuff? Why? What's he going to do with it?"

"He says to treat Wichita just like Istanbul."

"Guy must be from Mars."

"Well, he ain't from Kansas."

"Where **is** he from?"

"Who is he anyway?"

"As far as you're concerned, he's just a client. Take my word for him," orders the authoritative female voice. "We don't get to ask the questions. We just get paid to collect the visuals and make his movie. Mr George

O JERUSALEM

Commos will be very pleased indeed with our invoice and our receipt. Let's just keep Deus Ex Machina out of sight."

"Wow! Watch this! A tornado!" A televised image of a great funnel cloud appears on the largest screen.

"It's a whirlwind."

"Why do you want a whirlwind?"

"It's on the Christian Images List."

"'Then the Lord answered Job out of the whirlwind, and said Who is this that darkeneth counsel by words without knowledge?' That help you?"

"Yeah! Wonderful. Explains everything. A talking whirlwind!"

"Dub in that voice!"

"What voice?"

"The Big Boomer. In storage."

Switches flick. A bass bellows: "WHO IS THIS THAT DARKENETH COUNSEL? ... ."

"Now get your whirlwind into synch with Big Boomer."

"O.K., O.K."

"And work on it in the closet, please. I can't stand hearing too much of that stuff."

"What else we need?"

"Client says he needs a Preacher. Suggests . . . let's see . . . a guy called Jones. Famous radio evangelist. Also appears on TV."

"And cuuuue preacher! Look at him. Chiseled jaw. Arm up like he's going to smash that podium. Got that one?"

"Just a tick. Yep. Got 'im."

"The only question here is 'Will the client want it?'"

"Bung it into the collection jar in case."

"What's the client's name again?"

"Jack."

"Are we running security on him?" .

"We are. Constant updates."

"Could he be an agent? CIA? FBI? MI5? MOSSAD? Rogue FSB?" wonders an incredulous voice.

"Taps on the Agency and Bureau show no contact. No prints, face, name. Nothing. Clean."

"Stop worrying about him, children" says the older woman. "I know who he is."

O JERUSALEM

They fall silent. Bach organ chords sound.

"Hold on here. We gotta flash. Heads up! Breaking news from Syria."

Onto the multiple screens comes a single image: a large building belching smoke and fire from every window. Out through the roof come flames. Against a brilliant blue sky the square, squat, concrete beast is alive with oxidation. It moves, breathes up its own death, vomits out a dying misery. A window spits a bathtub; another window belches up a bed mattress. They hang like little tongues on the face of the building, which slowly collapses forward. A flaming man leaps through a forward-moving window out into space. Trailing smoke, he lands on the ground. The wall falls onto him. The inner structures are exposed—bones now visible in the bleak, blasting middle eastern sunlight—brighter even than the little tongues of flame that eat at inner corners.

The young people in the Darkroom watch, enraptured, breathing quietly in the glow of their screens. One voice asks: "have we eaten of the insane root that takes the reason prisoner?"

The Third Meeting: Wichita, Kansas
"Then I fell into the hands of evil."[3]

"WE'll make a *real* difference, *really* help the people there, body and *soul*," she trilled in breathless excitement. "And after what they've just did to us in New York and Washington, we really need to turn the other cheek and learn to love our enemies." Her voice was so childlike and whispery that the young reporter leaned forward to hear her better. When he did so, he caught her scent, a familiar sweet perfume suggesting fresh fruit. She sat beside him on the next stool, leaning her elbows on the counter-top. It was hard to look at her; it was impossible not to look at her. She was a large girl, despite her small voice—full-faced, full-bodied, long-haired, round-eyed—with all the beauty of youth. Her name was Betsey. She had an enormous smile. Her blouse fitted tightly over her maternal bust. A tiny gold crucifix bounced hypnotically between the third and fourth buttons, which strained against the contents of her clothing. He had trouble remembering what to ask her.

He forced himself to concentrate on the fact that she was headed for Afghanistan as a member of something like the Wichita Bible Saviour Team. He couldn't remember what they called themselves. His editor wouldn't like his not getting it right.

"Of course we'll have to change our name for security reasons," she piped. Her tiny, squeaky voice made it impossible to credit her ideas.

What would it be like to go to bed with this child-woman? The thought took his breath away. He fumbled for his notebook. The neon sign outside the café, located across the street from the Wichita Salvation Army Headquarters, flashed on and off leaving a red gloss on her cheek with each illumination. He felt a little drunk.

"How can you leave all your friends and family here?"

"Well, I don't want to embarrass you because I assume you haven't been born again, have you? Mr Smith? Have you?"

He hadn't and gulped while he shook his head.

"Oh, Mr Smith," she lamented.

"Call me Bob," he thought to say.

"All right, Bob." The innocent voice contrasted weirdly with the

---
[3] Smith, Robert, *Memories of my Kidnapping,"* (Wichita: Evangelical Press, 2031), p 10.

awareness she showed of him. She wasn't completely self-absorbed, like most of these people.

"But this is my *calling*. These people *need* me."

"Will you . . . will you . . . will you wear a veil in Afghanistan?"

"Not just a veil. I will cover myself from head to foot just the way the local women do. It's called a burka."

She couldn't be completely unaware of the effect that her physical existence had on the male half of the species, he realized. Even if she could not possibly be quite the babbling child that her voice suggested, he doubted she could have much sense of her public sexuality.

"When do you leave?"

"On Tuesday in two weeks. I can't *wait!*"

He noted down the date of her departure.

"What do you plan to do while you're there?"

"Well, we'll be doing the Lord's work, of course—but very carefully, quietly. If they ask us about our faith, then of course we'll tell them. We'll take Bibles in English, and we've had most of the New Testament translated into Pashtu. That's the native language?" She whispered at him questioningly to see if he understood what she was talking about. "The Old Testament is really a problem for us, by the way; we haven't been able to find a translation yet. But we won't be giving our Bibles away unless we're asked for them. Meantime, we'll be working with the Red Cross on a food distribution site. We'll have a trunk full of medicine with us, too. And I'm hoping to take and give away most of my clothing while I'm there."

Bob Smith imagined her doing a strip-tease in the desert, donating first her left glove to a goggled-eyed boy, then her right glove to another astonished native pre-adolescent, next her shawl to an adoring admirer, and now fingering the buttons on her blouse, deftly maneuvering around the little gold crucifix, which she twiddled in front of him. His hand trembled. This really wouldn't do. His fantasies about this voluptuous creature were becoming a real problem. He supposed she was probably a virgin, since most of these young Christian girls believed in chastity, or at least said they did. But Bob found that the more they proclaimed their chastity, the more it made him think of sex.

But he couldn't let on that he had any of these feelings. Actually, if he was honest with himself, he was afraid of her. If he said the wrong thing, he might really face problems. His editor had told him that she was the niece—or some other relative—of the Air Force General who ran the enormous base just outside the little city that called itself the "Buckle on the Bible Belt."

Her face glowed; her eyes were bright. She was certain of herself, her purpose.

"We will give the people what they need. Don't you find that giving is the . . . well, how can I say it? . . . *the* greatest, most *incredible* pleasure?" Bob shuddered at the word "*incredible*." She looked straight into his eyes, her ecstatic gaze imploring him to understand. He thought for a moment that maybe she was about to weep with joy.

He hadn't written anything at all in his notebook yet, except the date of her departure for Afghanistan.

"Don't you?" she asked again, leaning toward him. Yes! That was it! She was wearing a scent he recognized from memories of his mother. "Don't you? Bob?"

Didn't he *what*? He'd completely forgotten. It seemed that she was asking him a question that required his response. He sorted back through his short-term memory until he recalled: didn't he find the act of giving to be a pleasure?

She whispered pleadingly, "don't you, Bob?" He thrilled to the repetition of his name.

"I suppose so," he admitted, trying to be honest, but not really succeeding.

"Oh," she sighed in disappointment. She sat back and looked away. "I'm sorry. I forget. I forget you haven't yet really accepted Christ."

The soda jerk brought her the cherry milkshake she had ordered, with two straws. Briefly, over the odour of his coffee, he thought about sucking on the other straw, their foreheads touching. But he couldn't quite bring himself to, although she almost seemed to be inviting him.

Instead, he sipped on his coffee and took a deep breath. He steadied his pencil against his notepad and stared around the tawdry room for a time, looking at the chipped counter-tops, the dull bulbs burning in the dark interior, the sense of indifference and poverty in this little café. It was an odd place for her to sit. Yet her beauty was made all the more brilliant by the contrast with her surroundings. She'd spent some money on her clothing, he figured. Her scent wasn't cheap, either. Briefly, he wondered where the money for her clothing came from.

"Where do you live?" he asked? He was expecting her to mention an address in the rich part of town.

"We're the branch of the family from the *wrong* side of the tracks," she told him. We live out at 32 Dumdruddy Road, north of town." She watched him with amusement to see the effect of this news. He wrote down her address "But being from there doesn't mean we can't do good in the world, does it?"

There must be some scandal about her family, then, for her to live at that address and yet have an uncle (or something) out at McConnell who was a General. She didn't know he knew about her famous relation, specifically. The reporter in him wondered if this story might not have legs and walk into the Air Force. Then his editor would get interested.

"Can I ask you a question, Bob?" she whispered breathlessly.

"Sure. But I thought I was the one who was supposed to ask the questions."

"It'll be your turn in a moment. I *promise*," she said.

He waited, silent, for her question.

"Don't *you* want to do good in the world?"

He had no answer to her question. He wondered briefly if doing good might not sometimes be meddling in other people's lives without their permission. But that was a thought he'd save for later.

In a Darkroom

The Darkroom is full of high spirits. Music blares up, fades down: Dvorjak, New World Symphony.
"Now client wants Jewish stuff."
"New York Jewish stuff."
"Piece of cake."
"How many channels?"
"Broadcast, cable, and satellite, they're beyond number."
"Is there a dedicated Jewish channel?"
"Yep."
"Websites for Hasidic clothing. Clear JPEGs."
"Yep."
"Yep."
"Client's coming for another visit today."
"Really?"
"That's what herself told me."

A man wearing a yarmulke floats jerkily onto the biggest of the television screens. He is walking down a street in New York, being filmed from above. Other people pass him, but the camera follows the man as he moves away. Then the man walks backward toward the camera, stops, twitches left then right. A flashing line appears around his headgear. Abruptly, the yarmulke disappears from his head, leaving a large white hole behind. It reappears on another screen, rotates, has its black color slightly intensified, and disappears.

"Into the can with you."
"Yarmulke number 1,492," says a bored voice.

Hasidic side-curls are captured, detached from their heads, beamed from one screen to another, and stored. Stars of David appear, switch screens and vanish. Someone is monitoring a Friday night service, and the Rabbi is plucked from his temple. A scroll appears and goes into the collecting bottle. A manora, a mezuzah—symbols flit into being, are frozen, then stored away. The young people hum and chat while they work—relaxed, efficient.

The door wheezes open, and a shaft of light falls into the darkness. Two silhouettes—one male and one female—enter and their sharp shadows fall on the floor and one wall. When the door closes behind them, the intruders vanish into the darkness.

The older woman's voice says, crossing through the void, "So we call our policy the Beneficial Scheme."

A chorus of protest: "No, no way, not right."

"Does this mean you don't know quite who you are or what you're doing?" cuts in the Client.

"Well, you hired us. Apparently you like our work."

"True. But you're just hired guns."

"For us you're the Sugar Client."

"Sweetness, won't you join us?" the androgynous voice croons. "Become a member. Join Deus Ex Machina. We hear you might become a co-conspirator. Come and breathe with us?"

There is a sniggering in the background—the threatening expression of youthful exclusivity. "Well, if you could tell me what you are trying to accomplish," says Client, I'd be more than willing to consider joining you. But so far I don't have any idea. But what are you people? Simply anarchists?"

"Nothing simple about anarchy."

"Anarchy's chaos. From chaos comes Creation, then new order. We create the chaos."

"Who creates the order?"

The Fourth Meeting: New York City

"I tried really hard but failed to sympathize."[4]

"I love nothing," he said. "Nothing and no one." This was his answer to her small-talk remark, "Don't you just love New York?"

She felt herself respond to him as if he were an alien species. It was not as if he was an animal or in some way inferior to humans—in fact, he seemed to feel that it was exactly the opposite. She felt as if she was looking at some survivor from an ancient age when humans had closer contact with gods than they do now. It wasn't so much that she felt he was superior, but that she felt that he felt he was superior. Was that it? She couldn't quite put her finger on it. In any case, Chaim looked profoundly different from other young men. His clothing was only black-and-white. He wore a black hat and let his thin beard grow without trimming so that the long hairs trailed away from the edges of his mouth in the strangest, most revolting fashion; and worst of all he had those long curls of hanging down in front of his ears. She tried not to stare at them, and to look him straight in the eye. But it was hard to do—partly because he had a shifty gaze.

She opened her notebook. Thinking of herself as a "*shiksa*" (wasn't that what he'd call her?) she paraphrased his remark, which seemed important. "You have no affection for anything or anyone?"

"Correct. None." He stared straight at her, dead-eyed. One of his curls twitched. She had the odd feeling that this was an act he was putting on, that he was a passionate soul underneath the pretence of a numb exterior. "I have a purely objective attitude. Although I am a Jew, I have been trained as a physicist. I am a scientist. My grandfather was Albert Einstein."

Helen didn't remember whether or not Albert Einstein had had children. She thought for a moment and realized that he must be speaking in some figurative or symbolic way. "You mean you are the heir to his tradition?"

"Correct. Also I am his grandson." He touched the lobe of his left ear, and then looked at the tip of the finger he'd used.

He stared at her, apparently waiting for her to ask some further question. The only one she could think of was a rude question, suggesting that he was somehow illegitimate.

---

[4] Fuller, Helen, "Extreme Judaism," unpublished dissertation, Columbia University, 2011, p 1.

"Was your mother or your father his child?" she finally asked.

"My mother."

None of this line of inquiry made sense to her, and it didn't seem relevant. She felt confused. Again he touched his ear, and she realized that it was bleeding slightly. He looked at the blood on his fingers. It made her feel disgusted. Her mind drifted a bit; she could feel it sliding sideways, off the subject. The smells of coffee and freshly baked bagels created an opulent sense of wellbeing, of a vast, on-going culture, a world well managed, professionally maintained, busy, happy, rich.

"Won't you have something to eat?" She glanced down at the food between them, which she had ordered. It was a plate of lox and bagel with cream cheese. She had heard that Jewish people liked this food.

"No," he said, not 'No thank you.' How rude, Helen thought.

She proceeded to ask the questions that her Professor had suggested for her. She had them written out on the first page of her notebook. The subject of her interview with Chaim was to be a man called Meier Kahane, who was dead now. Jewish militants followed his cause. Why did they exist? What would they do next? Who supported them? Helen was a Columbia University graduate student writing her thesis about Jewish religious fundamentalists. She was acting under the direction of a famous professor, whose presence she felt hovering above the table, like a guiding spirit. Professor Friedman had arranged this interview, through his connections in Brooklyn.

"So, what about the Palestinians?" She suddenly blurted out then realized that she had been unforgivably rude. Oh dear. She should have worked up to the subject—it was what everyone wanted to talk to Jewish people about these days—but she hadn't been subtle and anyway, her question was irrelevant to the conversation so far. She felt herself blushing. Yet he didn't seem offended at all.

"What do you want me to say? We have no choice but to kill them," he shrugged. "Objectively, what else can we do? Is that what you want me to say? You have it. I say it. It is us or them—kill or be killed. There is a simple calculus of population. We wipe them out in our lands, and keep them out of Eretz Israel, or they breed like rabbits and drown us in their piles of flesh. It's not even mathematics; it's basic arithmetic. We must be clear about this." The clatter of plates and the buzz of ordinary talk around them provided a comforting static, a filler to the long silence in their conversation. He touched his bleeding earlobe again.

"So you believe in killing people?"

"Correct."

Her heart stopped. Outside the delicatessen the City's eternal sirens sounded. The sides of great trucks passing by alternately revealed and hid the view of the buildings on the other side of the street. Traffic roared; pedestrians hurried past at a New Yorker's pace.

"We must cleanse *Eretz Israel*. There must be no Arabs. No Christians. Only Jews. Only real Jews. No one else matters in Jerusalem. Rome for Christians. Mecca for Muslims. Jerusalem for Jews."

His face was not intense. It was dead. He made these statements without any sign of passion.

Then his gaze drifted downwards over her body, studying her as if she were some animal in a zoo. She could feel him mentally undressing her. She picked up the oversized laminated menu and hugged it to her chest so that he could only see her flushed face. His gaze came back to her eyes, briefly without apology. He wasn't in the slightest embarrassed by what he had just done. Yuk. She wondered if she was an antisemite. Maybe that disqualified her from conducting this interview, from writing this thesis. Maybe she'd chosen the wrong topic. She wanted to get up and run from the table.

The sirens outside sounded even louder. Her tape recorder turned and turned. He said nothing. Dishes clattered. A waitress called out an order "Three blintz specials. Side of cabbage." She was wasting her tape. She couldn't think what question to ask. Talking to this man was like talking into a void; except that the face of this void had a voice, an opinion. He was a vacuum that sucked everything into his own oblivion. Professor Friedman would not think much of her oral history technique. She blushed again. She couldn't help it. Oh dear. There must be some pill she could take, she would ask her doctor. It was so humiliating!

Finally she wheezed out, "What is your full name?" She hadn't even got that much out of him yet.

"My first name is Chaim," he said. She wrote it down.

"Chaim? C-H-A-I-M." She spelled it out.

"Correct. But a little Jewish girl like you shouldn't need to have it spelled," he observed.

She turned red, yet again. Should she should tell him she wasn't Jewish?

"Join us. Or you will die with the rest of them."

She couldn't look up from her notebook.

"And you will deserve it."

She wrote down "*I will deserve to die.*" Then she thought that was silly, because the tape recorder would have everything. So she began to erase it with the rubber end of her pencil. Finally, then, she found the courage to say, "I'm not Jewish."

"Oh," came his voice.

The rattle of dishes rang in her ears. She listened to the sirens of the city, rising and falling—just urban background noise. She stared into her notebook for a long time.

When she looked up again, he was gone. He had simply vanished. Then Helen felt hot tears on her cheeks. She was ashamed, embarrassed.

"You all right, sweetie?" asked the waitress, clearing away the plates. She could only nod. Her cheeks must be bright red.

"That yours?" came the waitress's question. Her hand appeared in Helen's field of vision, pointing to a little glass vial, which hadn't been there before. Through her tears she could see that it contained something small and pink, and that there was an envelope attached to it with cellophane tape.

The address on the envelope read "For Professor Friedman." The envelope was sealed.

In a Darkroom

Torrents of pictures whirl round disembodied heads. Eyes stare at screens. Fingers fiddle endlessly. The visual realm is often soundless, punctuated only rarely by fragmentary comments and odd scraps of music. The cinema, the video, the photograph, the frame, the cut-out, the fragment, the collage of men and women, trees and skies, landscapes, seascapes and cityscapes—images pile up in electronic memories, floating like dead leaves. The young people are skimming through the recent past, reviewing, revisiting.

"Hang on, hang on. Back up, back up. There's the client! Himself!"

An image of a young man appears on the screen. He is sitting on a wall, in front of the National Portrait Gallery, facing Trafalgar Square. A pretty, narrow-faced, dark-haired young woman is sitting beside him, watching him watch the protesters. He looks disapproving—of the proceedings, at least. She looks approving—of him.

"What to make of Client Man?"

"What indeed," says the mother-figure. "He'll be ok. Stop worrying."

"Why are you so loyal?"

"He's clearly not participating."

"He's observing. Taking notes?"

"Don't think so."

"Why not?"

"He likes being observed too much to do the observing."

"The chick?"

"Call her a chick once more, and you'll pay the sexist fine."

"Oh come on. Give us a break. We can't all make a complete break from every little bit of all of history."

"Sexism isn't history."

"What is it then?"

"It's now! In this room! In Istanbul! On the internet! It's everywhere, present, never-ending!"

"Okay. Okay. Anyway, the young woman is watching Client Man and he's too busy being watched to watch us."

"Right."

"So he's safe, you think."

"Yep. And he pays for equipment."

"True enough. And the body armor? See it?"

O JERUSALEM

"I remember it. Felt really good when it started to rain down truncheons on my back."

"Hold on. Here we go again. Old breaking news."

"Meaning?"

Images of parts of an airplane spiraling downwards appear on two screens. Everything stops. The bits hang, suspended. The nose is aimed downward, the body upwards. Then the nose spirals upwards, weaving an intricate pattern around the body, which rises. They meet in the sky. Then join together, become whole. A burst of light appears in the airplane's side. It flies backwards. A line of light grows out of its side and grows away from it. Then the clouds freeze and the airplane stops, hangs, unmoving, against the blue, just beside a cloud.

"Ready?" someone asks.

"Always," someone answers.

The missile flies forward into the plane. The plane's belly explodes. Its nose breaks away, spirals downwards.

"Where'd you find it?"

"Private archives. Amateur footage collection."

"Pan Am 103?"

"Rain down on Lockerbie."

"Rain down, you death."

"Wait a minute, guys. No missile in Lockerbie. That ain't Pan Am 103."

"No?"

"Nope."

"Wait."

"Waiting."

"Looking. Here it is. File note says it's ... a Gulf Air Flight from Teheran to Bahrain. Let's see. Missile is from US battleship in the Persian Gulf."

"Ah-hahh! Thought so!"

"OK. OK. Sorry. Sorrreeeee! But seriously. When you've seen one disaster you've seen 'em all!"

II

ISTANBUL: NIGHT JOURNEY

"The minds that we are considering themselves consider that words exist independently of any particular reader or listener. . . . Holy words come from God, not man, and therefore have noumenal status."[5]

"You will take tape to *Sabah*," says Muhammad. *Sabah* is an Islamic-influenced daily paper whose title means "The Morning." Ersan has lied to Muhammad and his Sheikh, saying that he is a reporter for this paper. Because of this lie, he believes, he has been granted the requested interview with this particular young Jihadist who might—just might—become a martyr. In fact, Ersan knows a reporter on the *Sabah* staff, and this friend has agreed to confirm that the newspaper may publish the interview. So Ersan's story is almost true. Indeed Ersan's journalist friend would like nothing better than to have the transcript of the ravings of a fanatic to edit and print—all without risking anything himself. Ersan feels confident of his "cover" story. Yet he has lied and he is nervous. He feels his left wrist with his right forefinger, seeking his pulse.

"Interview is end. You leave now," instructs Muhammad. With that, the waiter's hairy hand appears and turns the portrait of Atatürk back from facing the wall to facing the crowded room.

Ersan shrugs, and reaches out to shake the youngster's hand. Muhammad looks at the outstretched hand with surprise—either feigned

---
[5] Felsefenin, "The Phenomenology of the Sacred Word," in *Cognitive Structure of the Terrorist Mind,* op cit, p. 9.

or real—and looks back at the older man with blank contempt. Ersan understands: shaking hands is a western custom, in which Muhammad does not participate. Ersan shrugs and says "Iyi akshamlar," which means "good evening." It would be polite for Muhammad to say "Güle güle," which means something like "go happily." But the young man says nothing. He merely stares at the older man.

Ersan rises, backs away, and departs into the early evening. Will they just let him go now—now that he has met a martyr to be, a hero at the doorway to paradise? He wonders if he hasn't made a terrible miscalculation. Outside the café, Ersan glances back through the window to see what Muhammad and his minders are doing. The two bearded men are still sitting motionless at either side of the window. They seem to be looking only at each other. Suddenly, all the men in the room—except Muhammad and his minders—rise in unison, then sink back despondent into their seats. They are focused on something that does not exist in that room; they have surrendered themselves to worship a moving image invested with all hope and fear. Herr Professor Doktor Ersan Felsefenin shakes his head at the sad spectacle of his countrymen. He walks away from the shabby café, thinking how there is good reason for Muhammad's hatred of this passion for sport—the rules of football have replaced *sharia*.

For his part, Muhammad waits. He watches his two minders speak briefly on mobile phones, and then—storing away their black slices of western technology—each turns to look at the youngster under the television. First one and then the other rises to his feet and with slow dignity walks out into the street. The first will follow Ersan. The second will follow Muhammad. This was an important interview, and the Sheikh has arranged that both young Muhammad and his contact will be carefully monitored.

When Muhammad leaves the bright light of the café and turns into the darker street, footsteps follow. Muhammad's follower is making certain that Muhammad is not followed. Muhammad does not look back. Bright lights from the elegant shop windows fall in squares onto the pavement; the street lamps are not working in this section of Şişli, so that Muhammad passes from light to dark and dark to light as he walks. It is a neighbourhood of expensive, European-style shops, and Muhammad contemptuously looks away from the displays of western-style women's dresses and lingerie, from the shelves of sweets, from the piles of scarves and rugs, the hand-carved ivory, the little knotted collections of diamond rings and brooches, the cut-glass and crystal vases.

Dressed in their finery, five girls laughing with each other are walking toward Muhammad. Like him, they vanish and appear, vanish and appear in the successive pools of shop light. It is a Saturday evening, and the worldly, westernized Istanbul Türkyeli are celebrating their affluence. The girls are modestly dressed, and one even wears a blue silk headscarf. But they are happy, smiling. The group stops before a window filled with women's clothing; they point at the dresses, and giggle at the idea of wearing the garments themselves. Muhammad walks straight toward the group, and instead of stepping around them, he pushes his way through them, shouldering the girls aside so that they scatter like city pigeons. His face is dead. He believes that these people live in ignorance. They are obviously girls from Muslim homes, so they should know better than to parade themselves as sexual objects before the lecherous eye of the stranger; but these girls do not live as they should. Only one of them wears a headscarf, but it does not properly hide her hair. It is bright blue with a golden pattern on the edge. It is more fashion statement than modesty. Shocked—and yet not utterly astonished, because they have experienced such fanaticism before—the girls stare after the young man in his cheap, false-leather jacket. A man in a large turban and long robes floats past. They stand aside for him.

The girl who is wearing the bravely decorated headscarf has been bumped hardest, has been pushed up against the shop window. As she straightens up, her friends gather around her. Perhaps Muhammad wanted to punish her especially, for wasting her life with unclean friends. "Stupid peasant," she whispers loudly, catching her breath.

Muhammad and his Islamic shadow never hear her insult. Muhammad proceeds at his steady pace, in his straight line, walking through his own invisible dimension, rejecting all vanity, all delusions of worthless luxury. His purposeful walk says that he knows. His shadow follows and knows too.

Professor Ersan has often wandered the streets of Şişli. These are his familiar haunts; he has known them all—the elegant, Italianate arcades lined with shops that sell pastries, sweets, delights. He passes under a window where—he remembers—he once had a lover whose long hair trailed across the satin pillow. He catches the scent of coffee from a quiet restaurant, and recalls how they stared into each others' eyes at that very table in the corner of the window—so many years ago, long before he was married. His memory is vivid, but where that woman is now he cannot say. He stands for a moment, transfixed by his past. He yearns for her in memory, smiling to himself. The memory is cushioned softly in his soul, and he treasures it, like a jewel wrapped in satin cloth and nestled in some tiny, elegant box.

Suddenly, reflected in the shop window, he sees across the street—standing where other people are passing by—a motionless, robed, bearded, turbaned figure. His mood of contented memory shatters. The fellow is almost certainly one of the two men who were monitoring the interview. Ersan has known intrigue in his day, and would not be surprised if suspicion and conspiracy were following him now. He moves on, thinking once more how it was possibly a serious mistake to interview Muhammad.

When he stops again, he knows. The man is following him. He draws a deep breath to calm himself. His heart pulses strangely, and he feels in his jacket pocket for the medicine he just may need.

Muhammad's escort has left him now. No one else was following him. As instructed, Muhammad now reverses direction, and walks toward Beşiktaş. Across several vast neighborhoods of Istanbul, Muhammad retreats from the interview with Ersan. His Sheikh has arranged everything. Perhaps Muhammad knows why all this has just happened. Or perhaps he doesn't even ask himself the question, but only whispers *"Insha'allah,"* in a tone that tells you that for him this is not merely a word. For him it is a way of life. *"Insha'allah,"*—God willing. He is empty of everything but God's will, which he knows with absolute certainty, because Sheikh Abu has told it to him calmly, clearly.

It is impossible for anyone to say just what Muhammad knows or thinks or feels. He seems no longer to have emotions. His face is dead. His father, mother, and wife to whom he now returns, do not know his thoughts. They do not know his reasons for coming and going from the shack where he lives with them. He goes to the mosque; he returns. Five times a day. He says almost nothing. He reads his Holy Koran. He prays. He lies beside his young wife, but seems a world away, inhabiting another realm. She does not ask. She is not a prying wife; she is a decent woman; she submits.

Muhammad now travels toward his family, threading his way through the fifteen million people of Istanbul. They smell. They chatter. They gossip. They buy their food, their clothing, their household objects, and their newspapers. They watch their televisions, they cry out for their football heroes. They drink their coffee, tea and beer. They are all ignorant of Muhammad and what he knows so surely that the Prophet Himself—blessed be his name—could only be slightly more certain. This modern Muhammad slips quietly into the subway, a small, dark man among millions and millions of small, dark men. A Muhammad in the twenty-first century among millions who share this name. But only this Muhammad knows what this particular Muhammad will do. And only his Sheikh will tell him.

The subway in Istanbul is flooded with the stream of shoving, smelling, eating, farting, striving, humanity. Motionless, though traveling fast Muhammad arrives at the end of the great city's new rail transport system. Now he is above ground, with ramshackle two-storied board houses around him. The neighbourhood beside the Bosphorus was once grand; but now its paint peels and its boards warp. Yet there lingers a sense of affluence only a decade or two gone—odours of ancient wealth from a rotting Ottoman corpse. Once there was a Caliphate; now there is only western colonialism and commerce.

Muhammad waits beside the great water. He takes a ferry across the vast flowing channel that divides Asia from Europe, paying a few coins to the conductor, taking his turn in the queue of people, saying nothing, ignoring everyone, refusing to be lured by the temptations of this world—not the candy sold in the canteen, not the filthy food, certainly not the beer. He glares from his death mask at a man drinking a glass of wine at the bar.

After the ferry, Muhammad takes a bus, a big, square, rattletrap machine that seats fifty people, but onto which seventy-five are crammed. Two men sit on the roof, clinging to the luggage frame. Muhammad is among the first to push on board—aggressive in the crowd, shoving other people. Some women do not cover themselves, and Muhammad looks carefully the other way. The men talk only of this world—of the price of food, the markets, the weather. He breathes quietly and considers only what is *"Batin,"* hidden from fools. He focuses inwards, intense upon his certainty. He knows. He submits. He prepares.

Again and again, the bus stops and passengers get off; at each stop none or few get on. Then, after a time, Muhammad has the seat to himself. *"Hamdilillah,"* he says aloud, when his companion has left the bus. God be praised. The bus stops again and yet another group of unveiled Turkish women depart into the night. His eyes do not follow them. Muhammad travels onwards toward the end of the line. He sees a glimpse of the great flowing Bosphorus on his left. Perhaps he notices the crescent moon, or its fragmented reflection. It is an Islamic moon, after all. It is to be loved, adored—the eternal symbol of the vanished Caliphate, which lives on in the hearts of the faithful. It is one of the few things in this world that is still clean. Or at least it was, before the Infidel landed on it. His Sheikh says, however, that the first thing the astronauts heard when they set foot on the surface of the moon was the Muezzin's call to prayer. They were too ignorant to answer.

Ersan strokes his well-trimmed moustache and again studies his reflection in a shop window. He is not the only person looking at himself. That pathetic man who does not cut a hair of his facial growth is still following him. Ersan knows the type. They grow beards when they turn religious in middle age. This fellow is probably a member of the potentially illegal Islamic sect to which Muhammad belongs. He is devoted to Sheikh Abu, of whom almost no one else has ever heard. This sorry primitive believes that his Sheikh's own little world is the center of the cosmos. He "submits" to Allah by submitting to Sheikh Abu and to no one and nothing else. He does not possess the mental sophistication to notice that his submissive humility is a form of arrogance. Only he and his friends know Allah's will. In philosophical terms it is idiotic because *prima facie* self-contradictory. The memory of the strange Latin phrase distracts Ersan: "first face" it seems to mean. How could that make any sense? He'll have to look it up when he gets home.

If he gets home. He thinks briefly of his wife. She is waiting for him. He is going in the wrong direction. He practices his breathing exercises to steady himself. He considers the almost unlit street, and thinks how foolish he has been—all for the sake of an interview that he might or might not use for his book, that might or might not appear in *Sabah*. And what did his book really matter? Beside his life, it was nothing—not worth dying for.

He remembers what his doctor said. When you feel anxious, try to look on the bright side of things. When you feel frightened, use your rational mind to notice all the reasons why you are really safe. While you are doing this, breathe deeply and slowly through your nose, said his doctor. He breathes as instructed, and tries to think of the bright side of things. Such men as the bearded wonder behind him are generally not very bright. Also, he is not being followed by the police, who are sometimes smarter. Two good things

Then, almost without thinking, with the mad impulse that only a few times before in his life has come over him, Ersan turns abruptly and confronts his stalker.

"*Evet?*" he asks the man, looking him straight in the face. Ersan's heart is pounding. He cannot believe he has just done this.

The man glances quickly back at Ersan, and then looks down, away almost shyly. "*Hayır*," he responds. He shows no embarrassment, no hint of apology.

Ersan stares at but not into the man's eyes; the bearded one looks away. The Turkish intellectual realizes that, so far as this fool understands anything at all, they are not two males of the same human species communicating with each other. Instead, for this man they are one superior human who knows the hidden truth and keeps his gaze fixed upon the invisible world, and one sub-human, ignorant apostate. Ersan understands that so far as this man is concerned, he—Ersan—is not really human at all. He has lost his human status by capitulating to western evils.

"What do you want of me?" he asks in Turkish.

"I want nothing," the man responds.

Ersan speculates, tries out a wild guess.

"Who is your Sheikh?"

"Abu Abbas."

"Of course," Ersan says.

The man stands unmoving, his eyes fixed on his non-existent world in the middle distance behind Ersan. Ersan realizes—surprised at the canniness of his own impulse—that he has paralyzed the man with this unexpected confrontation. It is nothing the poor fellow has been prepared for. Rude Western frankness can serve a purpose sometimes.

"Take me to your Abu-bey," Ersan orders—stabbing in the dark at the opportunity to have an interview with a radical leader. Ersan steps back from the man, to watch the effect of his boldness. He has quite taken his own breath away. He has to admit to himself, in all modesty—but with the customary irony of his sophisticated soul—that this instinctive gambit may in fact turn out to be a piece of brilliant inspiration. The man might do exactly as asked and led Ersan to the Sheikh. He might get a meeting with the motivating force behind this small, virtually unknown group of fundamentalist operatives—these peasants come in from the fields but now aspiring to destroy the modern world. The blood is pounding in his temples as he awaits the effect of his tactic.

O JERUSALEM

The man turns about and begins to walk in a new direction, toward the Beşiktaş district. Ersan follows him. Their roles have reversed. The followed spy makes a brief mobile call. Ersan cannot hear what he says. Only once does the fellow look over his shoulder—as if to make certain that Ersan is still there. While he follows after his own shadow, Ersan tries to work out what is going on. The Sheikh through whom he has arranged for the interview with the foot soldier and potential martyr Muhammad, has also arranged to have him followed by someone rather obvious. Abu has also arranged to have Muhammad tape-record the interview himself, which seems like a reasonable precaution. These people are actually a secret organization that seeks publicity. Another contradiction, like arrogant humility.

Ersan wanders on into the night following his follower, pursuing a mystery through the shadowy streets. The neighborhood is now not as propitious as the Şişli shopping district. A pile of rotting garbage infests the pavement. He sees a scurrying rat.

Istanbul is a city of fifteen million people—with everything that such greatness means: filth, danger, excitement, hideous darkness, glowing beauty, terrible poverty, enormous wealth. Ersan loves his city. Sometimes, as in Şişli, he knows its intricate streets like the veins in the back of his own hand. Now, however, he is leaving the neighborhoods he knows, heading off through an unfamiliar neck of Beşiktaş toward the Bosphorus. Though he does not know it, he is following the same route that Muhammad has hurried through before him. The bearded man in front of him looks back again. He makes another phone call.

A siren sounds briefly down at the end of a long alleyway. The wailing vanishes; the police presence is fleeting. A large man lurches past Ersan on the pavement. The fanatic leading the way in front of him turns right. A child rises out of the darkness and plucks at Ersan's cuff, pleading "Lütfen, lütfen," ("please, please") and running along beside him. Without breaking his stride, Ersan reaches into his pocket for a coin, which he gives the child, who vanishes back into the shadows. Ersan still follows, though he wonders if it wouldn't be better just to stop, turn aside, leave the fellow and go home to Suhandan, to his wife, to his comfortable home. He's been drawn into a fool's quest. He's got his interview. He taps his breast pocket where the tape recorder is safely hidden, next to the little vial of heart medicine - why risk more?

Now the bearded man, like the child, vanishes into the shadows.

Logically, Ersan can assume that the proper direction of his pursuit will be straight ahead. But he is no longer certain. He had never really been certain of anything, he realizes. Was he intended to follow the bearded believer? A neon sign advertising a kebab house sputters and spits electrical sparks above his head. A drain has burst a few paces further on, and stinking water flows in the gutter.

Nothing works as it should in these wild, night streets. A wind whistles off the nearby Sea of Marmara, smelling of salty rain. The sense of some vast darkness just beneath the surface of things becomes acute. When you are with your family, within the walls of your own home, you have a sense of order, sanity, safety. But outside, on the street, you sometimes feel as if you might suddenly fall through a trap door into some underworld of shrieks and madness. You might be stabbed or robbed. You might take the last wrong turn into the mapless city and never find your way home.

This is not good for his heart. He decides to break off the pursuit. He stops in his tracks on the pavement and stares down the narrow side street to his left, looking for an intersection with a larger thoroughfare where he will be able to hail a taxi and go home to Suhandan. He sees headlamps of automobiles hurtling back and forth across a distant road.

That is the last thing Ersan sees for several hours. From behind he hears one sentence, in Turkish, which tells him "The Sheikh will see you now." After that, he hears voices speaking a dialect of Arabic that he does not understand. He smells the musty cloth bag someone has slipped over his head; he feels the gentle but firm hands of his captors on his arms and wrists.

By now, Muhammad is alone at the back of the bus. All the other passengers have left, except for a young girl not wearing a headscarf, who is sitting by herself near the driver. She glances over her shoulder at him, demurely, and perhaps he understands from her quick look that he has been noticed. Or perhaps not. It is impossible to know what Muhammad perceives. His inner life is hidden by his dead face. Perhaps he has very little inner life; perhaps he is emptied of all but his one purpose in this world. Nothing within him exists except his obedience. He is reduced to his cause. The rest is emptiness. Perhaps.

The girl leans forward to say something to the driver. Her smooth, plump arm is revealed, momentarily bared all the way to just above her elbow. The bus lurches to a stop, and she exits. Muhammad watches out the window. Perhaps his eyes are following the girl down a side-street. Perhaps not. The driver glances at him once, but asks no questions, makes no remarks.

Muhammad reaches the end of the bus line in time for evening prayers. The muezzin has just finished calling as Muhammad walks swiftly across the barren parking lot between the broken-roofed bus station and his perfectly domed place of worship. In the wind, a styrofoam cup skitters noisily across the pavement. Muhammad enters the outer precincts of the mosque, removes his shoes, kneels beside the fountain, washes his hands and his feet in the light of a single bare bulb, and joins the men who kneel and prostrate themselves, rise and spread their hands and kneel again. The peace, the order, the soft murmuring of prayer must soothe the young man after the turmoil of his travels. Yet his face is no different than before.

When prayers have ended, a man touches Muhammad on the shoulder. Muhammad apparently knows exactly what is wanted of him. He hands the man the little black tape recorder. The man vanishes. Muhammad leaves the mosque.

They have rolled the soft, clean material up over Ersan's mouth and nose so that he can breathe. Their hands are gentle, caring. The car feels luxurious—especially after the raw barbarism of the Istanbul streets full of trash, filth, and desperate humanity. With his left hand, he discretely feels the upholstery, which seems leather. The men around him say nothing. There must be at least three of them, the driver and two others. He takes his pulse—which is, surprisingly, quite steady.

"Where are we going?" Ersan asks, as calmly as he can. He is afraid that his voice may have quavered.

"You want see Sheikh Abu. He calls. Tell us bring you."

A mobile phone beeps, rings. How ironic, thinks Ersan, that these men who yearn for simpler times, before cars, planes, television, tape machines, plastic, the internet, chips, laser beams, nuclear bombs …now make such casual use of modern technology. The car and telephone they take for granted. Their grandparents believed in the same Allah, but needed no greater complexity than a staff to herd sheep and a bucket to carry water; now secular technocrats have invaded their peasant brains. The new devices should be unwelcome guests—digital Djinns; but these shepherds and farmers, have wandered to the city where they pluck the western fruits without fear.

Blind-folded, sightless, in his darkness Ersan thinks and thinks and thinks that now he almost knows. His quest is to understand their inner lives, their minds, how and what they feel. Tonight he will penetrate the mask of mystery.

After what seems a very long time, the car stops. Ersan suspects that they may have crossed the Bosphorus to the Asiatic side; at one point he thought he heard the mournful wail of a ship's horn sounding below them—as if they were traveling the great bridge between continents. But any certainty of his geographic location is impossible.

Gently, the men help him out of the car. One says in foreign-accented Turkish, "You see Sheikh now." They guide him through a doorway; then hands are fumbling with his feet, removing his shoes for him. They guide him through a second doorway, and he stumbles a little on the sill, and starts to lose his balance; but they catch him, tenderly. Then they remove the cloth bag.

It is almost as dark in the room as it was inside the blindfold. Someone strikes a match, carries the flame to a wick, steadies it. A larger flame springs up, and the hand holding the little flame expertly turns a lever on the lamp. The flame rises. The man's movements are practiced and efficient. He has lit lamps—and this one in particular—countless times before. He places a clear glass chimney around the flame. Behind the chimney is a burnished metal reflector that glares in Ersan's field of vision. The right hand adjusts the wick to a lower level. The left hand helps the right hand close the little leather box that holds matches.

This is all pre-modern: no electricity, no plastic, only woolen cloth, leather, wood. He smells the air. Perhaps the kerosene is modern. Or does the lamp burn animal fat? He cannot tell. Ersan begins to see walls covered in old carpets. The floor is earthen beneath kilims and cushions—he can tell from the uneven surface under his feet. There is no furniture except the low table on which the lamp sits. Just as his eyes focus on a rough-hewn wooden door, it opens—but only to blackness beyond.

Through the doorway comes the sound of gentle disturbance in the darkness. After a time, a man emerges, looking backward toward a second shape that becomes a man whose form appears in the dim lamplight: he is wearing long robes, is fully bearded, is wearing a turban and—strangely enough—is also wearing silver-surfaced, reflective glasses. The blind man is led through the door and toward the lamp. This is the Sheikh.

Nothing is said until the white-robed leader is seated on cushions behind the glow of the lamp. Ersan, hypnotized by the performance, has neglected to notice the other people in the room, who now number half a dozen, hovering around him—ghostly.

The Sheikh says something in Arabic, and a voice behind Ersan translates. "Abu-bey wishes to know if you would you like tea?"

"I would drink tea with my host if my host wishes to have tea."

A little flurry of translation follows. The old man twitches his hand in an almost imperceptible gesture of command. Ersan hears a door behind him open and close. Someone passes through it, invisible. A hand reaches into Ersan's vest pocket and removes both his tape recorder and his vial of heart medicine. The hand disappears into the darkness beyond the halo of light from the oil lamp. It then reappears to place the machine and the medicine on the table beside the oil lamp. The tape recorder is not operating. The Sheikh's trembling left hand hovers over the table to find the machine, the vial. His hand touches them like mere breath. Ersan listens to the rustle of the Sheikh's long sleeve.

Then Arabic again—but not an Arabic that Ersan understands.

The vial, in another disconnected hand, levitates its way out of the lamplight back to Ersan. Dazed, he watches but does not reach out. He is frozen here, in this moment, this place. After a respectful hesitation the hand forces its way gently back into the vest pocket of Ersan's new suit, within the silk lining of his elegant western dress. The hand pats his chest, to reassure him that his medicine is back where it belongs.

The door opens again and tea arrives on a silver censer swung on chains. The usual rituals ensue—practiced, elaborate, elegant.

"Şekerli?"

"Evet."

Cubes of sugar go into Ersan's tea. The glass comes to his hand. The Sheikh drinks. Then, suddenly, his face splits open into what at first seems like a smile. Or is it a grimace of pain? Ersan sips his tea politely, without tasting.

The conversation begins—always in two or three directions: Arabic to English or Turkish; English or Turkish back to Arabic. The Sheikh apparently speaks only Arabic. His retainers are sometimes more comfortable in English than in Turkish. Translations echo questions from mind to mind and back. Answers bounce about. Whatever their radically conservative orientation, several men are skilled linguists.

Is Ersan content with Muhammad?

O JERUSALEM

Yes. (Cautiously)
Is he not a lovely boy?
He is. (Still cautious)

An almost imperceptible gesture of command from Abu's left hand, and a second little black tape recorder appears—almost identical to Ersan's own machine, which still sits on the low table between them. Another small gesture, and a finger pushes "play." Ersan hears his own voice from the café interview, saying pompously "I asked merely for an interview. I have not asked a single question yet." Is this what his voice sounds like? Surely the volume is too loud? He thinks of his book, the publicity, the lectures, the interviews. He must find a voice coach to work on his delivery. Again, the Sheikh's mouth spreads out into what seems to be an enormous grin. Underneath the silver glasses, and in the middle of the spreading threads of his beard, his teeth glow Hollywood white. Are they false, or real? The tape recorder drones on, replaying Ersan's and Muhammad's voices.

So, it is now understood: both sides recorded the conversation; Muhammad has already delivered his version to his Sheikh. Ersan controls nothing and understands little that is happening around him. But this much is clear. The translations rush back and forth:

How did the interview proceed?
Well, thank you.
Your man at Sabah will be pleased?
He should be pleased.
Can you guarantee that he will publish?
Abu-bey, I can guarantee nothing. I am only the messenger.
We understand. But you think it likely that he will be pleased and publish what Muhammad has said?
I think it likely.
Good. Allah be praised. We wish to be understood.

Abu makes another gesture, smaller, even, than the blink of an eye. A hand appears to push the "record" buttons on both tape recorders. There will be two records of this conversation as well.

Suddenly, with a change in tone, an increase in volume, a flattening of intonation like a muezzin in the tower, Sheikh Abu recites in Arabic, and the voices from the darkness translate into English for Ersan:

And when we willed to destroy a city, to its affluent ones did we address our bidding; but when they acted criminally therein, just was its doom, and we destroyed it with an utter destruction.

The long flame of the lamp trembles with the sound of the voice so near. It flickers in the silver glasses of the speaker, like a pair of vertical slits of cat's irises in the giant artificial pupils of the lenses. The blind Sheik sees the invisible and only the invisible. Aside from polite utterance, the man knows only the Koran. The "we" is a royal, divine pronoun in the original but Abu calls himself and his associates "we." He and his men have become the "we" of the text, the collective voice of Allah. Ersan's scalp tingles. There is no debating this text. To these men, it is simply the unambiguous Word of Allah; they do not even think that the Word does not exist if no one speaks or reads it; for them the Word cannot mean more than one thing to more than one listener.

Abu's voice wells up again

And since Noah, how many nations have we exterminated! And of the sins of his servants thy Lord is sufficiently informed, observant.

Ersan stops himself making the apologetic gestures he had used with Muhammad in the café. His new vocabulary of non-committal shrugs and hand signals would be dangerous here. He must stay motionless; he must seem to submit. He thinks how the simple yet profound original Muhammad could not have imagined the multitude of nations that would follow in the centuries then still to come. If this were a seminar room at the Sorbonne, Ersan would say to his students that this sura does not justify genocide. He would mount a long but convincing argument that people today must not abuse a sacred text to suit their political purposes, to justify genocide. But Ersan says nothing. He closes his eyes. It is better not to see. Not to think. He almost wishes to have the felt bag over his head again so that the men cannot see his face, read his thoughts.

Ersan is sitting on the floor, palms upward on his knees, facing the Sheikh. It is the posture of prayer. Ancient habits return. The circumstance has forced him back into the appearance of belief, back into submission. He sat down a secret apostate; but perhaps he will rise a believer!

Abu emits a storm of sound. There is a flurry of words, a babble of languages. Arabic, Turkish, English:

When thou recitest the Koran we place between thee and those who believe not in the life to come, a dark veil.

The verse seems familiar. For a moment Ersan thinks that he has heard these words before; then he thinks that—no—this is Abu speaking his own mind. His voice fills the room, strident, aggressive, at odds with the delicacy of his gestures. The Sheikh has continued to use the first person plural. It does sound like another sura—if the translation from the Arabic is accurate. It has been so long since he read the Koran that he does not know if these words are what Gabriel said to Muhammad and Muhammad to the huffah, and the huffah to the scribes, or whether these are simply words that Abu has made up. The distinction between man and God is blurred. This is a phenomenon that he could observe in his book—if he lives to finish it.

There are three voices in the room: Abu's in Arabic, and two others, one in English, one in Turkish, conferring.

And we put coverings over their hearts lest they should understand it, and in their ears a heaviness.

There follows the flurry of tongues. The English-speaker behind Ersan asks, "are you among these unbelievers of whom the Prophet speaks? (Praised be his Name)." Now Ersan's moment of decision has come. He cannot acquiesce in full honesty to their simple creed. They have no sense of history; they do not know that language itself evolves. They reduce the ever-shifting human language to the simplicity of divine utterance. Ersan cannot accept their collapse of the one voice of God, and the many voices of men, into a single voice. Yet if he does not lie, they may kill him—despite what the Koran elsewhere says about mercy to the non-believer. His problem is that he is not a westerner ignorant of the Koran. He cannot be excused on the grounds that he has not had the opportunity to submit to the one great truth. He knows Islam, was born to know Islam. He submitted as a boy. He has heard the Koran time and again. He was raised beside—though not always fully within—the one and only true faith. So his non-belief is apostasy. He who has once believed and falls away from belief must die. To save himself, Ersan has no choice but to be a good liar.

He breathes deeply, feeling his heart pump hard, once, then flutter several times. He could pretend to have an attack of cardiac arhythmia, to slump side-wards onto his shoulder and seem to faint. His heart is beating loudly irregular. Yet how would they interpret his fainting? Would they think it the Will of Allah that this apostate should faint with fear before the Servants of the Lord? What would they do with his prostrate body? If his heart actually failed, would they simply stretch him out and let Allah's will prevail?

Ersan can hesitate no longer. The silence in the room strangles thought. He can hear the breathing of the others; he feels their waiting. He must lie, or pretend to pass out. His moment is now.

And yet his moment is not yet. Suddenly the young Muhammad enters the room. Ersan sees in the Sheikh's glasses the movement behind him; his moment of truth and danger has passed.

"*Sholom aleichum*," the Sheikh says. The youngster mutters something deeply respectful back to his master.

The voices in Arabic are slow and deep. He listens hard for the odd identifiable word, but cannot even tell what the subject is now. When an unseen hand touches him lightly on the shoulder and asks him in Turkish if he understands, he responds in the negative "*Hayır*," raising his head and clicking his tongue.

Now a manila envelope appears on the floor in front of his knees, and he is told to open it. Inside are high quality glossy photos in black-and-white. They look as if they were taken at a graduation ceremony of some kind. Several are group photos: formally posed lines of young men, always somewhere including Muhammad. Other photos show him holding a kalashnikov, praying, holding a broad canvas belt fitted with cylindrical pockets. Ersan tries not to react. Suhandan is always telling him how articulate his face is. He must practice the art of blankness. He must learn from Muhammad. Now hands put the photos back in the envelope and lean the package against Ersan's knee.

"For *Sabah*," a deep voice says behind him.

Ersan reaches out and touches the envelope with his forefinger, in symbolic acceptance of the materials.

Muhammad returns to his family. He leaves the rooms in the precinct of the mosque that are occupied by Sheikh Abu and his retainers, and walks through an area where old wood-frame buildings line a cobbled road of ancient stones. Under the bright moon their surfaces gleam, polished by the footsteps of a thousand years. This village has known the tread of pagan Greek, Jewish, Roman, Christian, Mameluke, and Turkish feet.

The young man's way proceeds beyond the old village to a suburb where new buildings are rising. They have been under construction for as long as Muhammad might remember—begun twenty years ago and never finished, so that their upper floors are roofless, gray concrete with metal re-enforcing rods sticking up toward the sky. People are camping on the ground levels without running water or electricity. Sometimes a low light inside gives the glimpse of a bleak room, with unpainted walls illuminated by low flames.

In the moonlight, Muhammad could see all this if he looked up from the pavement. He does not look up but only watches where he treads. He leaves the old village for a modern asphalt surface—pot-holed and gravel-strewn. No cars travel this road tonight, so he walks down the center, towards the end of the little village. The cheap modern tarmac, on its uneven substrate, gives way to a crushed-stone, single-track road that runs through olive orchards whose trees are gnarled into fantastic shapes, arthritic with age. Many are older than the village itself. This year the crop fell to the ground unharvested; now it is rotting back into the soil. The price of olives is so low that they are not worth picking.

The youngster passes onto a two-rut road running along under the face of a cliff that rises high on the eastern bank of the Bosphorus. The bright moon gives the only light. To his right and slightly above him are constructions at which he does not look. These are squared spaces claimed from the state of nature by hastily erected tiers of cheap ceramic building blocks sloppily mortared together and roofed over sometimes with plyboard, sometimes with corrugated sheet metal. The back wall of these buildings is the cliff-face itself. The first examples of this architecture are relatively elaborate, with chimneys poking through the roofs and sometimes panes of glass fitted awkwardly into only roughly rectangular openings in the walls. Looping along the cliff side is a heavy black cable that is illegally attached somewhere to the Istanbul power grid. Here there is often no electricity, and tonight Muhammad could see if he looked only the dimmest glow from a kerosene lamp or the flickering light of a fire burning low just outside a doorway—embers from the evening meal. Further along the path, away from the ancient village and out into what had been wild countryside until a few years ago, the homes that huddle up against the cliff become smaller and poorer and more precarious in construction. One has collapsed and been abandoned. The occupants of its neighboring hovels have scavenged for building materials, and one wall is almost entirely missing.

Then the path makes an abrupt right turn into a gulley that a stream has carved into the slope down to the great channel between the Mediterranean and the Black Sea. The walls of the steep little valley are soft stone. A stream trickles in the center. Peasants who have come to Istanbul from the countryside but have not found their places in the great urban miasma have made themselves a little community here, at the city's far edge. They have been enlarging natural caves and carving out new caves with the dogged energy of rural folk.

Muhammad's home is half a cave. His father has been renovating it for several years now, using the fractured stone he removes as the raw material for making front and side walls. Muhammad's father has been a brick-layer, and he has scavenged rejected specimens of those ceramic blocks used to make houses in this part of the world. So one wall is unplastered red blocks, each flawed in some way; one wall is but untidy rubble piled high. A sheet of corrugated metal is the roof.

His mother and wife cook meals over a brazier outside the mouth of the cave-house, just under the edge of the roof. The coals are burning low when the boy arrives. His mother wearily fans the embers and throws on a few bits of olive wood. Muhammad's wife is sleeping in the back room, the cave. Her small round form is just visible under a gray blanket. Muhammad's father—a tiny man, smaller even than his small son—sits motionless, wordless, exhausted from his day's work. There is no joy evident in their greetings, just a grim satisfaction.

Muhammad's mother calls to his wife to come and help serve the meal. She rises, groggy, and nearly falls as she stands. Once a girl of some beauty, her appearance is now disfigured by an enormous goitre bulging out of her neck. She tries to hide this with her scarf, pulling it tightly around the left side of her face and over the tumour; but the bulge is easily visible. Her name is Aysha. She squats beside the fire, and works to help her mother-in-law with one hand, as she holds her scarf over her disfigurement with the other. This makes her clumsy and Muhammad's mother is impatient with her, as she cannot both stir the fragments of meat in the pan and hold the pan at the same time. The pan tilts precariously over the fire, and cooking grease falls into the flames, which hiss upwards. The older woman grabs the younger woman's left hand, pulling it away from the scarf, allowing the material to fall to one side and reveal the tumour. Aysha glances at Muhammad; but he is staring into the fire, unaware of his wife.

Suddenly, a ringing sounds. It is Muhammad's mobile phone slicing the silence with its clear, imperative tone. Muhammad reaches within his false leather jacket, and answers the call—his gesture practised, efficient, his face impassive as always.

"*Evet*," he says.

He listens.

"*Evet*," he repeats.

He listens.

"*Hayır, Abu-bey.*"

He listens.

"*Insha-allah.*"

The conversation ends. The father looks at his son with flickering admiration. They eat without relish. A popping crackle of static from within the single room behind him does not startle Muhammad. A dull, blue glow from one corner of the cave-room flickers up and lights the inner darkness: the television has come on with the surge of returning electricity. To the left and the right, above and below them in the little gully, a few bare bulbs flash on. Muhammad and his family seem not to notice.

The awful event occurred as planned. Muhammad must have been delivered in a taxi to a busy corner of Istanbul. He must have walked a few last steps to the stadium. He would have been wearing loose-fitting clothing. He was small. He was hidden in the crowd that flowed through the gateway; he was swept along by the mass of men. Ersan could imagine it all. There would have been the great roar of enthusiasm as the victims appeared before their adoring fans. Press reports said that the boy leaped through the police lines and ran heavily toward the beloved crew—just as if he was one of the adoring, worshippers in the secular religion of sport. Then he, and everyone near him, ended.

In a Darkroom

In the video screens show a flutter of dismembered bodies—lying on the grass, slumped over the seats. Feet, arms, a head, a hand, a leg float past in endless cycles, on many screens. Someone yawns.

"Turkish cameramen really like this stuff."

"It's not just the Turks, you know. They'll sell these images down the line to US and UK papers. You'll seem 'em in the tabloids. It's all part of the acquisitive global brain."

"No cheers for the gruesome global brain!"

"No Hip-hip for the Silicon Chip!"

"It's just a football match—or was going to be. Why bomb a football game? Who cares that much about a silly game?"

"And the only people at the game were their own Turkish people. They weren't the enemy."

The maternal authority says with quiet resonance, "Well, they've figured that stupid football is the real opiate. You males of the species should be able to understand that." In the embarrassed silence someone clucks a tongue, making a small noise of disapproval of something. Images of carnage flow off the video screens and through the young people's minds. They sit passively collecting bloodied faces, eyeballs gouged out, a scalp hanging off a skull like a leather hinge.

Men and women in white coats clamber down the stands, carrying bodies on stretchers. Old women are searching, weeping, wailing. One screen shows a severed hand, which seems to twitch.

"Sparagmos, torn flesh," mourns a female, "male idiocy."

"Turks publish this stuff in print media too? Not just broadcast? Government allows it? Yep. Turks love media violence. Ankara just blocks the sex. But they do the violence. Just like we do."

III

WICHITA: BUCKLE ON THE BIBLE BELT

Nine time zones west of Istanbul—almost half a world away—Betsey had, without trying, managed to attract the attention of Bob Smith, the young reporter, for the *Wichita Falcon*. He had been pursuing her ostensibly for professional purposes. But his true motive was good old-fashioned lust, even leading possibly to love, marriage. Yes. Bob Smith had decided that, if he had to, he must marry Betsey. But whether or not she would have him was another matter entirely.

They met again just across the street from her "work," as she called what she did for love but not money at the local Salvation Army. Betsey wasn't a member of the "Army," so far as Bob could determine; but she had some affiliation with the "Sally," as the locals called it. In fact, he had not been able to determine just which denomination of Christianity she professed.

They were in the same dingy café where they had first met, with windows looking out on the busy street. The storm drains didn't work properly in this semi-industrial part of town, so that the water from rain had been splashed up by passing cars and trucks against the café window, leaving a filthy, hardened muck that no one had bothered to clean away. The dirt on the window turned the daylight yellow.

None of this mattered to the young reporter. He was ecstatic simply to be with her. It was unprofessional to keep manufacturing reasons to come to see her—but he didn't care. He had lied to his editor, saying that there was more to this local interest issue than just the story of the girl who'd won the contest to serve Jesus abroad. Bob had absolutely no evidence, but he knew how things worked, and he'd suggested the possibility of some scandal involving the beautiful girl, the handsome aging Pastor, the General out at McConnell Air Force Base, and the General's relations who lived on the wrong side of the tracks on Dumdruddy Road in a run-down, rented house. Some of what he had told his editor was probably even true. He'd again suggested that there might be some connection between the Salvation Army, the Reverend Jones's Church, and the Commanding Officer out at McConnell.

"So the Right Rev is in cahoots with the Big Bopper out at the Base, maybe? Needs to keep the illegitimate daughter out of the public spotlight? Suppose it's possible." The cynical old goat wasn't opposed to a fishing expedition. So he'd told Bob to keep poking around.

Of course Betsey wasn't illegitimate. Bob was sure of that. She was just poor, that was all. Her father—whoever he was—had apparently deserted her mother. That wasn't Betsey's fault. Anyway, it didn't matter. The *Wichita Falcon* reporter would have proposed marriage in a moment if Betsy had shown any interest in him. But he just couldn't figure her out. Her perfume, her expensive clothes, her run down home – where did she get the money? It didn't add up. And then Betsey herself was the greatest mystery of all. She dressed with all the elaborate care of a seasoned seductress—applying red lipstick, shimmering eye shadow, sculpting her figure with tight undergarments, slipping into skirts and blouses that revealed as well as hid. And yet, she seemed completely oblivious of her effect upon Bob, upon *all* men. He watched her in amazement, this Christian temptress. He watched, he waited, he yearned for a sign.

Now, in the dingy Wichita café where it was about three o'clock in the afternoon, and the television was playing images of some far away, catastrophe—it looked like a movie, except for flashing subtitles saying 'News Flash…News Flash'. Betsy was leaning forward on the counter, gazing at the television.

Bob glanced at the television and saw what looked like parts of a football stadium on the screen. Bits of clothing were strewn about behind the earnest reporter, who was barking into his microphone. "Absolute massacre! Incredible! Barbaric!" Bob lost interest in about five seconds.

The intensity of the broadcaster's hysteria, however, seemed to catch hold of Betsey's mind. Those *poor* people!" she sighed. Bob thought that no human voice could sound that way. She was angelic.

Now the television had turned to an advertisement for dishwasher detergent and Betsy turned her gaze to Bob, her wide eyes brimming with compassion.

"There was a giant *bomb*! *Hundreds* of people have been killed!" she mourned.

"Where?" He asked politely.

"I don't know just where it was. Someplace in the Middle East. Maybe Israel?"

She would be leaving for Afghanistan next Tuesday. Bob had only four days to figure out some way to declare his love. His hand shook a little at the thought.

"What are you doing for dinner tonight?" he asked, as she passed him on her way to the ladies. She raised a finger to tell him to wait; she'd be right back.

She was gone for what seemed a very long time. Now, alone again for a few minutes, his heart beat a little more slowly; his soul was a little more peaceful. He had learned a good deal,—despite his motives. He reviewed what he knew, just in case his editor asked. She was twenty years old, and therefore still technically a minor; it was just possible that making love to her would involve breaking the law—he wasn't certain about the legal statutes in Kansas, about exactly when "statutory rape" became legitimate intercourse. He was from Nebraska and the laws change when you cross state lines. He must check his facts. In any case, he'd happily have waited until she was of age. She'd be worth the wait.

But back to the point. When you asked her, it turned out that she had had many, many boyfriends, or that she had never had any boyfriend at all—depending on what mood she was in and—probably—on how you defined "boyfriend." He was afraid to define it too explicitly; it was none of his business; yet at the same time nothing interested him more. Was she, or wasn't she, a virgin. He hoped that she was.

Betsey had been "born again" about two years ago, when she came under the influence of the man she called "My Pastor," the Mr Jones who was the main preacher at her church. He wasn't sure of the name or the denomination of that particular church. It was just Reverend Jones's Church. There was something not quite legitimate about it, he sensed. He'd learned that the Rev Jones was an "Adjunct Officer" at the Salvation Army, though he wasn't a member. The young reporter had met Rev Jones last week, and the older man had looked at the younger suspiciously. The reporter remembered feeling uncomfortably observed. Of course the minister suspected his motives; but Bob knew in his heart that his own intentions were pure—well, purish. He was sort of lying to his editor, but that wasn't important. What really mattered was that he would be marrying this girl if she would have him. There was no evidence that she would or wouldn't. The righteous Reverend only considered the moral side of things. Bob remembered the older man's gaze boring into him.

Betsey had been selected to go on the Jesus Mercy Mission Abroad by means of a contest that a group of local pastors had conducted. The ministers each headed up a church that belonged to some Protestant denomination that Bob Smith had never heard of before. One was Followers of Christ; a second was Disciples of the Early Saints; a third was The Flock of the Redeemer. There weren't any Lutheran, Catholic, Methodist or Baptist churches involved. The ministers had got together to run an essay contest. The young man's editor had emitted an epiglottal snort on being informed of this selection method. "Spiritual push-ups, eh?" he'd observed.

The Rev Jones had nominated Betsey. She'd written an essay entitled "Why I Want to Do the Lord's Work in Afghanistan." Somehow she'd known a bit more about Afghanistan than the rest of the contestants—she'd said she figured that was one of the reasons she had won the prize. She'd handed in a neatly computer-generated printout of her winning essay. He took the copy she'd given him out of his pocket while he waited for her.

Betsey began her essay with a quotation:
Knowledge puffeth up, but charity edifieth..
Then she wrote in her own words, which weren't at all that bad. She wasn't stupid. She knew her Bible—that was for sure. She knew it better than he did—though that wasn't hard to do.

> This is my plea to be sent to Kabul to bring some physical relief and the secret but intense love of Jesus Christ to the poor, suffering people there. It goes without saying that I would do the Lord's work discreetly if I were selected to go to Afghanistan. The Lord works in mysterious ways, so that I would have to do His bidding in a very special and even secret manner. The obvious things that we would do together—because it wouldn't be just me—would be the distribution of food and clothing and medicine. We'd limit ourselves to this activity, at least on the surface, because the people there don't like

> Christians. I do understand that. I am sorry for them, but we must forgive everyone who has not yet seen the Light and knows The Way.
>
> The people there are all Muslims and they believe in the Koran the way we believe in the Bible. And it says in the Koran that Allah will be merciful to the "unbelievers" like us. So we have to be generous to pagans like them. It just makes sense, doesn't it? What's fair is fair.
>
> So we have to practice charity. We must give till it hurts, otherwise there's no real charity. The greatest gift we can give is not what we own but who we are. We can give our time, our love, ourselves.

Bob wondered if she had any sense of the implications here. When his editor had read this passage, the old cynic had snorted again, chewing on his dead cigar, leering down at the suggestive page as if there were dirty pictures on it, instead of immaculate typescript. The cub reporter was offended and decided that he wasn't going to share certain things with the boss any more.

Betsey's essay ended with a quotation:

> *Now at this time your abundance may be a supply for their want, that their abundance also may be a supply for your want: that there may be equality.*[6]

He wasn't quite sure what this meant, but it didn't really matter. It was basically all just about charity. He looked up from his reading as Betsey emerged from the Ladies.

"Did you write this before the bombings in New York and Washington bombings?"

"Yes. But they make no difference."

He made a note. He was about to renew his invitation when she looked up over his shoulder and her face went round with pleasure. He turned, and to his sorrow saw that the Rev Jones was coming to join them.

The girl descended from the stool at the soda bar and more or less

---

[6] Smith, op cit, p. 21.

flowed around the side of the reporter, glowing with pleasure at the arrival of the older man.

"Rev Jones!" she purred, producing, his name in her infantile voice. "You've never come *here* before!"

"Theah ah whole loads a things you doahn know 'bout me, girl," the Rev. boomed in an exaggerated southern drawl. Bob realized that this was the public voice the 'Rev' used from the pulpit and on his radio broadcasts. It wasn't his real voice, and was quite different from the tone and accent the older man had used in his office, when interviewed about the Afghanistan Expedition.

Rev. Jones clapped his hand on the reporter's shoulder and squeezed the muscle until it hurt. "May Ah join you, suh?" stage-whispered the preacher.

"Of course," said Bob politely.

"Bahrtendah!" called the preacher in his stentorian tones.

"Reverend Jones!" squealed Betsey. "This isn't a *bar*!"

"Let's pretend, girl!"

"Oh Reverend Jones," she giggled.

"Bahrkeep!"

The old man who had served them up their milkshake and coffee, came shuffling toward the booth. He didn't notice Rev Jones's little joke.

"Ah'll have a beer," proclaimed the preacher.

"Reverend! What's come over you?"

The waiter's gaze moved on to Betsey.

"Nothin' wrong with a little bit of the elixir of life now and again—everything in moderation, girl. What'll you have, son?"

The reporter had a beer as well. Betsey said she was fine with her unfinished milkshake whilst the two men made small talk.

The Preacher was a handsome man of about fifty, who still had his full head of blonde hair, which hadn't a touch of gray in it anywhere. He combed it straight up and back from his high, square forehead. He had such big hair that his head seemed impossibly large. The Reverend Jones could have been a minor movie star. He sat erect in his seat, his shoulders back, sipping his beer with pursed lips. As he savoured the drink, he exhaled with satisfaction. This wasn't the first beer he'd ever had, the reporter realized. Betsey might not understand this, but he certainly did.

"Can Ah he'p you with yoah story, son?"

"I'm sure you could, sir."

O JERUSALEM

"Well, what's puzzlin' yuh? Y'all keep comin' back fuh moah. So what seems to be the problem?"

"There's no real problem, sir."

"Ah'm right glad to hear it. But Ah'd like to know what y'all are going to say down at the *Falcon* 'bout our Jesus Mercy Mission Abroad." The great—or at least large—man waited for his response.

"Well, I don't know that I'm going to say anything in particular. Just give the facts, sir."

"The facts, the facts. That's good. What are the facts?"

He recapitulated what he knew. There had been about fifty entrants from Kansas churches. The Jesus Mercy Mission Abroad contest was organized by Wichita churches, but administered by Rev Jones. They would be sending the winners off to Kabul to distribute relief supplies to the natives, who didn't have enough food and medicine. Betsey had won the contest by writing the best essay about why she wanted to go to Afghanistan. There were four runners-up, who might also make the trip. Betsey was the only girl.

They would all be staying in some little village near the mountains for six months. Betsey would have to dress like the native women in those big things like tents all around them, because the people there didn't want to see women. When they came back, the members of the Jesus Mercy Mission would be reporting on their adventure to their local congregations.

"Right, boy, right. Nothin' else now?" The Reverend seemed slightly suspicious.

But no. There was nothing else.

"Good, good." Another sip of beer. Another savoring sigh. "Son, y'all down at the paper know 'n' ah know—'n' Betsey knows too—how it's awful awful easy to make jes' a lil bit a harmless fun of a venture like this one tuh Afgannystan. The whole thing sounds sorta like a goody-two-shoes square dance to a lotta folks. It sounds like the worst kinda liberal do-goodin'. An' there's nothin' sillier in the whole world—at least to the members of your distinguished newspaper fraternity. We all know that."

"True. But the official editorial policy of the *Falcon*, sir, is to allow local stories their own dignity. You do appreciate that, I hope."

"Ooooh yeah," he sighed out his assent in a small symphony of vowels and a long exhalation that indicated just how relieved he was to be reminded of this great wisdom in local reporting. "Ah know, Ah know, Ah know that good ol' boy who's your boss. Known 'im for donkey's years.

He wouldn't've survived here in Wichita if he'd let all that cynicism of his show up in his print. Ah know. Ah know."

The two men each took several more contemplative sips from their glasses of beer—with the young reporter politely following the example of the pastor, and drinking only when the older man drank. Betsey sucked on her straw, wide-eyed. Then suddenly, with a slurping whoosh, she vacuumed up the last drops of her drink, swallowed and said brightly, "Praise the Lord for cherry milkshake!"

The Rev chuckled.

"This 'ere young gal here deserves the best, 'cause she is the best. Aren't you, Bets? You're the Best Bets." He actually put his arm around her shoulders and squeezed her, pulling her body towards himself. Bob's heart raced; his breath stopped.

"Sooo what Ah'd really like, really appreciate, would be the chance to sorta—how shall I say it?—well, just have a lil look at ya'll's story before it appears in print. Ya'll think that'd be possible?"

Betsey looked up at Bob expectantly. She smiled, shrugged. She'd known all along. That's all there was to it. How could there possibly be a problem with the Pastor's seeing a draft of the story? The reporter agreed. The issue was settled, problem solved.

But there was still more. "Now young man, Ah've been thinking. As you may perhaps recall, we've got our Seven AM Saturday radio show? We call that SAS? That's bright 'n' early tomorrow mornin'? Right?" Bob nodded knowingly to hide the fact that he'd never listened much to this radio show; he tended to be asleep at 7:00 am on Saturday mornings. But he decided to nod, as if he knew.

"Well, then, good. How'd you like to come on the show and tell us about what y'all've learned from our beautiful young friend here?" He squeezed Betsey up against his side again. His arm was over her shoulders, and his giant hand was dangling down in front of her breasts.

"The point would be to have the whole community supportin' us in Afgannystan. Betsey will be out there representin' Christian Wichita and not jes' Mah congregation. The Air Force Chapel, too, of course—and also the whole Wichita Synod. Y'know what a synod is?"

He didn't. Then Rev. Jones taught him. After that he did know what a Synod was—sort of. Betsey sat across the table, bent a little above her empty glass, looking up from under her lashes, with the Rev Jones heavy arm weighing down on her shoulders. Nothing else mattered much. Saturday morning it would be. He would be rescuing Betsey from the Rev.

Next morning, Bob went to find the sound studio at Rev. Jones' church, in a shabby but respectable part of Wichita. Much of the city was like that: simple, clean, unpainted, but somehow respectable. These were good, decent folk—not rich, but not poor. The land their houses were built upon had once been ploughed fields. The reporter arrived half an hour early, thinking of that gold cross, imagining a brightly colored blouse, the hem of a skirt, the toe of a pretty shoe. He found himself outside a long-unused grain silo, a large concrete cylinder with a door at ground level. Betsy dissolved and reassembled in his mind's eye, a kaleidoscope of desire made all the brighter by the bleakness of the gray morning sky and the grim back alley behind the church where he'd parked his car next to the 100-gallon oil drums converted to garbage cans.

There were two other cars on the gravel beside the scraggly hedge. The new one, a Cadillac, and the old one, a Chevy, both had a bumper sticker that said, "In case of Rapture, this car will be vacant." Bright-pink, cartoon-sized musical notes adorned the words.

He went up to the door in the silo wall and pushed. It opened. He heard her voice, her laughter, far above.

"Oh Rev. Jones, don't, don't . . . ." For a moment he had the disturbing image of the older man excitedly tickling the girl with a huge forefinger. Betsey was giggling like a baby. Yet there was something assured in her voice. He sensed how the young woman controlled the older man. 'No Trespassing!' said her girlish laugh.

"Hellooooo ...," he called up to them, to let them know that he was ascending the steel spiral staircase that had been installed on the interior wall of the silo.

"Helloooo ... " she mimicked back. "We're up *here*!"

As he came up through the trapdoor into the studio that had been installed in the top end of the silo, Betsey was just settling an enormous pair of earphones over her lustrous hair. The cord ran away from her head to a plug in a console, and she was starting to listen to something. The pastor was fiddling with a dial. The Reporter could hear the music, in the earphones. It was rock'n'roll, not a hymn.

"Now I told you to stop that, Rev. Jones," Betsey remonstrated again as if to a child.

O JERUSALEM

"Sorry, ma'am," he said and flicked a switch. A great organ blasted out an enormous chord. Its harmonies flooded out to Bob from Betsey's headset. Betsy smiled and sighed. "Praise the Lord!" she cried. It was 06:50 am and Bob wasn't sure if he was awake, or dreaming.

"Okaaay," breathed the Pastor, turning pages. "Here's your script, young man." He was using his normal voice. He handed Bob a typewritten page. There would be nothing unrehearsed in this interview.

The reporter got his headset, too, and then the organ music faded out, and a basso profundo cross-faded in. "Welcome to the Seven AM Show. It's Saaaturday mornin'! Rahse 'n' Shine! This is the voice of the Jesus Holy Missionary Church. 'N' Ah'm Reverend Robert Jones!" This was his public-speaking voice. "Today we all ah heah with Miiiiss Betsey Barndale, the winnah of this yeah's Jesus Mercy Mission Abroad Contest. This year the Proselytiiizing Pilgrimaaage will be on the Untrod Path to Afgannystan. To interview Miss Barndale we have with us a representahtive of ouah very own *Wichita Falcon*."

Barry White! Yes, that was it, thought Bob. Rev. Jones sounded like Barry White born again, reborn in a white man's skin. Then in the special voice he adopted for scriptural quotations, the Preacher said,

"Though I speak with the tongues of men and of angels, and have not charity, I am become as sounding brass, or a tinkling cymbal."

The Rev knew that the people he wanted to attract liked their preachers to be from somewhere down home, not too educated, not from back east or out west or too far up north. They liked their preachers like themselves. They wanted the Rev's hypnotic cadences in local lingo.

"Good morning. Tell us a little about yourself, Miss Barndale," said Bob, woodenly reading the words that Rev. Jones had written for him. She was Marilyn Monroe teaching a theology course. Bob imagined radios trembling, exploding as she spoke.

"And though I have the gift of prophecy, and understand all mysteries, and all knowledge; and though I have all faith, so that I could remove mountains, and have not charity, I am nothing," she whispered," in an utterly infantile voice.

Bob forgot where he was in the typescript and stared at her, trying to understand what she'd just said, who she was.

O JERUSALEM

Afterwards, when he'd descended the spiral staircase inside the silo wall, Bob was allowed the privilege of following Betsey home. He had said that he wanted to interview her family "for background." He didn't figure they would agree; but he seemed to have passed some test. Standing beside his baby blue Cadillac, Rev Jones waved goodbye to them—as if he had now decided to bless their union. Bob could hardly believe his luck. He was going to meet Betsey's mother. A plan began to hatch in his mind. He drummed his fingers on the steering wheel with impatience.

He followed her out through the square grid-work of orderly streets—each main road precisely one mile from the last. He cursed another driver who came between them; he trembled with impatience when a traffic signal turned red just after she had slipped through it. She didn't pull over to wait for him, but her left rear brake light was broken, so she was easy to follow. He caught up with her. He could read the bumper sticker that proclaimed her status as one of the Elect. The big, pink, musical notes were light-hearted, however; Betsey didn't take herself too seriously. Her proclamation that she was among the Born Again was somehow meant to be funny.

She led him away from the working class sector of Wichita where the church was located, out past the stockyards and slaughterhouse. Beyond Eight Mile Road the four-lane highway dwindled down to a two-lane blacktop. A few more miles later they approached a strangely shaped hill that loomed behind a "No Trespassing: US Government Property" sign. Just after the sign, she turned off onto a gravel road. They pulled over to let a tractor pass them, and she waved cheerily to the farmer. He wondered momentarily what it would be like to be a person toward whom the whole universe gravitated. What would it be like to enter a room and find everyone looking at you. Betsey was the center of attention, male and female, everywhere she went.

Road ruts jolted Bob out of one reverie into another. He imagined Betsey's body bouncing hard on the seat, imagined her breasts floating gently up and down. Finally, the two cars arrived at the little house by way of the back garden, coming in through a broken board gate into a yard littered with abandoned farm machines: a rusting eight-blade harrow, a detached snowplow grown over by long grass, a radiator from a car tilting into a puddle of water, a wheel rim, a crank-shaft, a pile of giant, rusted nuts-and-bolts.

O JERUSALEM

She hopped out of her car before him, and waited on the unpainted boards of the front porch beaming beatifically as he came across the yard.

"What did you think of Daddy's little playground?" she asked.

This made no sense to him, but he didn't want to admit it. He hesitated, and then decided to ask, "Is this your Daddy's farm?"

"Oh no," she giggled. She found the question very funny.

"But Daddy kind of manages the land we took the detour just around. Didn't you like his little garden with the big fence?"

Bob hadn't noticed any garden at all. Laughing at him, she turned and walked to the screen door, which was hanging loose on its hinges. She started to giggle again.

In the kitchen the radio was playing, loudly. " . . . *charity begins at home but it doesn't end there,*" Betsey cooed.

"Amen to that, sistah," boomed the Rev Jones. "As the Good Book says, *He which soweth sparingly shall reap also sparingly; and he which soweth bountifully shall reap also bountifully.*"

Betsey's mother was sitting with her hand on the dial, fine tuning the scratchy signal. The woman nodded and raised a finger for silence as the interview ended.

"Thank you very much for the interview this morning, Miss Barndale," Bob heard himself say on the radio.

"Ooooh, don't you just *hate* it? Your own voice?" Betsey hugged her own torso and shivered.

"OK, famous daughter," said the mother, with a flat, weathered inflection. "Get yourself changed now so's we can get on with things here."

Betsey left the room, and he could hear her steps up the wooden stairs, which creaked under her weight.

The woman who Bob Smith assumed was Mrs Barndale was the physical opposite of her voluptuous daughter: fleshless, severe, and husky-voiced from smoking cigarettes. She lit one now—an unfiltered variety. The older woman looked straight at him and did not smile. She pinched a bit of tobacco off her tongue, and then got right to the point.

"What do you want to know, Mr Reporter? Betsey says you want to know things about us." Then she got up and began work around the kitchen—wiping down the sideboard, putting bowls away, storing tableware in a drawer, waiting for his questions to begin.

He wanted to know about Betsey's father, but there was no way to ask about that. He would have to stick to the business of Betsey's trip to

Afghanistan. He asked how she felt about her daughter going off to the other side of the world.

"It's a free country," said Betsey's mother.

Was she worried about her daughter's safety?

She looked blankly at him, with one eyebrow raised, the way you do when you're talking to the village idiot.

Did she think Christians ought to go off to bring charity to non-Christians?

"Now there's a question," she agreed.

Betsey came back into the room, having changed her clothes. Her tight jeans made it hard to focus on theological questions. Bob tried to put himself into his reporter mode, taking mental notes about the clean, barren room. The floor was unfinished wood. The table at which they sat had one leg too short and was propped up by a wad of folded paper. The cutting board beside the sink had a broken corner. Above a cheap print on the wall, showing Jesus Christ looking like a hippy with long hair, the wallpaper was torn. A pot was cooking on the stove. He noticed a microwave oven beside the radio on the counter.

"See you're noticing the unfinished kitchen," said the woman of the house. "Sorry about that. But we've just had—what should I call it?—a domestic re-arrangement. We've just moved out here. Hardly had time to make things decent. And Betsey's father hasn't been much help either. Not sure how we'll pay the rent."

Bob hadn't expected this confession and didn't know what to say. Did she imply that her deserting husband was not Betsey's father? He found her watching him, and he looked away, embarrassed. "That's off the record, of course, Mr Reporter," she added.

"Of course, Ma'am."

"If I was a drinking woman, I'd take to drink now," she continued. "But I'm not."

"Do you want me to call Daddy?" squeaked Betsey. In the radio interview her voice had been *nearly* that of an adult woman. But now she seemed to have regressed into earliest childhood, speaking like an infant just learning language. It was very odd—and very erotic.

"No Miss. You leave your Daddy out of this. I'm sure he's got enough trouble without you and me landing on his doorstep."

With that, she closed the door on the subject, and the young reporter did not have the courage to try to open it again.

Betsey started to lay the table for a meal, arranging knives and forks and plates. The childish voice called out: "Oh but things will work out, won't they Mother? The Lord *will* provide."

"Amen to that," said Betsey's mother, who looked at Bob again, awaiting his next question, blank-faced, a strand of pale grey-blond hair trailing across her lean, ascetic face.

"Did you ever think your daughter would grow up to do missionary work, Mrs Barndale?"

"It's all down to who you meet," was her answer. She apparently referred to Betsey having met Rev Jones.

"Did you get to the bank?" she asked her daughter.

Betsey nodded.

The older woman's mind turned to immediate and practical matters. She adjusted the flame under the cooking pot. She had no obvious religious fervor in her soul. He tried a frontal assault:

"May I ask if you've been born again, Mrs Barndale?"

"You may ask." But she gave no answer. He didn't pursue it.

"You staying for Saturday lunch?"

He looked at Betsey. He was staying.

The cook accommodated a guest—without comment. There wasn't much Bob could learn from her. She was exactly what she seemed to be: a single mother running a household, raising her daughter, and working her job during the week. She wasn't going to tell him anything she didn't want him to know.

"Melissa!" she called out through the ceiling to the room above. "Come down for lunch!" So there was another child, another daughter. She was firm with her children, without ceremony, without sentiment, without passion, even without maternal warmth, but narrowly and clearly focused only on what needed to be done right now. Nothing in her ordinary manner even hinted at her heroic, spectacular daughter. "What I don't know, Mr Reporter, is how I'm gonna manage whiles Betsey is off on the other side of the world. I really can't quite see it. Rev Jones says that he'll find us some help, of course. We sure are going to need it. Sure are."

There was a terrible, slow, deliberate bang-thump-bang-thump-bang-thump coming down the stairs above them. Betsey's sister Melissa appeared in the doorway and it was clear that the banging sounds had been her crutches hitting the floorboards and stairs. She was missing one leg from the knee down. Otherwise, she was as lovely as Betsey herself.

After a time he even had the courage to ask if the girls were twins. They obviously were. He didn't have the courage to ask how Melissa had lost her leg. They were identical in face and figure—voluptuous, blonde. But in manner they were opposites. Betsey smiled brightly, constantly. Melissa was serious, calm, modest. She never seemed to look up at the world around her. Instead, she looked down at the floor, then down at her plate. She said grace in a traditional way, head bowed. Bob couldn't take his eyes off her until he caught Betsey watching him watch her sister with a brilliant smile on her face. He stopped gawking at Melissa.

Bob concentrated on the food, instead—not knowing what to say. It was deliciously ordinary roast beef and potatoes. He wondered if Betsey was a good cook. He imagined her in an apron making his dinner. For one instant his hand touched Betsey's forearm over the salad plate. The down on her skin was like an electric shock. Bob forgot all over again about being a reporter. He remembered only his plan.

Melissa spoke her first and only words, "Thank you for the delicious lunch, Ma'am. I'll go back upstairs to my reading if you don't mind."

"That's all right, Melissa," said her mother.

The terrible thumpings returned up the stairs and across the thin wooden ceiling above them. Again, Bob caught Betsey watching him. In a little girl's whisper she confided, "Melissa's just about finished. She's somewhere in Revelations. She's doing the whole Good Book. For the second time now."

When leaving, Bob decided to take the shortcut that Betsey had used—out across the fields. He drove until he was certain that he'd gone the wrong way: a chain link fence and a locked gate crossed his path. Signs said "US Government Property. No trespassing." He began to manoeuvre the car around to go back. A siren went off somewhere beyond some bushes.

He didn't know where they'd come from. It was as if they fell from the sky, like science fiction aliens: white-helmeted soldiers carrying rifles surrounded him. One of them knocked on his window, and he rolled it down.

"ID, sir," said the man.

He pulled out his driver's license. The soldier made a quick note.

"What is this place?" he asked the soldier.

"Sorry, sir."

"What's here that's so secret?"

"No can say, sir."

"You guys Air Force?"

"No can say, sir."

Another man appeared. He looked at the Reporter's ID, nodded, and said, "Exit's that way, sir," pointing up the track through the fields that Bob had just come along. His curiosity was aroused, however, and he tried to linger. But the soldiers weren't having any of it.

"But what is this place?"

"Off you go, sir."

He heard a clicking sound behind him. It sounded like the machinery of a gun. Another voice spoke.

"Now. Go. No questions."

He went. Fast.

Bob had never done anything this insane before. Here he was, on a flight to Istanbul. He unbuckled his seat-belt and walked up the aisle into the business class section.

She looked up at him from her cushioned seat, at first uncomprehending, with the peaceful smile of a dreaming infant. Only after her eyes focused did alarm come into her look:

"What are *you* doing here?" she gasped.

"Reporting on you," he said affectionately.

"Whaaaat?"

"I'm sorry, sir; but if you don't have a Business Class ticket you may not come into this section of the plane."

He left her, saying "Come back to me in economy class when you wake up." Whether she was sufficiently conscious to understand that he was actually on the flight and not just in her dream, he couldn't tell. He also couldn't tell how she had managed to get an expensive seat. Was the Wichita Synod paying for this? Perhaps his editor was right, and there was something corrupt here. Maybe he'd have a story to file. Maybe the *Wichita Falcon* wouldn't accept the resignation he'd left on the editor's desk.

When she came back to his part of the plane to say hello, she explained that the check-in clerk in New York had given her an "upgrade" to Business Class.

"Wasn't that just so sweet of that boy?" she proposed.

Bob could see what had happened. There was no doubt that it paid to be beautiful.

The plane lurched in the air just then, and she reached out to steady herself with her hand on his shoulder. He could feel her warm hand through his shirt.

She whispered in his ear, her long, light-brown hair falling against his cheek: "This is the first time I've ever been in a plane! Isn't it *exciting?*" He agreed. It was exciting. "So the newspaper decided to send you along to cover our mission! Isn't that wonderful!" He didn't correct her. He couldn't possibly tell her that he'd quit his job for her. He watched her sway up the aisle back to her luxurious seat. He developed a passionate hatred for a man two rows in front who craned his neck to watch her walking away.

In the Istanbul airport she was joined by other members of her Jesus Mercy Mission Abroad team. He expected to see Rev Jones. But the preacher wasn't there; four young men joined Betsey and together they constituted the whole party. Bob stood behind Betsey and took mental notes—the reporter's habit still functioning fitfully. Yes indeed. Maybe he'd file a story after all.

He bought an English-language newspaper called *The Turkish Daily News;* it wasn't bad. Every once in a while you could tell that the people who wrote the stories weren't native speakers; but you always knew what they meant to say. It was reassuring. The paper covered recent events, especially the mass murder at the Istanbul soccer stadium. Some young man had run onto the field and blown himself up, killing several dozen other people—including a couple of players. Bob remembered the first he'd heard of the event, sitting with Betsey in the café in Wichita. Now he was here in the city where it had actually happened. Being here made him feel a bit different from his American friends and family.

A man holding a UK passport stood behind Bob in the line up to the check-in counter for the Turkish Airlines flight to Kabul; Bob tried to engage the Englishman in conversation, with no success at all. Further up the long line, Betsey and her new friends were gaily chattering away, happy to be together. Suddenly two men wearing enormous white turbans pushed past the westerners and went straight to the desk, talking very loudly in a strange language, and ignoring the other passengers. They had their tickets stamped and their baggage checked before anyone else. The Englishman made a slight clucking noise with his tongue. A policeman carrying a submachine gun passed by, looking at the reporter suspiciously. Two very fat ladies wearing long gowns and shawls covering their heads waddled past, pushing in front of Betsey, and positioning themselves as next to be served. But the little group of American Christians didn't seem to notice, much less to mind. Bob looked at the Englishman and finally got fleeting eye contact, followed by the subtle raising of an eyebrow.

A man pushing a very wide broom came by. He was dead-faced, functioning but mindless. Bob nudged a smashed styrofoam cup that lay on the floor into the path of the broom, expecting the man sweeping the floor to somehow acknowledge the gesture of assistance. But the man's eyes never left his broom.

Finally, Betsey and her friends, still chattering away to each other, reached the counter where their tickets were stamped. He watched the two male clerks and realized that they were the first males he'd ever observed who didn't seem to notice anything special about Betsey. They didn't stare at her. They didn't even sneak furtive glances when they thought she wasn't looking.

Bob followed. His ticket was eventually accepted—though he felt that the clerk was reluctant to let him on the plane. His passport was inspected—and he had the feeling that the man thought he was traveling under a false identity. Then he followed in the direction that Betsey had disappeared.

Women wearing black masks that covered everything except their eyes sailed past, ignoring him as they pushed forward in the crowd that was slowly filtering through a second checkpoint that made him feel a strong presence of some invisible and powerful authority controlling everything it could. A man wearing a long beard and a black turban shouldered him aside. The man smelled of stale perspiration—or was it even worse? Bob tried to hold his breath as he stood in the line, allowing himself to be sucked slowly onward toward checkpoint. People all around him were touching him, rubbing shoulders, pushing him. It was uncomfortable.

Bob began to feel that he was in some danger, that every man or woman he met was a possible enemy. Part of the problem was his height—he was a foot taller than anyone else except the Englishman, so people could see him. He'd never had any feeling remotely like this before. The small, dark men pushing their way forward to passport controls and security checks all looked like terrorists. He knew they couldn't all be terrorists; but he felt that they were. He knew that he was experiencing what someone had called "Islamophobia;" but he couldn't help feeling under threat. The departures hall was chaos. Not one person smiled at him. The security officer who checked his passport and re-checked his ticket must have spoken a little English, if he was able to read the documents; but the man did not respond to the reporter's overloud "Hello." He stared at the young American, then stared back at the passport. His lips moved. He was reading every word. He even got up from his stool behind the counter, walked to the next stand, said something to his colleague at the next desk, showed him something obviously suspicious in the passport, and hesitated over and over, clearly not wanting to grant permission to travel. Bob lost heart. Betsey and her new American friends had just been admitted through the gate into the secured waiting area. She looked back at him and waved. He would lose sight of her perhaps forever if they didn't let him follow. But for a moment he actually hoped he'd be denied entry.

Just then the officer smashed the passport on the desk with a heavy machine and stamped the boarding card. Without looking up, he held the documents out toward the reporter. He was off to Kabul whether he liked it or not.

Betsey had disappeared. She'd been there just a moment ago; now she and all her friends had vanished. He stood still and methodically checked every person in the departure lounge room: five men with black turbans stood in one corner; six men with white turbans stood in another corner. The women in their long black gowns and masks stood by the window, and several sad-looking, obedient, defeated children sat on the floor at their feet. Leaning against one wall, four or five unshaven, dark men were obviously thinking about doing something desperate. The air was thick with cigarette smoke. He thought to ask one of the airline people where the other Americans had got to. But there were no airline personnel in the room. The old black-and-white films he'd seen on the television late at night when he was a boy had shown Arab women wearing veils; and they'd all been exquisitely beautiful under their diaphanous coverings. The actual women near him looked fatly misshapen. He tried to find someone who would make eye contact with him, and who might tell him where the other Americans had gone. But he got no eye contact. The women who weren't wearing veils all had light moustaches. Their eyes were dull. They didn't smile—not at him, not at each other, not at their children.

But then, suddenly, Bob found himself staring at a pair of beautiful brown eyes that actually looked back. It was Betsey, now wearing one of those head-to-foot coverings. She was wearing a mask that covered her mouth and nose.

"We have to wear this," she said in her baby voice.

He looked for evidence of her voluptuous body under the long black gown. He could see the vaguest outline of her shoulders and bust, but nothing more.

"It's awfully hot under here," she said quietly.

The urgent animal attraction that he had always felt for was gone. Why was he following this dark-robed person to the ends of the earth, he wondered. When he looked into her brown eyes again he knew why.

Then a disturbance around the entry door distracted him. A turbaned man was being led through the metal detector by two younger men. The man being led wore mirror-glass sunglasses, and was obviously blind. He shuffled through the metal detector, led by his young attendants. A little group of women and children scattered in front of the blind man's advance. He wore long robes that hid his shape, and something inside those robes set off the metal detector, so that the guard had to search him respectfully with a metal-detecting wand. Whatever it was that had triggered the alarm was immediately obvious to the guard performing the search. He seemed apologetic and immediately allowed the long-robed figure into the waiting area.

Was this an "Imam?" Or an "Ayatollah?" The man was short but enormous—his long robes and great turban seemed to contain vast but ambiguous volumes. He consumed space, required distance, and set up an invisible perimeter around himself. He and his party arrived in the center of the room and began to rotate until they reached a certain orientation that satisfied them. One of the attendants was carrying a cushion that he put down before the great blind man; another had a small rug, which he placed on the floor. Instead of sitting on the plastic chairs, the enormous man at first sat back on the cushion and then knelt forward onto the rug. He held his palms out and began to pray toward Mecca. The old man's three attendants took up positions on the floor next to him. Bob had never seen a public prayer before, but he recognized the activity—rhythmic, hypnotic movements. The praying went on for some time and the room was hushed. None of the other passengers joined in; but several of them stood and stared. The Englishman walked quietly to the window to look out at the runways and the gray sky—as if trying to ignore the praying. Bob looked at Betsey. She held her forefinger up to her hidden lips, and watched the praying, round-eyed. After he had stopped, the old man sat on the floor and stared blindly into the room around him. You couldn't tell what he knew about the people around him. The young men at his side kept whispering to him.

The public address system said something loud and intrusive and incomprehensible. None of the other passengers made any special movement. Instead, they sat. They waited. The time for departure arrived. Nothing happened. No one explained. There was no one to ask.

Then, as if from nowhere, more dark-uniformed policemen than it was possible to count suddenly appeared. They carried submachine guns that they each kept pointed at the floor. Betsey was pushed back against the wall by two startled women in long black gowns who had made way for the police. Officers surrounded the huge kneeling man in the center of the room, weapons at the ready. It seemed absurd. What possible danger could he be? Two of his attendants argued with the uniformed officers, waving their arms and shouting incomprehensibly, as they stood around their leader. Two men not wearing uniforms now came into the room, walking slowly. One was middle-aged, wearing an immaculate, dark blue western-style suit. The other man was younger, hard-eyed; he wore a gray, rumpled, western-style suit. The room became very quiet.

The younger, grey-suited man walked to the kneeling figure, looked down at him, took his older companion's arm, and gestured toward the blind man with a questioning look. The second man, in the elegant suit, studied the kneeling figure for a very long moment. He plucked strangely at his own sleeve. He looked around at the blind man's helpers. Carefully nodding at each. No one moved and no one spoke. They all just looked at each other. Finally, the dapper man raised his head, made a very audible clucking noise with his tongue, and rolled his eyeballs upwards. The younger man shrugged in disappointment, and said something in Turkish to one of the uniformed policemen. The intruding mob of law-enforcers filed quickly, politely, with perfect discipline out of the room, leaving the blind man kneeling on the floor.

"Hamdillilah," said one of his attendants.

Everyone spent several minutes thinking his own thoughts. After a time, someone came up beside Bob.

"I think they were looking for the man who master-minded the football bomb," the Englishman said quietly into the reporter's ear.

They were on the plane, in the air, headed for Kabul. He'd been seated next to the Englishman—as if the people making the seat assignments had known that the two western men would like to be together.

"The young man who came in after the uniformed police arrived? Remember? Gray suit? Unpressed? Badly cut? He is the Chief Detective." The Englishman somehow knew.

"They thought this blind guy masterminded the bombing last week?" whispered the American.

"Yes. If I understood the Turkish, the man who was with the Chief Inspector—immaculate blue suit, remember? Well, apparently he had met the head of the terrorist cell, and could have identified him—*if* this had been the fellow."

The knowledgeable Englishman paused and thought. "It was odd. That elegant Turk hesitated for quite a long moment. Maybe he did recognize the blind Imam. Or thought he did. Or didn't want to say he did. Who knows?"

"Why did they think it might be this guy?"

"Who knows? Most of these terrorist cells have a clerical nucleus. The Turks are experts at fighting this stuff. All started with Atatürk. Back in the 1920s and 30s. A military man. You see his picture in every café in Turkey. Compulsory. Fellow decided to make a modern nation out of Turkey. Succeeded, a bit at least. But had to combat Islam to make it happen. Or at least tried to. Religious totalitarianism's still alive and kicking though. Bombing football stadiums, things like that."

"What's wrong with live and let live?" asked Bob.

"Nothing. For you and me."

"But not for them?"

"Turkish friends tell me we're naïve. 'Can't let these people take over,' they say. 'They'll run your life for you. Come into the schools, the kitchen, the bedroom. Religious totalitarians.' Educated Turks tell me we need to watch out for that."

"So we have to tolerate *their* intolerance of the intolerant."

"Good boy! Something like that." The Englishman actually laughed. He looked about himself—as if to make certain that they weren't being overheard. Then he worked himself into his seat, tilted his head back and nodded off.

Bob decided to try to visit Betsey in the rear of the cabin. But a steward rose up from the seat beside the curtain that had been drawn across the aisle, blocking the way.

He returned to his seat.

"That was a mistake," said the Englishman, without opening his eyes. Bob hadn't realized that the man was awake.

"What *do* your young friends think they're doing out here?" he continued in a whisper, his eyes kept firmly closed and his lips hardly moving.

The reporter explained about the Jesus Mercy Mission Abroad. Bob explained that they weren't going to try to convert people. The Englishman moaned softly. They were just going to help give out food and clothing. Bob explained how Betsey was going to dress the way Afghan women had to.

"Oh my," murmured the man.

"Really. They're going to be very discreet. They're just doing good. That's all. Surely that's ok."

Silence. Then the Englishman asked: "And where are the people who organized all this?"

"Rev Jones is probably going to meet us tomorrow evening in the Kabul airport. That's what Betsey said."

"*Rev* Jones?"

"He represents the Synod."

"*Synod?*"

"Yeah. The group of church people."

"I know what the word means." hissed the Englishman, irritated.

Bob wondered what the Englishman was doing on this flight to Kabul, and in the ordinary course of conversation, Bob's inquisitive temperament would have impelled him to ask. But there was something about this whole experience that was causing him to feel a lack of self-confidence. He felt trapped, confined. He looked out the window and saw, far below, only pale yellow rock fading into gray in endless lines of mountains separated by endless, empty valleys.

Finally, they landed. There were two doors to the plane; the men exited out of the front door and the women out of the rear door. The wind flung the women's long gowns out sideways from their bodies, and as he descended the men's stairs, Bob tried to see which one was Betsey, but he couldn't tell.

The airport arrivals hall was a vestibule to hell, with broken plate glass in half the windows and no glass in the other half. "Abandon hope ye who enter here" would have been an appropriate welcoming motto. He tried to remember where that came from—someplace in the Bible? In any case, there was no motto anywhere that he could read. He stayed close to the Englishman. He caught no sight of Betsey. The women passengers were being dealt with in another room.

The Afghanis had all crowded forward, leaving the westerners to wait behind them. Betsey's four male companions were behind Bob, last in line. They were unsmiling, serious, respectful. The reporter heard one of them say, very quietly, "And though I bestow all my goods to feed the poor, and though I give my body to be burned, and have not charity, it profiteth me nothing."

The Englishman turned and glared at the young American.

Another one said, looking straight at the Englishman,

"Charity suffereth long, and is kind; charity envieth not; charity vaunteth not itself, is not puffed up."

"For Christ's sake, shut up!" the Englishman hissed through clenched teeth.

The four young Americans stared defiantly back. The Englishman's pale face flushed.

Things did not go well. Sometimes he forgot that he had resigned from the staff of the *Wichita Falcon* and consoled himself with the thought that he would have a wonderful story to file. At other times, he simply wished he was back home in Wichita, in his warm, comfortable bed. Now he lay shivering under a thin blanket, and dreamed of thick blankets. He ate from a metal bowl and remembered china tableware—about which he had never cared before. He looked at a wall made of uncut stones that were stacked up precariously atop each other, and he remembered walls of painted plaster and patterned wallpaper that he'd never really cared about. He remembered windows with unbroken glass. Here everything was broken. Nothing worked. Nothing was easy. He learned quickly that this was not the place for him.

And as for Betsey, he had no idea where she was. She had simply disappeared somewhere in the arrivals hall of Kabul Airport. What was it called? Did it matter? Why did he even think about it?

The Englishman had been helpful initially. He had the address of what passed for a cheap hotel, and he took the young American under his wing. They arrived, and at first were required to share a room with each other. Despite the intimacy that this enforced upon them, and which neither man wanted, the American never found out what the Englishman was doing in Kabul. Then, a few days later, the Englishman simply disappeared too.

Nor did he ever see Reverend Jones in Kabul. One afternoon Bob did encounter the four young male charity workers walking in the street. They'd all begun to grow beards, and they were wearing native cloaks over their western shirts and blue jeans. They looked dazed and disoriented; but when he asked them how they were they responded

"Very well, thank you."

"Never better."

"I'm just in love with this place, aren't you?"

Had they seen Betsey?

No. But they knew where she was. She was living with a family of Afghans and couldn't be visited by anyone male. How did they know this? An Afghan friend had visited the family, and had asked the father. He had assured them that everything was just fine.

"You believe that?"

"Why not, brother? These are good people."

"Amen to that."

"They understand what we're doing here."

"Amen to that too."

A cold wind whipped the dust into their eyes. They huddled together. Bob wished *he* understood what he was doing here.

"We've got God's work to do," said one.

"Amen to that."

"Peace be with you," they chimed simultaneously and walked off leaving the young reporter shivering, conspicuous, lost.

In a Darkroom

The Twin Towers fall. History—filmed by the losers—repeats itself endlessly. The Towers reconstruct themselves, and fall again. The airplanes crash into the towers, the towers fall; the airplanes reverse out of the towers and fly backwards into the sky above the Manhattan cityscape. Recordings make the past an eternal present. There is no chat, no music, virtually no machine noise. It is almost possible that no one is in the room, just automatic video machines playing and replaying the event, trying by means of some electronic miracle to undo the done.

Soon the shaft of light falls into the room. The Client follows. Somewhere in a corner someone has flicked a switch—now there are words.

"It was as was foretold. Thus has it been. Thus will it be. St John was told to write the things which thou hast seen, and the things which are, and the things which shall be hereafter."

Someone throws the switch: silence again. The young people breathe again. The Client stares at the movie silently repeating itself.

"That was Reverend Jones," says a boy's voice. "Listen to him."

"Alas, alas, that great city Babylon, that mighty city! For in one hour is thy judgment come. And the merchants of the earth shall weep and mourn over her; for no man buyeth their merchandise any more."

"New York as Babylon? Whose side was he on?"

"The Big Apple of Eden?"

"Rotten to the core?"

"This your man, Mr Client?"

"He's on my list."

"Love your friends, I do."

"Alas, alas, that great city, that was clothed in fine linen and purple, and scarlet, and decked with gold, and precious stones, and pearls!" The vast voice of Reverend Jones obliterates thought; only the images of the falling towers remain. "And I stood upon the sand of the sea, and saw a beast rise up out of the sea, having seven heads and ten horns, and upon his horns ten crowns, and upon his heads the name of blasphemy." A pause sounded static like the cosmic background radiation. "And the beast which I saw was like unto a leopard, and his feet were as the feet of a bear, and his mouth as the mouth of a lion: and the dragon gave him his power, and his seat, and great authority."

"He's got his animals mixed up," says another youngster. "Should have been some kind of eagle or buzzard or something."

"It's certainly a beast we're dealing with."

"As bad as Bechtel or Nestle?"

"And I saw one of his heads as it were wounded to death: and his deadly wound was healed: and all the world wondered after the beast."

"World sure has something to wonder about," admits one member of the staff.

"They're using the Bible to understand this? That's great. The prophets two thousand years ago really understood how airplanes could fly into buildings."

"Mah Brothahs and sistahs," says Jones in a voice slightly less full-throated than the voice he uses to read holy scripture, and much more southern, "the Good Book tells y'all that powah was given to the beast to make war forty and two months. That's three yeahs 'n' six months. So for three yeahs and six months henceforth we shall be at waah with these people. Brothahs and sistahs, the Good Book tells us soooo."

The Client shakes his head in dismay. "This kind of crap is responsible for that catastrophe. I'll bet the Koran gives its believers something a lot like leopards with crowns! The madmen who smashed into the World Trade Center were certainly high on something very similar to Revelations!"

"Aren't you a little carried away?" asks the older female.

"Me!? Who's carried away!? Me?!" He points at the screens. The room is silent as the Twin Towers collapse for the umpteenth time.

"And Christians call their bible 'The Good Book'! Good Book! Now this kook and the whole tribe of Christian idiots who believe this crap, who can't separate myth from reality, are going to get their fellow delusionaries all fired up to go out and kill a bunch of Arabs. Real Good Old Testament stuff."

The authoritative female speaks for the first time and says very deliberately: "Sometimes you're just like one of these prophets yourself, running around a waving your arms. You'd have been a good Jeremiah. Remember him?"

The Client laughs bitterly in a kind of choked cough, and shakes his head. His shoulders slump down. Then he straightens his back and sits up.

O JERUSALEM

"I am going to make this movie," he says, slowly pushing one fist into the palm of his other hand. "Help me?" It is more order than request.

"Pay us," is the counter demand.

Someone finally plays music—American Gospel, the sounds of solace. "Swing low, sweet chariot, comin' for to carry me home."

"Is this editorial?" asks the client.

"Nope. Just needed it."

Black out.

IV

NYC-JERUSALEM: SCIENTIST-PROPHET

Helen left Professor Friedman's office with a renewed sense of purpose. The learned man had explained something more about Hasidism so that she didn't feel quite so ignorant about it all. The Hasidim were still pretty strange, of course; but at least now she knew that they were actually not all *that* ancient. She'd always supposed, without thinking about it, that the strange men in black hats were from another time. But now it turned out that Hasidism was a fairly modern sect. They had started up in the 1700s when a man named Israel ben Eliezer was the first "Master of the Name." It was somewhere in Poland, Professor Friedman had said—she didn't remember just where. That did make more sense than the idea that the Hasidim were very ancient. After all, that black top-hat could not have been made in Biblical Babylon. So her subject was modern, then—not ancient. Somehow that made it easier.

Swinging the new pink handbag her mother had bought her, she walked as quickly as she could down a block of Fifth Avenue, feeling like a girl just out of school. At the same time, Helen was well aware that the present moment—call it an inflection point in history?—was a very troubled time. Under the influence of her wonderful professor, she knew that it might be important to learn how very strong Jews would respond to the world trade center and the Pentagon being bombed. Now she would see this weird Chaim again, and resume the interview that he had ended by walking out of the delicatessen. Somehow, Dr Friedman had managed to convince the Jewish fundamentalist to let her interview him again. Something had changed his mind. She guessed that the Professor's brother, the Rabbi, had been helpful. It was all about who you knew, of course, and Professor Friedman knew so many smart people. Also, people had changed since the towers of the World Trade Center had been blown up, so maybe that had influenced Chaim too? She didn't know.

But she was very pleased that her teacher thought she could still do the job—despite her failure with the first interview. He'd said it wasn't her fault, and to tell the truth, she couldn't think what else she should have said. In any case, now she was better prepared. Professor Friedman had explained to her about Rebbe Schneerson who had influenced so many Jews before he died. What a name! So strange! How did these people manage to look and sound so—how could she put it?—inhuman? (That wasn't right.) Atavistic? (That was a good word!) Other-worldly? And now the title wasn't "Rabbi" but "Rebbe." She'd try to remember that, to be polite. It was clearly the same word; she didn't understand why they had to keep changing the spelling and pronunciation. Like Negroes became Black People and then African-Americans, changing their category every few years. It confused you.

Perhaps she could explain how Chaim and people like him thought, what they felt, what they were willing to do, what they believed their "historical function" to be. Professor Friedman said that they had a strong sense of history—only it was future history, which was an odd contradiction in terms. Maybe she could ask Chaim to explain it. She was a bit worried about meeting him again, but her parents were paying a lot of money for her education, and in any case to earn her degree she had to conduct a research project, and this was the task her beloved Professor had assigned her. If she could just do it, her self-confidence might really improve. That would be wonderful. The Self Esteem Counsellor she was seeing every week would really be impressed.

Helen sat waiting in the same delicatessen as the previous week, listening to the same sounds of traffic and sirens outside, smelling the same odours of food, feeling that same sense of the fabulously rich complexity of New York. What a privilege it was just to be alive in this particular place, at this particular pinnacle of civilization and progress. The life of the city was so robust that it just went right on, even after the World Trade Center catastrophe. Remembered images gnawed at her mind for a moment. She did wonder, sometimes, why she subjected herself to the anxiety and trouble of writing a thesis. Why bother, when she could just be enjoying herself? Why deliberately make herself confront difficulties and unpleasant people?

Chaim was not on time. Watching the street outside, she found herself studying a muscular young man in a tight T-shirt, with a shaved head to which a yarmulke was somehow pinned. She wondered how they managed to keep their little round caps fastened on—especially when they had no hair. The man was having an animated conversation with a small, older woman. Helen noticed this woman especially because she had a terrible black eye and a bandage across her temple. Her gray hair and stillness gave her a dignity as she looked up at the young man in front of her. He was waving his arms, as if explaining himself to someone who couldn't understand, bending down towards her in an almost threatening way. She stared up at him, unintimidated, shaking her head from side to side. The conversation continued for a few more moments, then, leaving the woman standing on the street, the young man turned and came in through the revolving door of the deli where Helen was waiting. He walked straight toward Helen's table, and stared at her — somehow, he was familiar. Then she felt his gaze inspecting her body.

"Hello again," he said, irritated and thrusting his face close to hers after it was obvious that she hadn't recognized him. "It's me again." He breathed at her over the table and then sat down without being asked. After a few moments of amazement, she realized: those were the same dead eyes as before, only now the beard and long hair and strange long curls beside his ears had gone. Now he was clean-shaven, transformed. Had he stopped being Hasidic? Had his belief collapsed with the Twin Towers? Had he decided not to be a Jew any longer? Would her interview be worth nothing now? And would she have the courage to ask why he had been so rude to her the last time they had met? And why did he keep staring at her breasts? She found herself incapable of asking any of these questions so she just said.

"Chaim?" Her own voice sounded almost strangled.

"Correct."

The voice was familiar. His gaze remained fixed on her chest. She clutched the menu to her as before, but his dead eyes continued to stare right through it.

Again there was food on the table, which she had ordered without asking him. Again he refused to eat any-thing. She wasn't hungry but Professor Friedman had told her to try to get him to "break bread" with her.

It was a way of establishing a "communion," he'd said with a twinkle in his eye. It was like the French word "copain" for friend. A friend was someone you broke bread with. Well, so much for friendship, she thought. She opened her notebook to look at her prepared questions, but she didn't have to ask any. Chaim did all the talking. He talked, as if he'd been instructed to talk, was inspired to talk, had plenty to say and had an absolute duty to say it all.

"You delivered my tissue sample to your Professor?" he asked.

"You mean your little glass vial?"

"Correct."

"You delivered it?"

She had.

"You have the results?" he asked.

Now she wasn't sure what he was talking about.

"You don't have something for me from Professor Friedman?"

She did. The Professor had given her an envelope for Chaim, which she dug out of her purse and handed to him. He tore it open and read what seemed to be a few lines written on a piece of notepaper, which he balled up and threw at the ashtray beside the salt and pepper shakers on the table. The wad of paper bounced off the vase that held a bouquet of tired yellow-paper chrysanthemums and skittered onto the floor.

"Tell your Professor that I want the results quickly."

"Why don't you talk to him yourself?" she bravely asked.

"I have my reasons."

She made herself sip her revoltingly milky, sweet coffee, which was a little hard to do with the menu clutched under her chin. If only she had worn something baggy and unattractive. Maybe that would have helped? But that would be like wearing Purdah, she thought, having to dress in frumpy clothes just because odious men like Chaim existed.

"Well," said Chaim, "Let's get on with it. Here's what you and your Professor want to hear. Got your tape recorder playing? Ready?" He waited a moment. "Even in the act of murder there is divinity. Divinity exists in everything, everyone—even you. You just don't see it in yourself. But I can see it." He peered at her face. For a moment, he actually seemed to acknowledge her existence as a human being, albeit some kind of curious sub-species of female, non-Jewish person. Or maybe it was unfair of her to think he felt that. Maybe he was just one of those geeky people who was completely socially incompetent. That was possible. Sitting across from him made her doubt every perception she had. She put the menu down in order to take some notes, but instantly felt him staring at her breasts. She hurriedly scribbled something then retreated behind her laminated shield again. He'd waited a moment, impatient. "It's just that *in you* the spark is very dim, very small." He looked her right in the eye, but still without expression. "The divine exists in every act, in the act of eating." He made munching movements but did not touch the lox and bagel on the table in front of them. "It exists in the act of fucking." He said this as if to shock her, and she was indeed shocked that he should use such a word with a stranger, and with such emphasis. "The little divine bit of light flickers up when you pay your money for this lunch that I won't eat." He made a paying gesture with his hand. "A divine spark lives even in the Negro criminal who steals things and beats people up here in New York. A spark flickers even in the Palestinian suicide bomber who murders us." Now he was whispering to her, as if conveying a terrible secret. "Indeed, for the bomber who kills himself and us, the spark is very bright indeed. He doesn't know it. He never imagines it. But he kindles a fire that lights the path to the place of the Coming of the Messiah." His dead eyes, usually narrow, widened theatrically and condescendingly to impress upon her the importance of what he said. Did he think her very dim?

"How do you know all this?" she ventured to ask, poking uncomfortably at a slice of tomato.

"I *feel* it," he said.

"But feeling isn't knowing," she whispered.

"You are wrong. Feeling is *better* than knowing. Feeling is simple. Knowledge is always complicated. People who only know things cannot act. But people who *feel* . . . *act*." He clenched his fist and studied the muscles in his forearm, flexing them. "This problem of emotion is what my scientific education never taught me. I've only just now understood it. I always thought that emotions weren't as important as knowledge. But recently I've begun to understand something: feelings are what make us tick. They are what make us *do* things, as distinct from understand things. And now we Jews must do things; we must feel. And what we must feel "—here his voice sunk to a whisper—"is *vengeance*."

She glanced at her tape recorder, which was still running. She hoped it was getting this. She would play it to Professor Friedman.

"That isn't what all Jews believe," she ventured. She was being a little perverse with him. But he provoked her.

"Well the world has changed a bit since Moses," he observed. "I have performed my *devekut* and have discovered my purpose."

"Your what?"

He spelled it out for her, and waited while she wrote it down: "d-e-v-e-k-u-t." He explained. It meant concentration, meditation. Focus on God.

"So you have some personal relationship with God?" she asked.

He sneered. She didn't know why. She thought of Rabbi *Schneerson*— *Rebbe* Schneerson. Did he sneer too? Perhaps it was something to do with Hasidism? She would ask Professor Friedman. She wished he was here or rather that she was there, in his office, safe. This was all extremely unpleasant. She wished the interview was finished. She wanted to leave. She wished he'd stop staring at her like that.

"Have you read what you call the Old Testament?" he continued.

"A little," she admitted. A dish clattered.

He sneered again. "Since I saw you last month, I have been reading and reading. I have read Torah ten times. I have read all night and all day. I have stayed awake by putting my feet into ice water at midnight, just the way the first teachers did. My window on the indwelling Presence is open now. The winds are blowing through me to the world."

He took a deep breath, as if his heart were racing. She tried for a moment to imagine what was going on in his mind, but really couldn't understand him at all.

"I learned a little something in English for you today." He closed his eyes and recited:

"And it came to pass in those days, when Moses was grown, that he went out unto his brethren, and looked on their burdens: and he spied an Egyptian smiting an Hebrew, one of his brethren.

"And he looked this way and that way, and when he saw that there was no man, he slew the Egyptian, and hid him in the sand."

He opened his dead eyes and stared straight through her. She glanced at the tape recorder and saw that it was turning quietly. That was about the only reassuring thing in her life at the moment.

"That's Exodus. The story of Moses in Egypt," he said

"So you are like Moses?" she ventured. "Isn't that a little . . . a little . . . " Words failed her.

"Correct. At least I can act." He looked at her with that dead face of his, giving nothing of his inner life away, except what he chose to reveal by words.

"I see the unseen, hear the unheard, know the unknowable."

A metal pot clanged in the kitchen. A horn sounded on the street. The tape recorder clicked. She saw him glance down at it, and realized that he was speaking not so much to her as through her to Professor Friedman. As a non-Jew and a woman at that, she was a kind of unperson to him; but at least her professor was a Jew, a real person and therefore worth communicating with. She was simply a medium. She knew she lacked self-confidence, but now she felt as if she lacked a *self*, too.

"Last year, my mother was robbed by some damned African." Chaim continued. "I will find that man who robbed her. And then . . . ." He clenched his fist.

"Just yesterday, she was mugged again on the street. Again by a black boy."

"The woman I saw you talking to was your Mother?" she asked.

"Correct." He stared into her eyes, defiant, as if waiting for her to question, or doubt, or comment. She couldn't say anything at all. "And the woman you saw is Albert Einstein's daughter. She has come to this—abused by thugs. The daughter of the greatest man the modern world has ever known punched in the face by an ignorant slob. And you do realize that Einstein may well have been the Messiah, only no one thought of that at the time?"

There was no response to make.

"Correct?" he demanded.

"I'm sorry. I don't know."

"Correct." He answered his own question.

"And many Jews died in the World Trade Center last month. But we will no longer be victims." He looked at her hard, and she felt for a moment that he was blaming her personally for everything that had gone wrong for Jews for the last two thousand years. "The blood that runs down the walls will no longer be ours. It will be theirs. We will fight back. And everyone who is not a Jew is a Nazi Arab."

He stared her up and down, making her shrink into her skin. He was a rude, disgusting man. Perhaps it came from his misery, or his obsession. Or maybe that was the way men in his world *always* looked at women—non-Jewish women. They wouldn't dare look at their own women so lasciviously. But Helen wrote none of this down, of course. She took no further notes.

"I will use all my science as a Rising Jew. I will bring on the end of the material world with material knowledge. I have chemistry and physics in my soul, and I shall mix them with the oxygen of my faith. Now that I understand what is needed . . ."

*C**hemistry and physics in my soul, and I shall mix them with the oxygen of my faith. . . ."* Chaim's voice repeated.

"Simple identification with the aggressor. But actually quite mad," said Professor Friedman, pushing the "off" button of Helen's tape recorder. "What is the world to do with a poor mystical soul like that?" He shook his head mournfully. She found herself shaking her head in harmony with her beloved professor. . "The poor boy! And you say he's shaved his beard and sideburns?"

"Yes. And he was wearing a tight t-shirt the way that low-class boys do on the street, to impress their girls."

"Or the other boys," said the Professor, *sotto voce*.

"But he's heterosexual."

"How do you know?"

"I know." There were a few things she understood that her Professor didn't, couldn't.

He looked at her with concern for a moment, and then breathed one of his long, meditative vocalizations: "I seeeeee." He stroked his little goatee and shook his head. "What is the boy up to? Renouncing Hasidism? What will his poor mother say?"

Helen remembered the woman on the street. She told Professor Friedman about her black eye and bandage.

"Yes. I know. Just yesterday Rabbi told me what happened." This was the Rabbi through whom the Professor had arranged the interviews. He was some kind of extremist. She wasn't sure what kind. But he had decided that Meir Kahane and the Jewish Defence League had not been clear-thinking and militant enough. When Meir Kahane died, this Rabbi had established the Jewish Offense League as "a further step in the right direction," said Professor Friedman, obviously quoting the Rabbi, but with heavy sarcasm. Sometimes they called themselves "Rising Jews." Apparently Chaim had joined this group.

"With Rabbis like this, we hardly need Islamic Arabs for enemies," he sighed. "September eleventh murdered reason. Now we see the resurrection of...of what rough beast? Of ancient horrors brought back to life from dark caverns within our souls."

Light from a high window fell into the dark study with oak panelled walls. Professor Friedman stroked his goatee and tilted himself back in his creaking leather chair. She had learned to love that sound, which meant that her teacher was thinking. This was what being a student was all about: sitting in the presence of someone cultured, erudite, who saw clearly, thought deeply. Around her master towered piles of books and learned journals; to one side of his desk the stack of students' papers, typed manuscripts, newspapers, magazines, grew into skyscrapers. Sometimes they cascaded down. When a pile fell, the old man would putter around, putting things back into some kind of order. But somehow the order of his mind never collapsed. He could always find answers, historical facts. He would see patterns, meanings, where no one else did.

But today he seemed stumped. He slumped down and wriggled in his chair like a restless child. For a moment, Helen thought he was going to break down in tears, so mournful was his face.

"Two-and-a-half-thousand years of history and even a bit of wisdom, and he has to go invent himself a new religion. Heritage is not enough. Not enough for our Chaim. He has to choose an aberration, create his own perversion. Half the Hasids don't even think Israel should exist. He's brought up Hasid. But he joins up terrorists who terrorize the terrorists. He leaves Hasidism for some improvement on Judaism. He knows the truth. No one else knows it. But he does. Isn't that wonderful." He was mourning. "His poor mother. I wonder what she knows."

Remembering suddenly, Helen asked, "What was in that little glass vial that he asked me to give you."

"Oh my girl, my sweet girl." He shook his head. She waited. He obviously didn't want to say, and just went on shaking his head.

"What was it?" Helen insisted.

"It was tissue."

"Tissue?"

"Yes. Human flesh."

"What? Whose?"

"His own."

"Why did he give it to you?"

"My girl, my girl."

She loved being called "my girl" in that paternal way of his.

"He wants us to prove that he's Einstein's grandchild."

"He said something about that. But why?"

"I guess because he thinks that if he is the offspring of a great genius, he will be himself entitled to greatness. Delusion of grandeur."

Helen stared at her teacher, not quite understanding.

"But how are you going to prove he's a direct descendant of Albert Einstein?"

"His note to me reminds me that Einstein's brain was preserved in a jar when he died. It would be possible to take DNA from that source and match it against Chaim's DNA—possible in theory at least."

"Can you do this?"

"I don't think so."

"So why does he think that you can?"

"Well, his Rabbi has told him that I know someone at Princeton, where Einstein worked, who just might be able to convince the authorities to permit a quick test."

"Are you going to try?"

"I don't know. It seems ridiculous."

She had to agree. What difference could it possibly make if this poor boy, as the Professor called Chaim, was the son of the illegitimate daughter of Albert Einstein?

The New York City Police realized nothing. A young black man died, his neck broken in an alley. There was no suspect. The usual mantra, "drug-related crime," got repeated—by the detective. The victim's mother wept—but even she was somehow unsurprised. Then another black man died, a week later—his neck broken in a similar way. Another detective investigated, thought "drug-related," made notes, turned his attention to other problems. A third man had his neck broken. The first detective investigated, noticed the similarity to the first murder, but said nothing, not even to his partner. There was a small notice in one newspaper for the second murder, but not for the first or third.

> The corpse of a black male, aged approximately 18, was discovered last night in an alley off 113th Street. No identification was possible. Pending the Coroner's Report, death was apparently by means of a broken neck.

Helen and Professor Friedman did not even know about the murders. Such people don't read that part of the newspaper. Only a major, front-page murder would ever get their attention. They spent their energies considering the awful madness of Chaim's theology. They considered how sick the subject of their study had become. They read a little, talked a little, thought a little. But mostly they went about their daily business and lived their ordinary lives.

The Professor read the beginning of Helen's thesis and talked to her about the problems that it raised. "My girl, I don't know if you should say that Chaim is 'sick.' Perhaps you should say that he has become 'evil.' Go back to the old ways of thinking. Evil used to be the explanation for everything that went wrong in the world but now sickness has replaced evil." He sighed. "Doctors and psychiatrists are the new rabbis. The virus has replaced the Devil. Some kind of evil organism has infected people and made them not themselves because modern civilized man is essentially good. That's what we think today. Or used to. Until just a little while ago."

Helen made a few notes. She drew a picture of the Devil, with horns sticking out of his head, then an equal sign, and a diagram of an amoeba. That was about the best she could do.

"It's all a mess," he mourned. "My girl, my girl, it's all a mess, the way we think today. Or rather don't think. Calling it sickness doesn't help. There is no remedy for Chaim. Or the Twin Towers people. We can't use a metaphor to cure a metaphorical disease—except in our imaginations. Our analysis is all just figures of speech. We're not dealing with the thing itself, or the people, or their acts. It's not reality. It's mere poetry. Nothing more. Smoke, wind, vague odors."

Far beneath them, like the sound of distant Atlantic surf heard from a high cliff, the traffic raged up and down Manhattan streets. The Professor had left his window open a little, as usual, and you could hear the world outside, far away, unthreatening, almost comforting in its distance. Helen retreated further into her comfortable easy chair.

Meantime, Chaim is loose in the city, murdering anonymous strangers just because they are young black men. Chaim gets to be good at death. He improves, develops technique. It is not his purpose to get caught because all this is just practice for the holy mass murder that is taking shape in his mind.

Every day he imagines a young Arab wearing a red-and-white checked head dress. Sometimes the figure that Chaim sees is holding a knife; sometimes he is holding a hand-grenade; sometimes he is holding a

Kalashnikov. Sometimes the figure sneaks around a corner. Sometimes he lurks on a rooftop. Chaim sees the man's dark face, his heavy beard not shaven for a week but not fully grown. Chaim grasps the young man by the neck and snaps it; Chaim slits the boy's throat; Chaim bashes in the Arab's skull. Then he returns to reality, takes a deep breath to slow his pulse and proceeds to make his arrangements. His moment of hot hatred goes cold.

He is quite rational, systematic. He knows that if patterns emerge detectives may detect him; so he varies his *modus operandi*. He murders one man in Seacaucus, another in Boston, a third in Atlanta. He is branching out, spreading his reach. The detectives in Seacaucus might talk to the detectives in New York; but the police in Boston are not likely to trade notes with the police in Atlanta.

The obvious thought crosses Chaim's systematic, inspired mind: all his sacred murders have occurred on the East Coast. To protect his anonymity, which is essential to his purpose—he must go to Cleveland, Detroit, Chicago, Los Angeles. His murders occur in the Midwest, in the West, and in the South. They vary in method, not always breaking their victims' necks. He has killed with the knife; he has killed with the gun; a favorite method has become the small bomb attached to the ignition of the victim's car. The victims are always young African Americans. Many, but not all, are Black Muslims, followers of Elijah Muhammad. Gradually various computers in various cities and states begin to "talk" to each other, and one or two murders have highly similar characteristics, so that a few detectives in widely spread locations begin to suspect that some itinerant madman is to blame. But none of the victims knows his assassin; none of the victims knows the other victims; no two of the victims live in the same community. Most—but not all—are Islamic. So Chaim, and only Chaim, knows what is happening.

But soon this must change. The world must know. He is ready now.

Chaim remembers Helen and her Professor. Helen receives a scrap of paper in the mail. The envelope has no return address, but is postmarked New York City. The note is unsigned. It says,

To me belongeth vengeance, and recompense; their foot shall slide in due time: for the day of their calamity is at hand, and the things that shall come upon them make haste.
 This in English for the little shiksa
 P.S. What of my DNA test?

O JERUSALEM

Helen is studying for an examination and fails to take the scrap of paper to her Professor. She has no way to answer the subject of her dissertation.

Chaim has now purchased his ticket and put his affairs in order. He sees his nightmare Arab every day: his dark eyebrows and unshaven cheek, his slumped shoulder and furtive walk down the alley between buildings made of ancient stone. He leaps upon his imaginary terrorist, and bashes his head with a satisfying squelch of soft brain tissue against the ancient stone of the wall. He breathes deeply and thinks calmly again; then he sends Helen another message:

Little Shiksa—
If I whet my glittering sword, and mine hand take hold on judgment; I will render vengeance to mine enemies, and will reward them that hate me.
Chaim Einstein

This time, Helen is thinking of other things. She has met a young man who interests her, and she thinks of little else for two days, until she learns that he is married. Then she retreats into herself, desolated, and although she emerges in good spirits a few days later, another week has passed and she has not communicated with anyone about Chaim. The Rising Jew takes his flight to Tel Aviv. Helen has saved both notes. She meets Professor Friedman, who has also received a single quotation—his in Hebrew. He puts Helen's notes on his desk, and places his beside them.

"No. Wait. Who's speaking? Who does Poor Chaim think he is? Let's see. Where's my Pentateuch?" The books go shuffling about, the papers falling, the dust is stirred. "Now where are these passages? I know I recognize them. Definitely Torah. Let's do it the easy way. Where's my concordance?" Books shuffle across the desk, and Helen waits quietly, a little bored, a little impatient, thinking mostly of the man who had betrayed her.

"Who does poor Chaim—wait, is this it?--think he is? No, not here. Foolish book," he scolds his scholar's tools. "Foolish little book. Awful great book. Barbaric Old Testament. In what forest of words has our Chaim lost his way, his mind? Now behave yourselves," he orders the dusty children on his desk. His lips still move but the sound has faded.

The light falls from the high window like a halo upon the white head of this wise man. Something in her heart is deeply perturbed; but the sense of peace in this place is powerful. She settles into her comfortable chair and waits. She almost weeps with gratitude at being here.

Her Professor apparently finds what he is looking for. He mutters over the text, following with a finger, his lips moving.

Hebrew comes out of him in little bursts, dying away with consideration. Then he remembers Helen, and English emerges,

And Moses spake in the ears of all the congregation of Israel, the words of this song until they were ended.

"This all looks like Moses. But Damn—," he whispers—"But this is so complicated. But, but . . . I should have been a Biblical scholar, not a social philosopher. What is it that Chaim's got hold of? It's vengeance. That we can see. But what is his particular confusion? Whose voice does he hear in his head? Whose?"

Suddenly Helen feels guilty that she hasn't been paying enough attention. She comes out of her stupor, and thinks clearly for a moment.

"Professor Friedman?"

"Yes Helen. One moment, please."

"No. Professor, I think it doesn't matter what his problem might be. I think we should notify the police. We know he's a psycho."

He stops, looks up, stares at her with recognition. He thinks. He picks up the telephone and hands it to her across the desk.

Now Helen hesitates. Is this fair? Should she be alerting the authorities to the existence of a madman just because he is mad? He hasn't done anything that she knows about.

"Well, maybe not . . . "   She hesitates, and never makes the phone call. Is it a crime to think you are Albert Einstein's illegitimate grandchild? She doesn't think so. She does nothing.

For his part, Professor Friedman spends an afternoon trying to figure out just whose voice the reader hears in his head when he reads the lines of a sacred text like the one that Chaim has copied out and mailed to him and Helen. He worries if the speaker is Moses, or God, or some disembodied being like the omniscient narrator of a novel. He philosophizes to Helen and even more to himself about the meaning of the passages that Chaim has selected. Holy text was never the subject of his scholarship; he never intended to become a Rabbi. He left that to his older brother. Maybe he should call Chaim's rabbi, whom he once met through his brother, and ask who is speaking the lines his deluded disciple has quoted. But Professor Friedman doesn't like his brother. He never calls him to ask. He certainly dislikes Chaim's Rabbi. And for now, his attention drifts to other problems. In the fog of thoughts the danger of Chaim drifts into forgetfulness.

Chaim's mother has noticed that he's acting strangely, that he's out of town frequently; but she's had her own sorrows and never dreams that she's mothered a one-man vengeance machine. So Chaim goes undetected.

And soon Chaim himself takes flight to Israel. His mother learns where he sighs with relief. Now he will be safe, with his own people. A good Jewish boy needs his own community around him.

Chaim, however, has his own plans. His violent black youngster who deserves violent death vanishes from his day-time reveries. Instead, the Palestinian who plans to send a rocket into Israel is lurking over his launching pad when Chaim lands on his back with hob-nailed boots, smashing his head against the casing of the launcher. The Arab boy's blood oozes down the leg of the rocket stand. Chaim experiences a thrill of pleasure. The Old Testament rings in his ears. He sits on the airplane, eyes closed, body rigid. Chaim imagines a mob of Palestinians carrying weapons: rifles, grenade launchers, rockets. Under the dull roar of the jet engines he hears: *Woe unto the inhabitants of the sea coast, the nation of the Cherethites! The word of the LORD is against you.* The red-and-orange sunset behind the airliner catalyses a searing fire of explosion above Chaim's hostile mob. A mushroom cloud rises toward the sky.

The plane lands in Jerusalem.

In a Darkroom

Skyscrapers implode, explode, tilt, totter and plunge on every screen. No tall building stands safe in the sky.

"Now come our final days," croons the androgynous voice.

"There goes the Sears Tower," one mournful voice observes. "Steel and concrete rain down on the windy city."

"Let's have our anthem," suggests a voice. If Deus doesn't have a policy, at least let's have a song.

Organ chords sound. A male voice begins to sing, at first very softly: "Mine eyes have seen the glory of . . ."

A building leans slowly to one side, its silhouette crossing before an outsized moon. Its fall is slow. Flung from the building into the sky, a body flails its arms and swims toward death against an orange sunset.

"That Pittsburg?"

"All the tall buildings come tumbling down."

The Battle Hymn of the Republic grows louder and the disembodied voice sings ever more triumphantly: "He is trampling out the vintage . . ."

The door opens and the Client enters, panting. He has to catch his breath before he can speak.

"Where the grapes of wrath are stored
He hath loosed the fateful lightning."

"What the hell is happening?" the Client interrupts in a gasping voice.

"World is ending. The crazies were right."

"Of his terrible swift sword . . . " The sounds of marching feet provide accompaniment to the song.

"Here comes Dallas!"

A glass-and-steel image smokes and crumbles.

"Glory, glory hallelulah, glory, glory hallelulah," comes the hymn, still louder.

The Client has caught his breath. His face is lit by the screen he leans toward. "Wait a minute, just a tiny fraction of time. You guys are making all this up! A movie all your own. Are you highjacking the whole world's mind?"

"Ah-hah! Eureka!"

"Some people think they know what's real."

"Some people really know what's real."

"And dreaming makes it real."

O JERUSALEM

"Soo o o o " breathes the Client, exhaling. "It's real that you're imagining it. The world is ending in your dreams. You create dreams?"

"Maybe soooo . . . ." croons the Androgynous character. "Maybe so."

Mine Eyes have seen the glory
Of the Coming of the Lord
He is trampling out the vintage
Where the grapes of wrath are stored
He hath loosed the fateful lightning
Of his terrible swift sword
His truth is marching on
Glory, glory hallelulah
Glory, glory hallelulah.

V

A SACRED CHILD

Just a few months after the skyscrapers fell, an absolutely unbelievable event occurs. It's the kind of momentous appearance that sacred scripture records for all eternity: a magical child walks into the world. He's about three feet tall. He wears saffron robes. His head is shaved so that his rounded skull has an especially infantile quality—although he's not precisely an infant. He's a cartoon baby. He's quite extraordinary to all concerned except one little Hindu community near Benares, India, where he is actually rather ordinary. In the Ashram it's quite common practice for impoverished but idealistic families to give their children to the monks. But in the Western—and especially British—media there is a motif of moral disapproval when they report on this story. The tabloids in London at first imply that the child has been sold into religious slavery. The subjugation of the child's individuality to the discipline of life in an Ashram only increases sympathy for him. On the world's television screens he is the ultimate wonder: tiny, brightly colored, clear-speaking. He appears first on Indian television, with his simple message in Hindi: "Peace or death; this is our choice. Especially Hindus, Jews, Christians and Muslims must choose."

The child says it in English, Hindi, Telegu, Gujarati, and even Urdu: "We all must make peace. Or we die."

The television pictures show the child's room, the barren walls, the simple mattress on the floor. He leads an ascetic, holy life. And he is only—how old? No one knows. The adults in the monastery smile mysteriously when asked about the child's age, name, origin. He might even be an old man who is very small, pretending to be a child.

Though he appears to be prodigiously fluent in several languages, when the cameras are rolling and the microphones live, the nameless child says nothing but this: "we must make peace or perish." He has not memorized the words exactly, but speaks the idea a little differently each time. Yet it is always the same idea, a variation on the theme of global salvation: *peace among all people or death for all humans.* It is really not possible that he has simply memorized sounds in languages he does not understand. Doubters suspect that someone may be training him to perform, like some intelligent animal, constantly reprogramming him. Or maybe the child is genuinely able to think and say these things. Nobody is certain about anything, except what the Child says: "Death or Peace. Peace or Death. We must choose." And no one can quite say just how and why this particular little being has become so suddenly famous.

The *Hindustan Times* gives a little more depth to the story, though they are not able to discover the boy's parents. The reporter is responding to the charge that the child is not just an orphan, but has been abandoned or, even worse, sold into the monastery by unloving parents. This is a false accusation that will be made by westerners who do not understand Mother India. What matters, of course, is the message of peace, and the warning against war.

Other Indian newspapers pick up the story, which spreads throughout the Subcontinent. Editors smile mysteriously and print the photograph of the round head of the child who proclaims the logical necessity of "Peace or Perish." Soon it becomes apparent that the nameless boy has somehow also learned Hebrew, Arabic, and English. Perhaps it is only because he has watched television broadcast in these languages. He clearly knows what is happening in the big world arena. A wandering free-lance reporter with connections to *The London Times on Sunday* appears on the scene. He is stuck for a story just now because no military murders in Kashmir have occurred for almost two weeks during a lull in the spasmodic border war. From the point of view of the local people however, it seems the itinerant British reporter has appeared as if by magic in the little village Ashram near Benares.

The reporter is no mystic, no pilgrim, no believer in anything much. Instead, he is a sceptic—a rational doubter—as his prose asides make repeatedly clear. "If one supposes," he sometimes begins his paragraphs. "The faithful believe," he reports, suggesting that he is not among the faithful and therefore deserves credibility in the world's faithless circles. He interviews the boy, and files a story. In his view, the child has decided to do what the United Nations, the Pope, all the Archbishops, all the Imams and all the Rabbis rolled together have all failed to do—or even tried to do. The boy wants to get the world's leaders together to work to control the madness that has begun to take over the world. Adults in the Ashram can be seen in the background of a photo in the *Times*: they are smiling; they may even be laughing; they seem to encourage the media feeding frenzy.

The nameless child has what the *Times* reporter calls "more than his fifteen minutes of fame." Soon, the Englishman suggests gloomily, the child will vanish. But the boy uses his moment on the world stage. He makes a very brief, impromptu speech in English into the reporter's tape recorder. He refers to several of the most recent atrocities committed by the Palestinian Liberation Army, the Provisional Irish Republican Army, the Egyptian Islamic Jihad, the Israeli Defence Force, the United States Military, and—for obvious good measure—by certain Hindu extremists. Then he says, "This must stop or we will all die." Afterwards he will not respond to the reporter's questions, but only smiles into the man's purring video camera and repeats his message. Thus the boy is reduced to a single idea. He exists only as that idea, as a floating signifier, a logo of Peace. He has no other identity.

The reporter speculates that the boy may be a kind of "puppet" for some unknown group of naïve idealists and within a week, a BBC camera crew appears (they happened to be in India anyway, making a film about the Bengal Tigers in their shrinking natural habitat). At the urging of the *London Times* reporter, the five-man, two-woman BBC crew make a short side-journey to the almost-nameless village monastery, where the child is proclaiming his message. They are all ready to assist at the boy's grandeur, even if a little tongue-in-cheek. They do not dream what awaits their efforts.

The child has vanished. Has he been kidnapped by Islamic militants? That is the rumour. He has been taken to a secret hiding place near the Taj Mahal. As luck would have it, a tiger is marauding nearby, so the BBC crew are going there next week, and will investigate the boy as well. It can be done cost effectively, so why not?

The *Hindustan Times* prints the story of the boy's kidnapping, and the Indian media launch a frantic search for the child, in the most public way. They don't find him. Finding no nearby real tiger, however, the BBC claim they've been told where he has hidden or been hidden, and go to the spot near the great temple, under cover of darkness, swearing secrecy to their sources. Lo! Their information is correct. In some nameless, hidden cavern, the BBC interview the child, surrounded by Mujahiddin—boys little older than himself—all of whom brandish kalashnikovs. The story is so much better than a furtive Bengal Tiger in the wild! The BBC crew transmit their report to London with trembling fingers, sensing that they may have a real "scoop."

The interview plays on the evening news in the United Kingdom.

"Hello. This is Malcolm Bainbridge of the BBC. We're here in an undisclosed underground location, somewhere in India, interviewing a remarkable young man, whom you see here beside me.

"Tell me your name."

"My name is of no importance. Only my message matters."

"And what is that message?"

"The nations of the world have a simple choice to make now. They must make peace with each other, or we will all die. It is very simple. Peace or death." He speaks with an Oxbridge accent.

"Is there anyone who has told you to say this?"

"Everyone and everything tells me to say this.

"I see. And who are these people here in the room with us?"

"They are my friends. They are people who agree that we must make peace with each other or we will all die together." The jihadis all nod; whether they understand English is unclear.

Suddenly, there is a stirring in the room. The boy looks out of the range of the camera and waves, as if to a relative who is coming down the garden path.

Blackout. The monitors go blank. The abrupt termination of the BBC interview is explained by the fact that Al Jazeera, has its crew waiting to film its own interview. Everyone hurries to file the story, make an impression, be the first. The Arabic television news media are simply next in the queue and now arrive for their interview with the Nameless Child who has the authority to terminate his time with the BBC..

Al Jazeera carries essentially the same interview as the BBC, with the child saying the same thing in Arabic—fluent, serene. He speaks with a Saudi accent. The only difference is that to the Arabic audience it seems that the child has joined the mujahedeen, not been abducted by them. It is even suggested—though not stated in so many words—that the Nameless

One has declared his intention to submit, to become Muslim. An Imam comes into the interview just at the end—avuncular, affectionate toward the boy.

A certain Saudi Prince is listening. His heart is full of anger and grief for what is happening in the world. He is outraged that the United States is heard frequently to observe in the news media that most of the hijackers who destroyed the World Trade Centre and part of the Pentagon were Saudis. Other buildings in the United States were bombed by people who were not Saudis. He wants this known. He will not allow his nation to be seen as a terrorist war-monger. He vows that he will attend any international meeting that the child can arrange. He will go to any ends to re-enforce the message of the Nameless One. Buying a five minute spot of time on Al Jazeera, the Prince announces his intention to the world.

Then the impossible happens—again. The Nameless One is stolen/liberated from his captors by a mysterious and successful "snatch." Some people call it a kidnapping. His liberating kidnappers are a group of unknown military wearing black balaclavas, and speaking fluent but heavily accented Arabic. The *Hindustan Times* reports victoriously that this has been a "great success of our heretofore humble intelligence services." This will teach the world to respect Indian military capacities. However, the young men who have been entertaining/detaining the Great/Small Nameless One report that the re-kidnappers were Mossad agents—Israelis who have descended out of nowhere to "steal" the child. They have only been pretending to be Indian intelligence.

For their part, the Israeli government instructs an official to insist that they know nothing. This official happens to be a man who has understood the connection between entertainment and political office: he has adopted the signature image of the lollypop—for some reason mimicking a long forgotten TV detective in the USA. He thinks that people will find this amusing. He waves his red candy and officially but unofficially reports to the media that his government is entirely innocent of any kidnapping; he suggests that the "snatch" of the nameless child has actually been conducted by the CIA. From Washington, the Central Intelligence Agency does not comment on such matters under any circumstances. However, off the record, someone supposedly in the White House suggests that this operation has "all the hallmarks of the former KGB, perhaps a rogue FSB operation." No one believes anyone about anything.

The nameless boy (thenceforth christened the Sacred Child by ironic western reporters) is now reported to be in Tel Aviv, giving the same interview, with the same message, now speaking perfect Hebrew: "You must make peace, or die. You have no choice." The newspapers and television channels all carry the story.

Nobody knows exactly where the Sacred Child is; but no one doubts that he is living in some publically secret place. Peacemakers in Tel Aviv watch the career of this child, especially a man called Edward, who runs the Jerusalem Arab-Israeli Friendship Foundation. The Child's message, and the Saudi Prince's promise, offer a slim but real chance to save the world. No man of good conscience could pass this by.

The man of good conscience opens the door to his office in Jerusalem. Edward is a distinguished retired journalist who has grown disgusted with what he sees as the hysteria, hypocrisy and superficiality of the press. He has become permanently distressed by the dire state of the human race. His tiny, book-crammed room with space only for a desk and three chairs is the headquarters and only office of the Arab-Israeli Friendship Foundation, founded and run by Edward, and funded (very modestly) by a small group of American liberals in Boston, Massachusetts, where it is still possible to have naïve hopes for the future. Edward keeps the location of his office secret. Because he has Arab friends, he has Israeli enemies; because he is Israeli he has Palestinian enemies. His office window looks out over the Temple Mount: the Al Aqsa Mosque, the Dome of the Rock, where Abraham almost murdered Isaac, the site of the Second Temple, which Herod and the Romans destroyed, the spot from which Muhammad leapt on his horse to heaven—in short, the theological omphalos of half the world.

As Edward enters, the telephone rings. A voice says, "You are in your office."

Edward, amused by the idiocy of this remark, replies, "Yes. I have just answered my telephone. This means I am here."

"Good."

A protracted silence follows. This pause may have electronic reasons. Edward has learnt to accept that his phone conversations are probably tapped and recorded. Yet this pause is so ludicrously long that it pushes Edward's patience to breaking point.

"Can I help you?" he snaps.

"Yes. You can," the voice replies. "You know of this crazy child?"

For a moment Edward doesn't know for sure which crazy child the speaker may have in mind. It could even be one of his own four children—who have all done insane things from time to time. However, the speaker probably refers to the Indian boy who has supposedly been kidnapped and re-kidnapped.

"You mean that Hindu child?"

"Yes."

"Yes. Obviously I have heard of him."

"Yes. Would you like to meet him?"

Even Edward's unflappability is tested. He searches for the right response, calms himself and says: "Wouldn't everyone?"

"Perhaps not. But would *you*?"

"Yes." He decides to make this simple, and to suppress his sense of irony.

"Good. Be at the Dung Gate in fifteen minutes—just where Ma'Ale Ha-Shalom meets Ha-'Ofel. Stand with your back to the gate, looking south up Malki-Zedek. A car will come." The speaker hangs up. Edward is convinced he's just been talking to an intelligence agent. Who else would have the nerve to be quite so melodramatic?

So, having just entered, Edward exits, locks his office door and heads for his rendezvous. He is looking south into the hot roadway full of hooting traffic, when a small black Volvo pulls up behind him, and a voice says, "Get in." He turns around to see the car door open and, without asking the questions he probably should, he gets in. The glass is so darkly tinted that he can barely see out. But within there is light for—behold!—the miraculous boy is perched on the upholstery, little legs dangling. Edward is struck dumb. What does one say to a Messianic Man-child? His paternal streak takes over:

"Are you all right?" he asks.

"I am very well," says the boy, in his best British. The child looks him straight in the eye, and says, "I have asked to meet you. Prince Ibn Saud gave my jihadi friends your name when I was with them in the cave."

This seems so completely improbable that Edward just listens.

"He said that you would be able to help set up a very public meeting between him and some important Israeli."

"Which important Israeli?"

"He said you should choose."

"I?"

"Yes. You. He said so."

"Why me?"

"I do not know."

Edward now has a choice to make. He can dismiss this whole episode as an obvious fraud, with which he can choose to have nothing to do; or he can decide to pretend to take it seriously, at least for the time being, and arrange for some contact of his—say perhaps that strange man with the lollypop who is or pretends to be the Minister of Culture—to meet with the Prince.

What's to lose? Why not? Arrange a great public event. Manipulate history. Play minor deity. What the hell. Of course, it's also a fabulous opportunity to make an utter ass of himself not just in public, but in the annals of history. He could be immortalized as yet another hopeful idiot! Be remembered that way? Oh! Damn it! Why not? Better than being remembered as a hopeless idiot.

Edward agrees to the child's proposal that important people should meet and talk. The boy gives him a telephone number on a printed calling card that reads "Peace or death." The child commands the chauffeur in perfect Hebrew, to take Edward back to his office. He is deposited on the street in front of the building that houses the Arab-Israeli Friendship Foundation, where there is no name on the door, because that would be madness. He climbs the stairs to the office.

His office door is wide open. Cautious, he peers in without entering. Someone may be standing behind the door. Someone may have planted a device under his chair. It may be a listening device. It may be a bomb. Edward likes to say that he has no secrets of his own, that he will keep secrets for others, if they request it; but he himself has nothing to hide. So a hidden microphone is perfectly all right. On the other hand, any bomb he has certain objections to. Breathing deeply he walks backwards down the stairs and then, once on the street he calls a security service of his acquaintance.

The security men arrive with de-bugging and de-fusing equipment and Edward explains what has happened. They look at him quizzically and then pat him on the shoulder. What a fool of an idealist he is! But that's why people admire Edward and why he has grown accustomed to affectionate gestures from relative strangers.

Ten minutes later the security guys emerge from the building, smiling and shaking their heads. They have found nothing, they say casually. It does not surprise them. It does surprise Edward, who shakes his head for a different reason. Someone has been in his office. He remembers locking the door when he left. No one else has a key. Someone has expertly picked his lock.

He ascends the stairway again and finds the office door still open. But this time there is a man sitting at *his* desk, in *his* chair – a man who theatrically extracts a red lollypop from his mouth. Edward recognizes the Minister of Culture. Edward knows much more about this man than the Minister knows about him. Edward knows that the Minister is the worst kind of politician, the kind who pretends to be foolish but actually has an insidious side, a man who promises everything and delivers nothing. He entertains people, fooling them. He waves his lollypop around in order to suggest that he is fun and funny. After his rise to prominence as a television quiz-show presenter, he capitalized on this popularity to run for the Knesset. This man has capitalized on the confusion in the public between entertainers and politicians. His campaign succeeded largely because he accepted illegal contributions. So he is clearly—in the opinion of the serious-minded man of good faith—utterly corrupt. In particular, the Minister with Lollypop is the idiot who has promised to rebuild the Second Temple—or, to build the Third Temple—on the site of the Dome of the Rock. This is not only a false promise, it is a dangerous false promise. No one Edward knows takes it seriously; but he does worry that some fanatics may be deluded. So nothing that the Lollypop Minister says can be taken at face value or accepted as truth.

"Our mutual security colleagues agreed to say nothing to you, my friend," the Minister says to Edward, pretending to apologize.

"Why?"—Edward waves his hand expressively at the whole rigmarole of secrecy and deception.

"Why bother with all this, my friend? You wish to know?" The lollypop goes back into its mouth.

Edward nods. Yes. Why all the bother?

"Well, when this famous Sacred Child telephoned me and suggested that you'd perhaps be reluctant to help us arrange the meeting. It might be dangerous. So we thought we'd make certain you were safe, first, my friend, and then stay one step ahead of the game and arrange things for you so that it would seem as if you had arranged them for yourself. Then the Prince will be more likely to continue to come to the meeting. And—my friend—you will have all the glory and none of the work. Think of it!" Back goes the lollypop.

"Prince?" Edward slowly takes everything in.

The Minister explains about the Saudi. It all begins to make a at least a dim sense. This is a government operation that is supposed to look like a private operation. Edward wonders—but only for a second—if he should let himself be used. "Proceed," he says, sitting down opposite the Minister. Edward feels like he's being interviewed for a job he never applied for, and which he is certain he does not want. Sitting in Edward's swivel chair and sucking meditatively on his candy, the Minister of Culture apparently considers in rational fashion the circumstance created by the Nameless Child.

"If we can make this meeting happen, it will certainly bring us a bit of legitimacy amongst our Arab friends," he says.

"That's not what the boy wants, I don't think."

"My friend, do we care what he wants?"

"Shouldn't we?"

"We need to care what we want." Such a popular minister with his comic cover personae knows his own secret minds with absolute certainty. The minister tilts backwards in Edward's chair so that it creaks alarmingly. He stares with calculation at his rhetorical victim. But Edward can see that he has no real choice in this matter. He must agree to assist, be helpful, allow himself to be used.

The Arab-Israeli Friendship Foundation announces the historic meeting of the Important Saudi Prince, the Israeli Minister of Culture, and the head of the Palestine Liberation Organization, who will gather together under the auspices of The Child. The meeting will take place on Sunday next, at a location somewhere in Jerusalem yet to be announced for security reasons. Many international dignitaries will attend as witnesses to the agreement that must be reached. The four important people will gather to sign a document endorsing the Child's Message: *we must make peace with each other or we will surely all die together.* Just one sentence. The combatants will then sign. There will be nothing binding or legalistic about it. This will be a purely symbolic act—both powerful and vague.

"It should threaten no one," says Edward over the telephone to his Boston sponsors. "What harm can it do?" These particular philanthropists are dubious. It seems like a crack-pot scheme. He tries to re-assure them and hangs up doubting that he has. He leans back in his tilting chair, and waits.

The telephone rings. It is a Palestinian connection of Edward's, using a long-established code to tell him that a telephone link to an important Arab personality has been established for him. This is the kind of thing that Edward has often tried to do, but never come very close to accomplishing. He takes the call. It is no less a personage than the Saudi Prince in Question, who says, "You must understand how difficult this is for me. I could meet with the Child. I could meet with the PLO Chief. But I cannot meet with your lollypop countryman without risking my life. And I have heard the rumor that the Pope himself might attend. Of course there will be several Rabbis. I wish you to know how nervous this makes me."

Edward expresses his appreciation. The man clearly has some courage. He has been inspired by something.

The meeting is actually to take place beside the Dome of the Rock, just outside the Al Aqsa Mosque. The world's media must be present—filming, commentating—or the whole event will be wasted. Everything important is public, Edward reflects sardonically. Faith is an inward quality, but these modern religions are radically public, external, dramatic. So the trick to this symbolic reconciliation will be to gather together the print reporters, the radio men, the television camera people, the glamorous blonde anchor women—the whole mad, over-ripe corpus of the traveling press carnival—in a place not far from the Sacred Meeting Place where Abraham didn't kill Isaac (or was it Ishmael?), where there had been at least one a temple and maybe two, where Muhammad leaped up to heaven on the back of his horse Burak (with a woman's head). Apparently. Anyway, the actual location will be kept secret until the very last moment. The media may arrive only seconds before the helicopters begin descending for the meeting. Only then can Israeli security be responsible—or so Edward has been informed.

All sorts of odd little things have begun to happen. The strange clickings in his telephone are hardly a surprise. He takes them as a tiny testimonial to the importance of his endeavor. Because his basement office has a toilet in the closet, several reporters, who have figured out where he operates, come to Edward's door to beg the favor of his plumbing. He hears their waters falling, their sighs of relief. How absurd it all seems! He wonders if great historic moments—the signing of the Magna Carta, the drafting of the Declaration of Independence, the meeting of Roosevelt,

O JERUSALEM

Churchill and Stalin at Yalta—were accompanied by such ridiculously mundane shenanigans offstage.

His telephone rings and it is a call from his friend in New York: Professor Friedman has a problem. His brother, a Rabbi, is afraid that a young Hasidic man who has gone to Israel is dangerous to himself and others.

"My student and I have been getting Biblical messages."

"Biblical messages?"

"Yes. Quotations on little scraps of paper about vengeance—from the Pentateuch and elsewhere in the Old Testament."

"About what?"

"Vengeance. As I said."

"I see."

"No, Edward, you don't see. This boy is a Hasid who has cut his hair and his locks. He has been lifting weights and he wears muscle shirts. He's gone way beyond Meir Kahane and the Jewish Defense League. He has recently claimed to be the grandchild of Albert Einstein, and he's given me a sample of his own flesh in a little jar for me to arrange to have tested at Princeton, where they keep the remains."

"You're kidding."

"Unfortunately not."

"Are you able to do this?"

"Well," Professor Friedman hesitates all the way across on the other side of the world. He sighs. "I guess it isn't entirely impossible to have someone check to see if there is a DNA match with Einstein. But you have to have a good reason. I don't have a good reason yet."

"What would be a good reason?"

Again, the Professor sighs. "Sometimes," he breathes in a hot whisper down the telephone line, "Sometimes I think our boy Chaim may have been killing people, but I don't really know so I haven't called the police. Yet. But if we please him by testing his genes, maybe we can communicate with him and possibly make sure he isn't murdering people."

Edward thinks about this for a moment. Then he asks, "Why are you calling me? I'm nowhere near as good as the police."

"I'm calling you because I want to ask you a terrible favor."

"Yes?"

"Would you go to visit the boy, where he's told his mother he's living, and give me your report?"

The project is just curious enough to tempt Edward. And anyway, he could do with a break from anxiety over global conspiracies for peace inspired by a Child. So, Edward takes down a Jerusalem address from his friend in New York. Then, off he goes, through the blasting sunlight, down a dark alley, through a doorway, into a courtyard, up a set of stairs, down a hallway and up to a closed door. He knocks. No one answers. He knocks and calls. Still no one answers.

"Chaim? Are you there? I'm a friend of your rabbi. Chaim? Chaim?" His voice echoes around the empty hallway.

Edward's reward for his good deed is silence. Yet silence is a good thing, he thinks. There is so little silence in the world. He should be grateful for the gift—especially in this case, at this time. No response to his knock certainly makes his life easier just how. And he could use a little relief just at present. After a few minutes, when he knows that he has done his duty and that no one will answer the door to his knock, Edward leaves the deserted, clean, dark hallway. He has tried to do a favor for his friend in New York, who is brother to the rabbi who is concerned about Chaim; that is all he can do. He shrugs and returns to the sunlit world, squinting into the blaze.

In the busy street, just outside his office building he is accosted by a whisper: "Don't turn around. You wished to speak to me? It is Chaim here." Edward feels a hand on the back of his neck, steady, firm, preventing his turning around to see the face.

Edward begins to laugh at the cloak-and-dagger stuff. Boys will play their games, he thinks. Chaim plays his game—a faceless voice behind him, an invisible hand on his neck, an invisible danger in Jerusalem.

"I have been studying."

"Yes. That's good, Chaim. Your mother will be pleased to learn it. So will your rabbi and also Professor Friedman."

The hand pushes him forward. The youngster is not normal. He thinks of the famous Jerusalem Syndrome: some religious people go mad when they arrive in their holy city. He has never met a sufferer before; he thought they were always Christians. Perhaps they are sometimes Jews. In any case, Chaim is his first. In silence the boy steers him into an off-street courtyard. He finds himself blinking in the white light.

"I have been studying the Pentateuch," his voice says in his ear. "And other books."

"Better yet." It seems a good, noncommittal thing to say.

"I have also been studying the science of explosives."

"That is not quite so good, Chaim."

"Not just chemical explosives."

"Nuclear explosives?" asks Edward, sardonically.

"Yesssss!" Chaim hisses in his ear. "And even better, I have acquired an anti-aircraft missile. Shoulder-mounted. Very accurate."

"That's really not very good," says Edward. He laughs quietly to himself at the absurdity of the madman's claims. They are so outrageous that the fail to be frightening.

They are crossing the courtyard and entering an archway back onto another street. Chaim has guided him past the way back to his office. Never mind. Ten more steps and there will be people to witness this madness. They reach the opening onto a crowded square; Edward feels safe.

"What you think does not matter," the boy whispers.

"Thank you."

"Your humor is effete. Self-inflicted irony is only for old-fashioned Jews."

"That is also a wonderful thing to say to someone who comes to you only to do your Rabbi and your mother a favor."

Chaim ignores this. "I have been studying how to blow things up."

"Chaim, Chaim. That is so sad."

"To blow big things up. Not just cars or buildings."

"How much bigger do things get?"

"Much."

The hand on his shoulder holds him in the dark shadow of the archway back onto the street. The whisper in his ear grows louder, to compete with the noise in the street ahead of them.

"The bigger the explosion, the greater the joy. It helps to bring the Messiah. This will solve all the world's problems."

"Indeed it will. With a big enough explosion we would have no more world left to worry about. That would do it."

"Yes. The final explosion. That will come when a nuclear scientist becomes a theologian, or when a theologian becomes a nuclear scientist. I am the grandson of Einstein, and I can bring the Messiah."

"You will do *what*, Chaim?"

"I am the Scientist become the Prophet. Behold not me but my Works. I am not the Beginning or the End but the Beginning of the End."

Edward is pushed back out into the street, blinking again in the brightness. The hand has left his shoulder.

"Chaim? Are you quite mad?" Maybe this isn't the thing to say to a madman, but Edward can't help himself. What he says does not matter; for when he turns to confront the enraptured voice, no one is there. The darkness under the archway is empty. He turns again and before him, in all directions simultaneously, flows the chaotic crowd of ordinary, apparently sane people who are buying food, household supplies and newspapers. Perhaps one of those people is Chaim. Or perhaps the boy has gone back into the courtyard, or disappeared into one of the doorways under the arch that Edward had not noticed. He cannot tell where the sad young man has gone. The mad young man. The bad young man? Edward stands in the blinding sunlight, wondering just how dangerous Chaim really is to himself and to others. The notion that he can produce a nuclear explosion or an anti-aircraft missile is a pathetic delusion. And what had Chaim said about Einstein? Edward isn't sure he can remember. But in Chaim's fierce grip, Edward sensed real danger. What should he do about it?

Soon, however, Edward is distracted by other matters, by another child. By another Beginning of another End.

In a land not so very far, far away from Jerusalem, trapped in a civilization made a very long, long time ago, a very junior, ex-reporter called Bob Smith, from a country about as far away as it is possible to get in time, space and understanding, is still desperately seeking the girl he still passionately desires. The young reporter has filed no dispatches back to Wichita from Afghanistan. For one thing, he has no means of communication with Wichita. For another thing, he has no means of writing anything down, since his laptop was stolen from his room on the first day of his residence in his hotel.

He feels suffocated by heat and dust. The four Christian men from America, whom he met in the Kabul streets every day for the first week, have vanished. Even indirect knowledge of his beloved Betsey has ceased. She may no longer be in Kabul. Plumbing has become monumentally important. Squat toilets have caused him severe constipation. He has developed a rash that torments him in a part of his body he normally ignores. He just wants to go home to Wichita, take a normal shit, and have a bath.

But suddenly he becomes the subject of a negative miracle. He answers a knock on his door, and a vision appears. A blind man wearing reflective sunglasses under his turban feels his way with delicate fingers along the broken dusty molding inside the door that cants crazily inwards from the frame. The Reporter has the crazed notion that he has seen this figure before—perhaps in a dream, or in a bad late-night movie. Behind the figure, two young men carry kalashnikovs. The figure is smiling at him—though it is hard to know if it is a smile of greeting or simply a grimace.

One of the Kalashnikovs says, "You carry message."

Bob comprehends nothing. More Kalashnikovs appear and gently push him before the grimacing visitor, who speaks a tongue unknown. A Kalashnikov translates: "Allah does not permit meeting. We explode it." Then Bob is handed an envelope.

"Open!"

His fingers tremble so violently that he can hardly obey. He stands in the room surrounded by Kalashnikov-carrying boys, and all he knows for certain is that he itches and smells. His nose is running. His rash is raging, as if someone has poured sulphuric acid over his buttocks. But with a supreme effort of will and some iron-man clenching, he finally manages to wipe his nose with his sleeve, conquer the desire to scratch himself, and open the paper.

After a long paragraph in a script incomprehensible to any average Kansan, the paper says: "Allah does not permit this meeting." Nothing more in English; much more in the language whose very letters he does not recognize. One of the Kalashnikov says to him, tapping the envelope, "Take to Jerusalem."

He stares into the blind man's face. He sees nothing but himself gawping in the silver surface of the sun glasses.

"If you deliver message, Christian friends live."

He feels the room reeling around him, as if he were drunk.

"If you fail, Allah permits death."

The Kalashnikovs suddenly seize him, blindfold him, bind him, push a large envelope inside his shirt. Then they roll him in a dusty-smelling carpet, bump him down the stairs, and throw him into a moving vehicle. Bob loses consciousness for a time, then feels himself being lifted again. He hears machinery and guesses that he is now in an airplane, perhaps in the cargo hold. He hears doors closing, jet engines starting. He feels the rush down the runway into the air, the slow climb, the leveling out and finally peace—almost like the peace of death. At length—cocooned in the carpet, just able to breathe—he remembers where he has seen the old man before: the departure waiting room in the Istanbul airport, where the turbaned Holy Man was accompanied by the young guards. That policeman came in with another man. They looked at the old man and jabbered to each other in some strange language, then shook their heads and went away. The scene replays itself in his mind.

Then he knows the kinetics of landing. He has the experience of cargo. He is dumped, dragged, lifted, dumped, prodded. Briefly, he feels the roll of carpet being pulled back. Someone takes his pulse from his neck. There follow several long hours of miserable waiting, followed by quick episodes of lifting, dropping, rolling.

Finally he is released from his carpet chrysalis, unbound, but left blindfolded. Someone reaches into his shirt to locate the envelope he carries. Now he is placed upon his feet but falls backwards. Someone catches him, tenderly. He is leaned against a wall, but slumps. He is placed in a chair, and prevented from falling off by steady hands upon his shoulders. Water is poured on his face, into his mouth. He fails to drink. He loses control of his kidneys. He is subjected to a stream of water all over his body.

A long wait follows. Then his sodden, listless body is guided into the rear seat of a car. The blindfold is removed, and he sees young men wearing masks in the front seat. Bob groggily peers through the tinted car windows and discovers that he is being driven through the streets of a strange city—he can't tell which. One of the men in the front seat hands an envelope to the masked man sitting beside the drenched Bob in the back seat. The car stops. The door is opened. The envelope is placed in his hand. It is the same envelope he has brought with him, he thinks dimly. Someone says, loudly, "go Arab-Israeli Friendship Foundation, upstairs in front when you leave car. Door number 11."

Bob stands unsteadily in the sunlight. The car vanishes behind him. He is the wretched messenger, dripping on the dry cement pavement, before a neat, well-painted doorway in a dingy, unpainted wall. Clutching his envelope, he opens the door and descends the dark stairway to door numbered 11.

"Good god, man, what's happened to you?"

He can only shake his head at Edward's question. He has no idea what has happened to him. The messenger has no message. He only clutches an envelope, and leans, bedraggled, against the doorframe. Edward telephones for help.

After the doctor has departed, and Bob has drunk a coca-cola, experienced the luxury of using a toilet, and been told the city of his location—Jerusalem—he remembers. "They said 'Allah does not permit this meeting.'"

"Yes," says the kindly man across the desk. "Your written message says the same: 'Allah does not permit . . . .'"

Edward asks Bob "What labyrinthine lunacy have you been caught up in?" Bob remains speechless.

Edward telephones to tell someone about the young American and his message. He says to Bob, who does not understand, "The Minister's secretary says that she will call the American Embassy." Then the two sit waiting—the one wet and dazed, the other troubled and bemused.

The American charge d'affairs appears in the doorway and takes Bob off to the safety of the American Embassy. He has served his function. He will return to a hero's welcome in Wichita, Kansas, USA. He has had no will of his own; but he will nevertheless be heroic. His editor will re-hire him. He will sell his story down the line to all the wire services he can find. He will be a noble victim. He will sign a book contract. He will be rich and famous for more than his wonted fifteen minutes. He begins to intuit these results. However, the great love of his life has vanished into Afghanistan. The world will know—though the world may not understand—what has happened.

Meanwhile, the Sacred Child remains faithful to his purpose, though Edward relays to him the warning that Allah forbids him to meet the Prince and the Minister on the Mount. Edward says nothing of the preposterous threats that Chaim has suggested. Neither the Minister nor the Prince responds to the news that 'Allah does not permit.' The Palestinian connection to the Saudi Prince reassures Edward that they have relayed the message, but that the Prince will defy augury and attend. All that Edward knows is that the meeting of the Prince, the Magic Child, The Head of the Palestinian Authority, and possibly other important people as well as the Israeli Minister is still scheduled for high noon today and that the Child will come dropping down out of the sky, by helicopter, to the meeting whose location is still being coordinated by invisible powers.

Edward calls the Minister of Culture, who reassures the Director of the Arab-Israeli Friendship Foundation that he stands ready, with the many other VIPs, to appear on the scene of reconciliation once The Child has landed. It will happen in less than an hour.

At eleven thirty, Edward steps into the blazing light and heat. It seems entirely improbable that the course of history will now change, that there will be some grand *rapprochement* between governments, religions, peoples. The whole thing feels grandly ridiculous. He is a fool. Still, isn't there the ancient tradition of the wise fool? Sometimes an innocent—a helpless babe in the dangerous world—makes a great contribution. He tries to think of an example, but can't dredge one up, unless it be the Christ-child who, as a nominal Jew, Edward doesn't interpret in quite the same way as other Christians do.

He is walking toward the Temple Mount and the crowded streets are full of people who do not know that the world is about to be miraculously altered for the better. The Jews and the Arabs with whom he brushes shoulders are mutually oblivious that they are about to be saved from their fates of mutual annihilation. When he hears a helicopter in the sky, Edward actually starts to giggle with glee. He turns a corner and sees the slope of the Mount with its crown of the golden dome over the rock that is the center of three whole worlds. He catches a glimpse of the chattering aerial insect banking above the narrow street, passing from right to left. He even thinks that he has caught a glimpse of the saffron robes of the Sacred Child inside the fishbowl glass cockpit.

Edward turns a corner and loses sight of the side of the Mount. He turns another corner and regains a glimpse of the flank of the acropolis, just as the helicopter passes over again on its final approach. Edward roars with laughter. He feels crazed with happiness. He comes out into an open space, beneath the vast cloudless sky, as the helicopter begins to descend—filling the emptiness with gobbling, chattering machine menace. The aircraft comes into view like a monstrous insect above the dome of the Al Aqsa mosque. The fingers of the dark evergreen trees point upward, emphatic.

A line of yellow light rises from somewhere beyond the golden dome to meet the helicopter, which explodes in a brilliant fireball, its black fragments raining and crashing down upon the paving stones of the sacred precinct. His own laugh chokes Edward, who sinks to his knees. He kneels, staring into the sky, a hundred yards from the Wailing Wall, where the black-coated Hasidim pray. They have stepped away from the wall and are staring up into the sky, wondering but unaware of the importance of what has just not happened.

The saffron colored robe of the Sacred Child flutters downward on the hot winds of the holy city—the autumn leaf of early death.

In a Darkroom

The orange robe of the magical child floats down on every screen in the room. Then it flies back up to the helicopter, which chatters off backwards into the distant sky. The very flow of time seems to go backward, then forward. Down and up goes the saffron-colored robe.

The Voices contend with the Client. He proposes that everyone should do something extreme and outrageous in response to this extreme outrage. The various voices cannot think what to do. He is the fiery believer; they have become the cool doubters. He is impassioned in atheist outrage; they are dispassionate in a conviction-free nihilism.

The Client stands in the center of the room and preaches into dark corners: "All right, so we can't convince the True Believers to give up their organized insanity. All right, so people need delusions to live. All right, two or even three thousand years of accumulated nonsense looks like wisdom to the masses. They don't know reason; they don't know science; they don't think for themselves. They just parrot what they're told to believe. All right. I concede all that. All right, all right, all right."

"All right, what?" asks the older female.

"All right, instead of giving up the organized madness of religion, we at least get the collectivized crazies to talk to each other."

"It'd be hard to get them to listen to you," says one voice.

Music up. Gershwin 'It 'aint necessarily so, the things that you're liable, to read in the Bible, they ain't necessarily so...' It cuts off hostility, dampens debate, gives pause—time to think.

The television screens now all show the same scene: wreckage on the wide terrace of the Temple Mount.

"God speaks again" says the Client. "Good old, reliable catastrophe Mr God."

An amplified voice from the ceiling of the room synchs with a larger-than-life mouthing face on one screen, "Well, Peter, it seems that loss of life has been minimal. It appears that only the helicopter pilot and this eccentric Hindu child have been killed. Of course this is very unfortunate, but..."

They all stare blankly at the latest horror. Someone giggles. Someone coughs. The Client goes on shaking his head—a metronome of dismay. Suddenly he emerges from his trance. He starts to smile a crooked smile. From the center of the Darkroom, where a pin spot suddenly illuminates him, he blurts out: "That's it! Bingo! Eureka! The idea of an Interfaith Conference has been killed in one small child but reborn in a million minds. It dies now to live forever. It has not perished but is disseminated to every corner of the earth!"

"So your idea rules?" mocks a nasal voice.

"It does! Just look." The client's pointing hand appears disembodied in a beam of light. "That boy's image is universal now." The BBC has caught the moment of impact, when the missile hit the fuselage and the fireball vaporized the child. The intense explosion leaves an afterglow on the screen, a white blankness.

"Quick death, anyhow."

"Quick immortality," says the Client. "The child is dead; long live the child's idea."

VI

CANTERBURY: ATHEIST AND ARCHBISHOP

"My uncle, who's actually the Archbishop of Canterbury, would love to meet you," she said as she sat down opposite Jack, in what had become their habitual cafe. She waited a moment to see what effect this information might have on him. "The Archbishop absolutely loves the idea of the Interfaith Conference." She spoke quickly because she felt foolish promoting herself as a relative of a famous person. Normally she hid the fact. She had certainly conducted a sustained course of deceptive modesty with this devout atheist. "Don't you remember what you suggested just yesterday? A conference? The three monotheisms? Get them to talk to each other? Like what that wonderful Indian boy proposed? Only bigger?" She prompted him.

He seemed not to have heard her. He was focussed on his telephone. A newsfeed had his attention. For several days now, the papers, the television, the radio, the internet had been full of the exploding helicopter above the Al Aqsa Mosque. Who had fired the rocket? Israeli rumors were that Palestinians had yet again exploded their chance of peace; Palestinian rumors were that Israelis had blown up the helicopter to prevent peace—as they always did. Egyptian newspapers said it was the work of the CIA. Hindu papers said it was the work of Kashmiri Islamic militants. Everybody's worst enemy had committed the atrocity. So far as Emma could tell, Jack was following the blame game with careful attention. Who did it seemed more important to him than any solution to the world's great problem of various and conflicting faiths.

"These idiot religions," he railed. "These damned delusions are literally blowing things up. The crazies have hijacked the whole world. Belief blown out of proportion. Soooo—" at last he looked at Emma — "it's time to blow Belief itself up. Belief with a capital B. End mysticism. Stop nonsense. Abolish religion. Marx was wrong. Religion isn't the opiate of the people. It is the fissile material of the fanatic!" He stared at her with wild green eyes, his anger righteously roused.

She wanted to laugh but didn't. Instead, she calmly repeated "My uncle the Archbishop would love to have tea with you next week and talk about all this."

"Thank you very much. But why should I have tea with a man who is effectively responsible for mass murder?" Jack exploded.

Now Emma was furious. She felt like getting up and leaving him to stew in his bitter atheist solitude. "Isn't that a little extreme?" she retorted—pushing her chair back, away from the table—getting ready to walk away from this suddenly awful man. She'd never before been offended on her uncle's behalf. Instead, she was usually irritated by the Archbishop's unimpassioned, detached calm when there was so much to be upset about. The old man would talk quietly away in his elegant, oak-panelled surroundings, discoursing in carefully sculpted sentences, pronouncing all his vowels and consonants with clarity, promoting the need for tolerance, forbearance, patience. Every once in a while he would murmur about how the Lord works in mysterious ways, about how we mere mortals cannot understand God's purposes. He seemed quite content to dwell in the mystery of things. The Archbishop had often infuriated her. Yet now she wanted to scream at the young man who was exactly what she once had wished her Uncle to be: furious, impassioned, driven by a sense of injustice. Emma stood up as if to leave the café. She took in a deep breath and let it out slowly. A calm came over her, like a magic spell. Her anger subsided. She guessed that this was what older people called "growing up," losing the rage, acquiescing, quitting the fight. She was suddenly amused at her own reversal of roles: she was adopting Uncle Richard's attitude of patience, forbearance. This atheist character friend of hers catalysed an eruption of patience, a spasm of toleration. She laughed at herself and sat down again.

"What are you laughing at?" he asked suddenly. She realized that he had in fact been watching her when she thought he was completely self-absorbed, and she felt herself blush.

"Yes?" he prompted again.

"Don't worry. I was laughing at myself," she explained.

She expected him to ask why she was laughing at herself, but he didn't. Perhaps he didn't care why; or perhaps it was because his phone was yet again echoing the explosion in Jerusalem. It was the soundtrack of the week, like an overplayed pop song. Bang, bang. Pop, pop. Bits of helicopter fell about for the twentieth time. Out of the blue sky that saffron robe would be fluttering down like a leaf toward ancient pavement. She did not need to see it all again.

Jack looked up from his phone. She had his attention again—for the moment. He seemed to be studying her. Then he was back on his soap box: "Religion causes death, invites death, seeks death, wants death. Religion *is* death." She suddenly felt like stroking his hair, smoothing his brow, hushing him like a child. *There, there.* The poor soul was straining after blasphemy as hard as he possibly could.

"Perhaps you'd like to debate this with the Archbishop?" she suggested yet again, even more mischievously. She was starting to enjoy teasing him.

He glared at her for a moment. His mobile rang. A new ringtone. 'Somewhere over a Rainbow' this time. Curious, and curiouser, thought Emma. Every time a new ringtone. When she commented Jack simply said

"Yeah, I'm always changing my tune. I can, so I do. Technology's my god – it's *real* invention, man-made, miraculous, but real. Unlike Him up there."

"My uncle loves technology." said Emma. "And he believes in 'Him up there'. The two aren't incompatible. Perhaps you'd like to discuss it with him?" she kept trying.

"No thank you. I need to talk to God himself. That particular big slob is the real problem that we ought to straighten out. Let's get a committee together and go have a word with Him. No, better yet, let's organize a posse and go arrest the big bastard in the sky. Or maybe a SWAT team should take Him into custody for psychiatric evaluation. He's got some sado-masochistic, paranoid-delusional tendencies. He should be locked up somewhere safe, and the key thrown away. This God fellow is dangerous to human health and life."

Emma laughed a little despite herself. She wasn't easily shocked, and she wasn't religious in any conventional way, but once again, she was offended by Jack's militant, dogmatic atheism.

She rose to his challenge, saying "You need to talk to God, then? Shouldn't you just pray? Do atheists pray? I would have thought not."

She refrained from paraphrasing that bit about atheists only praying in foxholes. It would have been as unfeeling to him as he was being to her. But Jack was a little more self-aware on this subject than she expected. "It's a funny thing," he admitted. "I do have these vestigial tendencies. I was raised atheist, and I'll die atheist. But I do have a strange way of talking to God. I don't pray, exactly, but I curse using the Lord's name, and I make exclamations like 'Jesus!' when I'm surprised or offended. After my time in the Middle East, I sometimes find it very convenient to say 'Insha-allah,' and 'hamdilillah.'

"Or maybe it's because you are secretly—hidden even from yourself—a believer?" she ventured.

"No, I don't think so." He seemed to consider her suggestion. "Atheism is natural to me. I'm entirely comfortable with it. I'm never tempted give in, submit, join up, start praying, counting beads, any of that stuff. And I tell you: it gets easier all the time to see that religion is simply evil. This last little episode in Jerusalem proves it."

"But evil is itself a theological concept," she blurted.

"Yeah. But fight fire with fire. Call evil *evil*. Use words religious people will understand. Religion is *evil*." His trembling fist raised up six inches above the table-top and she expected it to smash down resoundingly. But he stopped himself, frustrated in self-control.

This time, however, Emma's inhibitions gave way. She reached out to touch his forehead. The effect was immediate. He looked up at her and grinned, awkwardly. She knew perfectly well that she really wasn't here for a theological discussion. She was here for more fundamental reasons. She wanted to eat of the *real* tree of knowledge. Taste the flesh of this impossible atheist. He would only have had to touch her hand, and she'd have yielded. She began to sense that this man would be her greatest infatuation yet. Her head swam. She took one long, deep breath. But, instead of saying, "Oh! Just shut up and kiss me!" she went back to suppressing her truth, feigning an interest in Him up there, or Him not up there, wondering over the rainbow.

Jack's phone rang once or twice more with messages from his anonymous friends " . . . *dreams really do* . . ." Yes. No. That was all he ever said. Never, "That was mum," or "That was work," or "That was my girlfriend." Did he have one? Emma didn't ask. But he did begin to apologize for the interruptions, "Sorry about that. What was I banging on about?" As if he needed reminding! Was he laughing at himself? Just a bit? Did fanatics have senses of humour? Emma couldn't work him out.

All of a sudden, with no immediate context, he blurted out, "Let's go meet your uncle! What the hell! Why not? Let's go take tea with the mass murderer himself!" Emma flinched. But there was no going back now.

They'd taken the train down to Canterbury together, holding hands secretly in the space between them on the upholstery, like a couple of teenagers. Jack told Emma a bit more about himself. He came from "a little town you never heard of in Nebraska." His uncle had left him some money that he was using to make a film, and... "that's enough about me. I hate talking about myself."

As fast as the countryside flew past, it wasn't fast enough for either of them now. They found a little hotel near the Cathedral. It was expensive but Jack didn't care. Emma's heart was pounding in her ears as they ascended to the luxury of the private room.

Jack turned off his mobile. Emma had him all to herself...over and over again. She smiled wryly. Jack was... how could she put it...he was beyond belief! *For what I have just received may the Lord make me truly thankful* she mused. Nevertheless, even as new lovers, they could not make love for thirty-six hours without stopping. So they went for a long walk through the town and out into the countryside beyond, holding hands, high on chemistry, their fingers dovetailed with desire. On the way back to the hotel, they stopped in front of the great Cathedral that towers over the town. It was surrounded by scaffolding on one side—"Religion under reconstruction," quipped Jack. "It could use a little deconstruction, too." He waxed ironic on the subject of rotting stone and mouldy timbers as they stood for a moment on the pavement watching the workmen high above. One man rappelled down the cathedral tower wall, as if it were a cliff on a mountain face. They craned their heads back, faces turned up toward the heavily clouded sky.

"Patching up these broken religions would be just about as risky as that, I guess," Jack said—watching the daredevil above them. He sounded sympathetic, wistful.

At last they were sitting together in the outer waiting room of the Archbishop's office. "I don't know what this will accomplish," said Jack. He was smiling shyly like an innocent child as he sat on the bench. His skin was so white and his hair was so black. And his eyes! Green to the point of glowing. Emma checked herself. Instead, she took his hand again, and squeezed it. Thank you. I love you. Later.

Mrs Brumley, the perfect secretary, ushered them into the splendor of the *sanctum sanctorum*, which was precisely as it always was. Nothing here changed—as if the office furniture itself participated in eternity. The faint smell of wood polish, the heavy brocaded curtains, the subtle shades of peach, plum and cinnamon fabrics, the magnificent gold cross, the chandelier catching the light from the vast bay window—made of clear glass now that the stained segments had been temporarily removed for conservation. That and the fresh flowers were the only things that had changed. Spring daffodils, red tulips, Lilly of the Valley. Uncle Richard dressed in an ordinary dark blue suit, rose and came forward to meet them; they settled into their comfortable chairs while the charming Mrs Brumley served tea and fussed over them. Jack refused to take any tea and rolled his eyes with impatience once or twice as she and Uncle Richard expressed their preference for sugar or milk or lemon. Emma threw him a furious glance. She wasn't sure if she believed in God just at that moment; but she knew without doubt that she believed in manners. They were the bedrock of civilization. Without both God and manners, what was there? Anarchy? She would give Jack a good talking to later. Finally, when she and her uncle finally had everything that was wanted, she began by saying, "Well, Uncle Richard, my friend Jack is troubled in his soul about how religion is getting used for the purposes of murder."

"Aren't we all?" asked His Eminence, smiling, raising his hands, palms upwards.

"Well, Jack has concluded that religion is *the* modern evil. He thinks religion is not just an excuse but actually the cause of mass murder."

Jack raised his eyebrows, tilted his head and grinned crookedly as if apologizing. The Archbishop beamed from behind his enormous desk, quietly, projecting wordless good feeling. It was something he did extremely well. He sipped his tea, then called out to Mrs. Brumley about some special cakes stored in the cupboard. So the cakes had to be found, put on a plate, and offered around, accepted by His Eminence and by Emma but rejected by Jack, and finally placed on the table. Emma watched Jack squirm and drum his fingers on his thigh, impatient to be getting on with the important conversation. He did not seem to understand how people revealed themselves in gestures. Uncle Richard's left cheek swelled out with delicious cake, he shook his head sympathetically at the young atheist—as if to say "poor fellow, he doesn't know what he's missing." At the same time did seem to be sizing up the opposition, wondering how best to handle this particular God denier. The tea ceremony was as much tactical as tasty and, in a perfect world, Uncle Richard had once said, all important meetings would take place at teatime. Meanwhile, Emma settled back into her armchair and watched.

The opening act concluded, Uncle Richard came around his great desk and sat with them around the coffee table. Jack sat forward, on the edge of his chair, alert, as if at last taking advantage of this opportunity to talk seriously to an important person. He reached into his pocket and switched off his mobile. He began to speak: "Sir. First of all, I'm sure I must thank you for taking the time to see me—or, rather, to see us. I'm sure if it weren't for Emma you wouldn't have found yourself free."

Emma's heart sank; Uncle Richard coughed a little over his biscuit. "Quite right," he was saying. "Quite right. I can't make myself available to every passing stranger. Obviously. But I do want to stay in touch with what you young people are thinking, how you feel. It's pretty obvious the Church of England isn't terribly successful these days with folks your age. You youngsters think we're stuffy, a bit old-fashioned, too involved with form for its own sake. Despite our every effort we look unfeeling about the plight of the—how shall I say?—civilization's discontents."

"I'm afraid it's gone well beyond that for me, sir."

"Please don't call me 'sir.'" The Archbishop interrupted, gesturing again, now with only one hand, palm up, toward Jack—creating a silence, a space for speech.

"Well, I was raised an atheist. And it's become clear to me that the Church has not just become irrelevant to modern life. It's worse than that. None of you church people are making anything like a sufficient effort to stop your followers from committing the most barbaric acts of mass murder. You simply completely fail to teach the simple truth that we are all human beings . . ." Jack went on and on and on, spilling his fury. Uncle Richard listened politely. Jack said something about life being more important than faith, instead of the other way around. He proposed the old saw that man had invented God, instead of the other way around.

Uncle Richard smiled. Emma knew that he had of course heard all these arguments many times. Jack paused for breath. Any rejoinders? There were none, so on he went preaching the atheist creed that millenarian sects were dangerous to the survival of the human race. Life was so miserable for some people that they needed to believe in their 'God-given right' to an idyllic afterlife. Paradise was imaginary payment for real suffering. He had the Islamic Jihadis as much in mind as the Christian believers in the imminent coming of the False Messiahs, then the real Messiah, The Rapture, and all the rest of it. At one point he said, "They really think the Messiah's sitting right offstage just waiting to enter on cue." Emma realized that Jack did have some familiarity with various holy texts. He seemed to know more about holy writ than she did.

He came to what Emma thought was the end of his peroration: "You church and religion guys have gotta stop 'em, even if it means admitting that you've been telling lies for two thousand years and more. You gotta stand up and say, 'Sorry folks, we got this backwards. God exists in our heads, not us in His.' Call off the wars that we helped you start up, and forget about all those simple-minded solutions to the great problems of the day that we taught you. We got it all wrong. There's no such thing as God, paradise, or hell. We've looked into it, and we realize we're wrong. And in any case, you ain't getting into paradise by killing each other. Sorry." Then he stopped. Emma glanced at her Uncle. The Archbishop was pondering the young preacher. Bemused? Amused? She couldn't tell. Perhaps he'd simply switched off. Jack could be such a windbag when he got on his atheist hobbyhorse and rode roughshod over anyone listening. Uncle Richard must be wondering what on earth Emma saw in him. She was beginning to wonder herself. She wanted to apologize.

Then a figure caught her attention. A man was clambering up the scaffolding opposite wearing what looked like a long black scarf. It billowed and flapped in the breeze and suddenly disappeared round the corner of the parapet like the tail of a huge rat. Emma shut her eyes and resigned herself to whatever it was she'd got herself into…Providence? Fate? She couldn't find the right words for anything at the moment. Unlike Jack, who, after a brief pause for breath, had once again turned his rhetorical tap on full and scalding. There was something strange and artificial in his pleading now, Emma thought —as if he was protracting the moment. It reminded her of that radio program in which the contestants were required to speak non-stop, without hesitation, deviation or repetition, for as long as they could. At one point Jack was concocting a verbal cartoon, gesturing up at the sky out the window, and calling up at "Yahweh over on that cloud, God in the middle there, and Allah over on that piece of cirrocumulus. You're each in a huff pretending the other two don't exist." Then he looked back at Uncle Richard and begged, "Come on now, that's about what it amount to, doesn't it?" Still, the Archbishop waited and said nothing—listening, munching on another biscuit.

Jack banged on, insisting that religions have developmental stages. "Islam is in an adolescent phase, aggressive, male hormonal, verbal but non-literate and thoroughly out of control." (Look at the adolescent who's talking, thought Emma.) "Judaism is a bit past middle age and kind of tired, and your Christianity having reached a ripe maturity, is now entering its mid-life crisis." American muscular Christianity, in particular, is an atavistic regression to an infantile state and wasn't much better than Islam; "in fact it was worse because it was armed to the teeth." A glob of spittle popped out of Jack's mouth.

Finally, finally, the Archibishop intervened—or tried to. "What," said Uncle Richard, "about that idea of having a grand meeting? Between leaders of the various faiths? What the Hindu child tried to do? Only on a much larger scale?"

"Yes, right," said Jack dismissively. "I must ask you. Have you talked to the Pope recently? How about a Rabbi or two? What about finding some Imam or other who can say to his boys, 'Now hold off a bit. These Christians and those Jews happen to be human beings exactly like you.' What about laying hands on some Rabbi and tying him down in a chair next to some Islamic guy and forcing those two madmen to talk to each other? Let's tape their faces together and make them breathe each others' halitosis. Let's have a new kind of anti-conspiracy conspiracy."

"All excellent suggestions—excepting maybe the very last," admitted Uncle Richard. "A little difficult of execution, but excellent nonetheless."

"I'm sorry, Sir," said Jack, sitting back again in his chair now. "I am sorry. Until very recently, we atheists have been a quiet lot; we let you believers get away with it. But we must begin to speak out now, because if you leaders of religions keep looking inward towards your own followers without paying enough attention to the relations between religions, then you're going get us all killed. And that's not fair to the great quiet minority of atheists. Or maybe we're even a majority nowadays."

A sudden rush of wind and a crash of shattering glass: a man on a rope came swinging rather awkwardly and slowly through the great bay window. He broke bits of frame and several panes of glass as he made his entry. He slid clumsily across the polished acreage of the Archbishop's desk, scattering documents, pens, bottles of black, green and navy ink, Post-its, paper-clips, a copy of The Tablet, and a vase of freesias before landing on his feet against the sofa in the corner of the room. Mrs. Brumley poked her head in the door to see what all the commotion was about, and added a final scream to the Ropeman's overture.

"Sorry about that mess," said the masked man, gesturing at the havoc in his wake. He was wearing a cloth stocking cap, a balaclava, dark skiing goggles, army fatigues, heavy boots, and—most remarkably of all—a long black scarf that had unfurled behind him in his flight through the window. In one of those odd perceptions that occur in moments of crisis, Emma remembered thinking that the long scarf was a real danger to the ridiculous acrobat.

"Message for you, Mr Archbishop Sir, from the Gods themselves. I've just been up in the sky visiting 'em. I represent Deus Ex Machina!" He pulled a leather wallet from his pocket from which he removed large white pieces of card. "My calling card," he announced with a flourish, as he handed one to each of the four spectators. Emma could not help herself, and looked at the card, which read, "Deus Ex Machina. The mechanism of progress." There was no contact information.

"Really," said Mrs Brumley. "Really. I'll call the police." And she exited, closing the door behind her.

Emma was standing behind her chair; Jack was sitting; and Uncle Richard was absent-mindedly standing up and dusting broken glass off his shoulder. Mrs Brumley re-emerged through the door, pushing past the intruder to help his Eminence, who said ironically, "I assume that you have called the police."

"I have indeed tried, but the line seems dead."

There was a loud click. The masked Ropeman had locked the door. He sat down in a straight-backed chair, arms folded, waiting.

Emma saw that Jack was still sitting looking at no one, his chin perched on his fingertips in a prayer-like posture. Mrs Brumley, meanwhile, had dusted down the Archbishop and was bundling him back into his chair; Emma resumed her seat. Thus the five of them contemplated each other, until the masked man broke the silence.

"I have something for you," he intoned. Out of his backpack he took a black package, which he unzipped to the sound of ripping Velcro. He produced a scroll of paper tied with a black ribbon, which he handed the

Archbishop. He next produced a video camera, whose buttons he pushed with expertise. "Read the manifesto," he ordered Uncle Richard.

The Archbishop took up the scroll, untied the black ribbon, and found that the document was ceremoniously sealed with wax. Mrs. Brumley, rummaged about on the floor, retrieved the ornate letter opener, and delivered it into the waiting palm of her beloved boss. Then, while the Archbishop fumbled with the seal, she busied herself trying in vain to make things neat again, but also shooting withering glances at the Ropeman who was sweeping the room with his camera, eye to the viewfinder. Still, Jack had hardly moved.

"Read it slowly," the emissary of the gods said to his Eminence.

Uncle Richard began, "I, Archbishop of Canterbury, do hereby declare a PLAGUE ON ALL OUR HOUSES." But here Uncle Richard just couldn't go on. He started to giggle, then theatrically guffawed. "Oh dear, I think they call this corpsing in theatrical circles," he spluttered. "I . . . I . . . just can't go on." Then Emma began to giggle, and lo, Mrs, Brumley too! And yes, yes, even Jack was grinning!

A thudding sound occurred in the corner of the room. A knife appeared stuck into the wooden panelling. The intruder's black-gloved hand pointed at the weapon, which vibrated in the wall. The room fell silent. There was no more laughter.

"Everyone listening? Now that we're all taking this seriously," Ropeman said, "let's start over again. Please read."

Uncle Richard got to the same place and collapsed in the same way, holding up his hand in protest and apology. "My dear young man," he interrupted himself again. "You really can't expect anyone watching your film to think that I think this. It's beyond belief. I really am very sorry, but you are . . . ." A second knife appeared in Ropeman's hand—as if by magic.

"Very well," said the Archbishop. He cleared his throat, composed himself and, in his professional pulpit voice, he read out the proclamation:

All the following institutions must participate in an interfaith conference. We have been inspired by the magical child who was just a few days ago idiotically murdered. The participants must include representatives of the following creeds:
    Hindu adherents to the various major cults
    Conservative, Orthodox, and Reform Judaism
    The Greek and Russian Orthodox Churches

The Catholic Church
The Church of England
All branches of Protestant Christianity
Shiite, Sunni, and Wahhabi Islam.
FAILURE TO APPEAR WILL RESULT IN A PLAGUE ON YOUR HOUSE!
This is the program of *Deus ex Machina*.

The Archbishop looked up from the proclamation and smiled calmly. Something about it actually seemed to reassure him—though for the moment Emma could not think why. "Is that all?" he asked, spreading out the parchment on his empty desk. "Is there anything else you'd like to order up?" he enquired with impish irony.

"That's all," said Ropeman. He quickly closed his video camera and stored it in his backpack with practiced, deft motions. Then, with a smart, sharp, powerful movement, he inserted the blade of his second knife into the frame of the closed door in such a way as to prevent immediate exit from the room. "Thank you for your time everyone. A wonderful performance, Archbishop. I do hope the rest of you enjoyed the show," he said, and walked back to the window. He took hold of the rope that he'd left dangling on the sill, and with a curt nod to them all—it reminded Emma a bit of the Fat Man in the poem "The Night Before Christmas"—he vanished, his long black scarf trailing dramatically behind him, catching on the radiator for a second, before finally sliding off over the window ledge into the late afternoon sky. For several moments they didn't dare move to the window to see where he'd gone. When Emma did get there, the rope was dangling all the way to the ground into a clump of early-blooming forsythia. Ropeman had vanished.

"A simple-minded anarchist, do you think?" Uncle Richard asked. He was addressing the question to Jack.

"I expect so," Jack replied, "though I'm not sure how simple." Emma inspected Jack's face, angrily remembering how he had just sat there, calmly, doing nothing. Guilty. Guilty, was her verdict.

Uncle Richard seemed to have concluded the same; Mrs Brumley was also glaring accusingly at Jack. "These friends of yours are not acceptable, I'm afraid, young man," she said.

Jack looked at Emma with a calculation that she'd not seen in him before—or at least not noticed. "I do apologize for this rude intrusion," he said. "I admit that I do think I know group who plotted this little bit of protest. But I certainly did not tell Deus Ex Machina to do this. This was their initiative—entirely."

"Well, if you do know this idiotic madman, you certainly owe me an explanation. Immediately," snapped Emma, livid.

"Emma. Temper, temper," said Uncle Richard.

"You stay out of this for the moment," she ordered her uncle. "Well?" She demanded to know again, looking at Jack. "And did you speak to anyone about our meeting with Uncle Richard?"

"I might have mentioned it once or twice."

"Once or twice?" Emma exclaimed, by now feeling completely betrayed and used.

"But I swear I never thought they'd arrange this little performance for us."

"Little performance?"

Then Jack started to smile. She thought he was going to laugh. She looked at her Uncle. He was shaking his head, with a very slightly wry smile.

Meanwhile, Mrs. Brumley was trying to get the knife out of the wall. After a few moments, Jack re-discovered his inner gentleman and rose to help. He pulled the weapon out with a sharp jerk of his hand and then turned, holding it, to face them. They shied away. He looked down at the knife in his hand and shook his head.

"You're holding a weapon, young man," said Mrs Brumley.

Jack turned the knife around so that the handle pointed toward Mrs Brumley and handed it to her with a chivalrous gesture. She accepted it without taking her eyes off his face.

"Who was it, Jack? Tell us!"

"Well, I certainly know about *Deus Ex Machina*, but I'm not sure of the identity of the particular young man. I think I recognized the voice though. With a little research, I could perhaps give the police his name. If you wanted."

"We certainly do. And we'll give them your name as well," said the outraged Mrs Brumley.

"Now Mrs Brumley, patience and tolerance please."

"I will not have any of that toleration nonsense from you today, your Eminence," she complained, rolling her eyes to the ceiling.

Speaking with great deliberation, the Archbishop said, "Let's see what we should do with this parchment. Let's have it framed and hung on the wall, Mrs Brumley. THE OFFICIAL PLAGUE ON ALL OUR HOUSES. Very impressive. A good lesson in intellectual humility."

"We will *not* have it framed. In fact, you should stop fingering it at once. It will be evidence in the investigation and trial. You and your insane friends, young man, are in serious trouble. Look at this mess. Destruction of property. Assault. Trespassing. There's almost no crime you haven't committed."

"Murder?" asked Jack.

"What did you say?"

"Murder? Have these people committed murder?"

"What are you talking about?"

"Really, Mrs Brumley," said Jack, "These *Deus Ex Machina* characters are basically harmless pranksters. No one's been hurt."

"Not hurt! Are you out of your mind? We have been invaded. Our privacy has been . . . ."

"Now now Mrs Brumley. Let's please sit down and have just a little more tea and think what to do," Uncle Richard suggested.

"Your Eminence," she spluttered at him, "How . . . ."

He made a gesture of command and she finally obeyed. He gestured also at Emma and Jack, who resumed their seats.

"Let us consider together," he said, almost in the tone of voice he might have used in delivering a homily. Then he raised his hand to prevent Jack's saying whatever it was that he seemed about to say.

"What are they going to do with that tape?"

Again he raised his hand to prevent Jack speaking.

"Not until we have tea before us."

The ritual was performed again, but this time the Archbishop would not accept that Jack should not take tea.

"It is positively rude, young man, to turn down tea—especially under the circumstances."

So Jack slurped tea. The telephone mysteriously came back to life, but the Archbishop decided not to call the police—at least not yet.

Mrs Brumley was not best pleased.

In a Darkroom

A rush of air. A flash of light. Jack enters. The door slams. "Okay," Jack the client says quietly. "I never asked you folks to turn into terrorists for me. What do you think you're doing? And who's the acrobat on the rope?" Any effect of his outrage is softened by his quiet smile and nearly silent chuckle.

"No one here is acrobatic," says the older woman. "Do NOT worry about that, my son. Just recognize that we have our ways and means. Our Deus Ex Machina is just your ideas, Jack, grown up and left school. Out of the mind and into the world!"

"Flash! Theological Flash! Yet one more replay!"

The Archbishop appears first on one screen, then another and another—until finally he is looking in on the darkness from all angles. Slivers of broken glass glitter in his hair. Perhaps his hands tremble very slightly. He appears either to be about to laugh or to be utterly terrified. He reads the proclamation ending with "PLAGUE ON ALL OUR HOUSES" in his official-sounding voice.

"There's no art to find the mind's construction in the face," sighs a young scholar.

A later segment of the broadcast originates from a newsroom. The Archbishop now looks composed, august. The whole Darkroom listens intently. He comments that the "Plague on All Our Houses" manifesto "is rebellious in an adolescent way. However," intones the head of the Church of England, "these young people do have a sense of urgency that we all should share. They are quite right to say that we religious leaders have not done enough to make peace in the world. I therefore would like to take this somewhat unorthodox occasion to announce that I will convene a meeting as soon as possible to plan for a Grand Religious Summit. Representatives of all the Major Faith Communities will be invited to attend both the preliminary meeting and the full summit. The preliminary meetings will take place in Church of England offices in London and Canterbury. We will not procrastinate," says His Eminence. "We will not speak empty words and take no action." The television people have given him only ninety seconds of air time, so he hurries right along. He has already contacted the Pope, and certain key rabbis. He has sent letters to an Iranian Ayatollah, and to several important Mullahs in Jordan and Afghanistan. He has invited various Saudi clerics. He has been in consultation with the Dalai Lama. He has spoken at length to various American Evangelists. Hindu Priests are on his list. The Archbishop's last moment of ordinary media-projected fame is his remark, "The Sacred Child is dead; but long live the child in all of us."

The screens go dark. "Well, "says Jack. He bows his head in thought for a moment. "I've got to go see some people about all this," he announces.

"We don't think you really want to leave us just yet," says the older woman. "Now, let's see . . . " she continues as if consulting a schedule of events. "We have to finish a previous job. You wanted Yahweh?"

"I did," says Jack brightly. "Give us the God of the Jews. He comes first."

"Oh. Okay. Good choice."

Clicking sounds, a buzz of static, a hiss of cosmic background radiation. A shrill whistle, ascending through the painful high pitch—up and on, dying out above the range of hearing. An African-American basso:

"**In the beginning God created the heaven and the . . .**"

"No, no!" snaps Jack. The voice ceases in mid syllable. "That's not God. That's somebody talking about God. Get us God, please."

"Who cares, man? It's all the word of God."

"Wrong. Sometimes God speaks, and sometimes prophets speak. It's different voices. Listen. It doesn't all pretend to be the word of God. I've done my homework." He pulls a small book out of his pocket and waves it at the Darkroom I general. He fumbles for a moment, searching through several pages. Then he announces, "Drop down three verses in your digitized holy wisdom, and you'll get the big boy talking in his own voice—or anyhow, in translation."

Hissing, static, buzzing. Then a loudness: **Let there be light: and there was light**."

"Cut the 'and there was light' bit. That's narrative commentary, not the Big Guy. Just have the Big Bopper's words. Nothing else."

"Anything you say, Mr Big yourself. What's next?"

"Let's see. Try verse six."

Booming echoes reverberate. "**Let there be a firmament in the midst of the waters, and let it divide the waters from the waters.**"

"Huh?" says one voice.

"Never mind," says another. "It doesn't have to make sense. After all, it's only God talking."

"Yeah. He's got poetic license. Issued it himself," says a young male. "How 'bout the voice?"

"It'll do. Pompous. Over the top. Good stuff," he says. "Now we have to go public. Let's get those CGI Gods up and running now! The premiere showing will be soon!"

VII

TRIAL OF THE GODS

After the Canterbury fiasco, Emma was at first determined to throw Jack out of her life. However, when she talked to him again, he seemed genuinely contrite about what had happened. He insisted that he had not masterminded the *Deus Ex Machina* coup de théâtre, although he admitted he probably knew the people who had. Emma believed him. She wanted to. Jack was certainly cagey about his life, but that didn't make him a liar. And when she remembered that night in Canterbury, her body leapt to Jack's defence. No, she couldn't give up on him just yet.

Her anger with Jack was also tempered by her Uncle's optimistic opportunism. That was the only way she could describe the Archbishop's attitude. He did not seem at all humiliated by the broadcasts of his recitation of the Deus Ex Machina proclamation "A Plague on All Your Houses." Their phone conversations astonished her: uncle Richard's had resolved to capitalize on the fiasco. He was like a born-again Christian, a resurrected believer, determined to make something good happen in the world. He seemed determined to leave his mark in the pages of history. He could have taken the easiest course to his imminent retirement and just carried on attending to business, going through the motions of his role. He was a solid, reliable performer, Emma realized, but so far his life was without historic importance. He explained to his niece how he had grown piously slack in high office with the relentless bureaucracy of management. The more involved he'd become with the Church, the less connected he was with God. He was like a husband always too busy with work to tend to his marriage. He'd reached the top rung of the ecclesiastical ladder, yet had lost touch with the core of his life. He couldn't remember the last time he'd tested his faith in action. What had he 'fallen in love with' all those years ago as a young novitiate? Why had he stepped on the ladder in the first place? In many ways, he admitted that Jack was right: Christianity had become just another self-interested business, and he was no more than Chairman of the Board, totally out of touch with the shop floor. In Jack's burning atheism, the Archbishop apparently recognized a remembered fire in himself. It was time to rekindle it. It was time for action. It was time for the global inter-faith conference. It was time to carry the message of the Sacred Child from India: Make Peace or Die.

"You know," Uncle Richard said to Emma one morning, when she was in his Lambeth Palace office, "we believers have an advantage. We think that God is good and that God exists and will do good things for us. And we Anglicans especially think that God will help those of us who try to help themselves. So for us there's hope. But, Em, there's something that bothers me greatly. I want to know how these poor atheists can have any hope? I don't see it. If you live by empiricism, you have to despair over the evidence that current events provide. And we know what despair does to us. So your friend Jack . . . " He shrugged, staring at the shifting shapes of clouds beyond the Palace window that has been so quickly repaired with clear glass. "So I feel it's my duty to give even the atheists a bit of hope." He leaned back in his creaking office chair, put his feet up on his august desk and smiled at her—a dazzling smile. She could see why he had become Archbishop. Every once in a while that became apparent.

The telephone rang in the outer office, and Mrs Brumley came on the intercom. "That Mr Foote rang up; but I'm afraid I took the initiative and told him to simply go away and leave us alone. It's none of my business of course, but . . . how can I put it? . . . perhaps it would be a good idea if Emma and Jack should cease to be an . . . (ahem) . . . item. I think that's the word. Anyway, just a thought, Archbishop. Sorry to intrude. Please forgive me." She hung up.

Uncle Richard looked at Emma. "She is a bit meddlesome," he whispered. "But she means well." He peered over his glasses, raised his eyebrows and looked into Emma's heart. How well he read it! He was tacitly advising her to stay with Jack. She easily forgave his opportunism. He agreed to schedule and announce the screening of a film that Jack reported he had produced. His spirit of compromise and accommodation was immense. After all, he was tacitly taking Jack's advice in setting up the interfaith conference, and he was communicating through him to the shadowy Deus Ex Machina protestors to try to ensure that they would not disrupt the proceedings. Her breaking off with Jack might somehow jeopardize prospects. Her relationship with Jack was a kind of eddy beside the stream of events; or maybe it was an example of how the puff from a butterfly's wing can cause a hurricane on the other side of the world.

But in her own defence, Emma vowed to assert her beliefs and attitudes against Jack's, the next time she saw him. So she said, "Don't you think that if believing in God makes people happy, then we shouldn't interfere with their beliefs? Hasn't religion been *the* major human mode of thought for several millennia? We really can't ask the human race just to pitch overboard everything their ancestors believed. And if we just accept it, and get on with our lives and think about something else, isn't that better?" She put her head on Jack's chest and listened to his heart beating its own time.

"I'd agree with you," said Jack, stroking her head with one hand, the remote control already in the other "—maybe—if it wasn't so obvious that religious faith is doing more harm than good in the world. Look at all the wars it causes."

Emma hesitated for just a moment, and then decided to say what she thought. Jack did it; so why shouldn't she. "Don't you realize how brainwashed *you* are, Jack, by the news. You are manipulated by the supposedly rational, impartial Media Gods? Everything you think is colored by your News Fixes. The chimes of Big Ben, the BBC Radio 4 pips are your call to prayer. You switch on the news as often as a Muslim prays, and your Reverend News Readers preach the same old litany of woe every time. They never preach good news, or mention the amazing things church people do quietly, every day. That isn't news, is it? And anyway, how do you report belief? Most common belief is silent, invisible in people's hearts; but every day it nudges people towards kindness, selflessness. Every day, *because of God*, (whether he exists or not!) people choose *not* to murder, but to forgive. But that isn't news! Where's the blood and gore in simple belief? Where are the guns and tanks and macho swaggering and all the melodrama of catastrophe in quiet prayer? I reckon, without religion, there'd be *much* more killing in the world. Without religion there'd be too much catastrophe even for the news to cope with!"

Jack said nothing but just carried on changing television channels, hunting for news. New takes on the same old news. CNN, Sky, BBC, Channel 4 all variations on the Morning News at Six!

"And, anyway, you can't just abolish religion with a wave of some magic wand," said Emma talking to herself. "And even if you could, what would that accomplish? In an overcrowded world, competing communities are trying to live on the same little patch of land. So people try to commit genocide. They'd do that with or without religion. It's social Darwinism, survival of the fittest. What about the massacres in southeast Asia? Remember Pol Pot? Have you forgotten Russia under good old atheist Stalin? What about Mao Tse Tung and the Cultural Revolution? Religion had no role in those slaughters."

"Not directly at least," Jack retorted.

"Oh! So you're listening! What do you mean, 'not directly'?" She poked Jack in the ribs so that he flinched like a child being tickled. He dropped the remote control, which she grabbed. She pressed 'Off'. "What do you mean, *'not directly*?'" Emma mimicked his phrase, angrily.

"Well communism was a religion for most of the people. It's just that the State replaced the Church; the leader replaced God. The Russians got it all wrong. People were supposed to have the same blind faith in the bureaucracy that they used to have in the clergy. There wasn't really much difference between the Niceaean creed and the communist manifesto. They were both articles of idiotic faith. And that just might explain why the communists indulged in murderous purges. They were just doing what the Old Testament describes the Israelites doing to the Canaanites. Communist politics was just religion by a different name."

"Oh come on now!" It was more than she could take. She yanked her share of the sheets around her and sat up. "You're blaming everything that goes wrong on religion—even the things done by militant atheists. And your bloody anarchist friends go rampaging and looting in Milan. It's not religion's fault that man is violent. It's just human nature."

Emma grabbed a pillow and whacked it on Jack's head—hard.

"Christ Em! That hurt! Just look how violent religion's making *you!*" He grinned at her.

"No, *you're* making me violent because you're as bloody-minded as the most bloody-minded believers! Your atheism is just faith by a different name.

Jack rolled away from her and shrugged, grinned, shook his head ruefully.

O JERUSALEM

Emma's phone rang. "Hope I haven't woken you, Em?" It was Uncle Richard, ringing to give her the latest progress report on the Interfaith Conference. He was optimistic. He had arranged for a preliminary interfaith conference for the purpose of laying plans for a full-fledged meeting. He had invited a select two dozen religious leaders to meet with him in London, at a comfortable hotel in Kensington. Most had even accepted.

"And tell Jack, schedule wise, we shall be opening festivities with that film that he says he has produced. A gala performance in the Odeon Swiss Cottage. Tell Jack. Must go, I've got some Turkish chap on the other line."

"My god," said Jack. "There's actually hope."

"Yes!" thought Emma, "even for Atheists!"

The preliminary planning for the conference begins on a rainy afternoon in north London, without great publicity. The media aren't interested in peace-talks without politicians, or movies without film stars. Nonetheless, in a Platonic cave of modern cinema, various religious dignitaries, an atheist, an agnostic, and a few reporters sit in darkness whilst ideas take shape on screen. Confusions of light spread upwards and outwards to illuminate dimly a vast chamber. Clouds obscure any ceiling; mists hang on cliff-like walls; spray boils up from the base of a distant plunging waterfall. It may be somewhere in the Himalayas, with no roof at all. Or it may be the interior of some unbounded cathedral or temple. A dream world exists but has not been fully created—a vague landscape.

The audience sees a bench so long that it has no beginning or end. On that bench sit, or rather hover, three giant figures of whom only segments are visible, both because they are obscured by mists and because they are so huge that they are almost impossible to view whole. As the scene shifts from left to right and up to down, we see a giant head here, a great arm there, and an enormous blank-gazing eye like the ocular orb of a whale or a long-extinct dinosaur. At one point a great shepherd's crook the size of the bole of an old oak appears, held by some partly visible hand. A great screen blocks the view from the front of the figure furthest to our right. He is hiding, or trying to. Only parts of him appear from behind the screen. At first the figures seem to be statues; but then an arm moves, an eye swivels, the shepherd's staff tilts, a moustache end twitches. Music deep as an earthquake rumbles up into the range of hearing. Harmonies slowly emerge in a cosmic crescendo.

A distant explosion becomes an echoing voice that bellows slowly at a painful volume, with a confusing echo: "I protest . . . *test* against having been summoned here against my judgment . . . *ment*. All present should remember . . . *ember* that I . . . existed . . . first, . . . *first* . . . *irst*!" Through swirling mists we see the gnarled wooden staff rhythmically moving up and down, marking time, eternal rhythm, as the voice booms emphatically, "I existed first . . . *irst irst*." The sound is bouncing off cliffs, rising, falling, fading out of meaning into a buzz and hum in the ears. Then the enormous staff rises and points threateningly at the two other presences who sit obscured in fog far down the bench, way beyond human measurement, beyond earthly notation. "You two are modern . . . imitations . . . of my greater antiquity, . . .,*iquity*." The staff trembles. Lightning leaps off the hook with jagged arcs and dances over the two distant figures, who seem quite unperturbed by the firebolts that spark off their bodies.

Behind the audience in the dark cave, rise sounds of shuffling feet and impatient coughing. A door slams. Someone has arrived late, or is leaving early.

The scene of the film now pans and trolleys in the direction pointed out by the trembling, tree-trunk-sized staff.

"And who are you?" thunders a second voice from behind its protective canvas. A dramatic parting of the mists momentarily reveals the cavernous source of this voice, a mouth the size of the Hoover Dam, hung with the uncut beard of eons. Tendrils droop down from chin and lips, curling down out of sight below the bench over which he sprawls. The beard must be a matter of some principle. It would weigh down his head, trip him up, tangle in his feet. And not even a god could comb such a beard! When the mists swirl away we see from the side that his long robes flow over the granite bench into rippling silk pools on a transparent or even bottomless floor. Cushions, hundreds of them, float around him. He lounges gracefully as he asks again, "Who are you?" His voice is imperious, fearless. He speaks with absolute clarity.

"I never name my name . . . my . . . ever . . . name . . .," replies speaker one, his crooked staff trembling with fury. Its knobby top has been blackened and burnished by eons of use.

A voice in the dark audience protests in some language not English. Specific words are indistinguishable; but someone is offended.

The camera pans away from speaker two for a quick roam around the landscape – mountains, caves, mists, a monstrous lamb, a flaming bush, sulphurous geysers spurting up, up, up through the ceilingless sky. Then it pans back again to show that a third speaker wears the head cloth of a Bedouin Sheik.

Light refracts into rainbows and mysterious luminosities.

"Not good for my heart," someone in the audience says quietly.

The flat intonation of the muezzin's call to prayer utters unintelligible syllables.

"Is that Arabic?" a puzzled member of the audience asks.

A band of yellow light falls from some spotlight hanging in the outer stratosphere upon the third male figure, who is partly naked, suspended in elegant repose in the middle of the bench. His muscles flex and his toga-like robes. His body oozes male strength. He is Mr Universe, before the universe, a being honed to perfection. He too has a beard which seems to have been neatly trimmed by some cosmic barber. "You two are both important but wrong." He now wears a Palestinian red-and-white–checked kaffieh to replace the Bedouin headgear.

This amorphous figure, with his millinery pageant, booms: "I will have mercy on you and all presences visible and invisible who have preceded my revealing myself to this world; but I will have mercy *only* when you acknowledge that I am the Truth. You two are partial wisdoms only. I am the absolute truth. The One. You both dabble in polytheism and evil images that ensnare the eye and delude the mind. You see angels that are half human, half winged birds. You worship saints who stink of unclean animals. My followers rip out the eyeballs of anyone claiming sainthood. There is no such thing. There are only prophets, and after my prophet, no more prophets. He gave my final word. Submit. Surrender. Obey. Only then will we have justice and peace."

"There is nothing partial about me . . . !" roars Speaker One. "Why should I cease upon some midnight hour? . . . *ow* . . . *er* . . . ?" The staff explodes and becomes a giant sword lashing the air, lopping off mountain tops that erupt with liquid heat. Thunders sound in distant valleys. Lightning splinters the sky. The mists compose themselves as storm clouds. Electric charges leap and crackle. A fireball flies towards the front of the screen, as if about to burst into reality.

Gasps from the auditorium!

But the imaginary fireball can't leap into the audience.

Wow! Strewth! Bloody Hell! But also laugher, coughs and cries of 'Blasphemy!' 'Ridiculous!' 'Drivel!' in English, Italian, Turkish, Yiddish, Arabic.

O JERUSALEM

The middle presence again gives utterance: "Now now, my friends. Let us learn to love each other." He floats up between the other two, supported by a mob of winged tubby-tots that multiply under him like overgrown protozoa in time-lapse photography. Their wings flap whimsically and they squirm and wriggle and giggle. Some carry trumpets, some harps—but it is all purely for effect because this giant defies gravity. "Let us learn to live in harmony. Let us learn to accommodate. Let us learn to love each other." He repeats himself from some comfortable Nimbostratus.

A loud thud sounds in the darkness behind the audience. Either it is a blow struck by a fist, or it is one of the cushioned doors striking shut as another viewer exits the auditorium. A grunt and another blow follow. It could be a spring-loaded, upholstered seat closing.

But the movie plays on. In the back of the dark cinema cave real people cough, groan, make more remarks in various tongues. Who wrote this garbage? Is this meant to be funny? Where's the action? What is the point? I'm out of here! Excuse me! Excuse me! From the rear comes the clear comment: "Satchma! Satchma!" A swinging door bangs. Embarrassed laughter ripples about in the dark.

"Ahmaghanast!" says a very deep male voice.

"And God said 'Let this be over'!" sighs another.

But the film is not over. Out of the mist comes a line of figures that parade before the bench: one has the head of an elephant, another waves eight arms about, a third displays the head of a bird, another is an exquisitely formed woman with wings. Sphinxes come by in a phalanx, bodies of lioness, head and chests of women, wings of bats. A half-man half-lion swaggers past. The mists swirl faster; the wind whistles louder; the bench tilts and the great beings seem to slide about on it during the time of the earthquake.

"I'hm vury much afeared Ah've got somethin' better tuh do than listen tuh this 'ere nonsense," growls a bass voice that might have stepped straight out of the movie. The sounds of more people standing, hinged seats creaking, a swinging door.

The blade of a long, curved knife pierces the cinema screen from behind and slits an opening into the flow of clouds. STAB! STAB! STAB! Right through the eye of Mr Universe. The few remaining people in the audience laugh and gasp, unsure if this latest plot development is intended. Is this real knife in a real hand part of the movie? The hand reaches through the opened slit in the screen, holding a cigarette lighter. Flick. The screen begins to smolder and melt, then suddenly bursts into flame. Smoke pours through the beam of light from the projector.

"This blasphemy will cease!" a voice announces on the speaker system. Reality has hijacked cinema.

Afterwards, Emma remembered that the house lights briefly came up, revealing a shrunken audience –Jack and Uncle Richard, several rabbis, three or four priests in clerical dress, a Sikh in his grand turban, an Imam from a south London mosque. In the back row two newspaper reporters were snapping photos and scribbling notes.

Then the lights went off again and the PA system announced: "The makers of this film will not be permitted to project their filth." But the film continued to play for a moment or two longer on the damaged screen before the images of the great deities went up in smoke. Emma sat, staring blankly into the darkened stage behind the burned-away cinema screen. She, Jack and Uncle Richard did not know what to do or say.

A fire alarm had sounded. But when firemen came bursting into the auditorium, wearing yellow, rubberized overcoats, the fire had died. She walked with Uncle Richard to the lobby, leaving Jack sitting stubbornly alone. Emma couldn't quite remember what happened next, but Jack appeared in the lobby. He was breathing deeply, rolling his head around on his neck, trying to relax, whilst policemen and firemen mingled with the small and thinning Premier crowd. She put her hand on Jack's shoulder to calm him, and sensed hot flesh beneath the cloth. He petulantly shrugged off her gesture, shoved his hands in his pockets and brooded. For once he was lost for words.

Other hazy memories: the American preacher lurking in one corner, a great scowl on his face. Images two stony-faced long-robed Islamic clergymen floating through the exits. A rabbi laughing with a pretty girl in front of the deserted sweets counter. A Turkish professor standing beside a man who, she had learned, was head of the Arab-Israeli Friendship Foundation. Mrs Brumley, ploughing through the loose police line to hover solicitously over the Archbishop.

Jack did his vanishing act, again. A policeman asked her mechanically, "Do you have any idea who the perpetrators might have been?"

She had too many impressions, all vague. The lights went off and on several times, and then suddenly, Jack came bursting through a doorway crying, "They've stolen the film. Officer! Officer! They've stolen the film!"

A dazed little man emerged through the same doorway. She later understood later that someone—the "perpetrators," as the police were calling them—had raided the projection room, blind-folded and gagged the projectionist, then pushed him into a storage closet and locked the door. The perpetrators had ripped the DVD out of the machine, and escaped onto the roof. It was a planned theft, with at least two people involved, one to set the screen on fire to distract everyone's attention, and a second to overpower the projectionist and steal the film. Jack had gone to retrieve his film, and found it missing. He'd heard muffled sounds in the closet and rescued the projectionist. She remembered Jack saying "They're on the roof. I'll bet they're still on the roof." He hurried off.

Various policemen continued to circulate through the lobby, asking questions. The guests all seemed quite eager to talk—exactly the reverse of some similar scene in the traditional murder mystery, Emma thought, where the all guests are murder suspects who stonewall the beleaguered police. She remembered a young man standing beside the blonde American Preacher, frantically scribbling notes. The Turkish professor later told Emma that the young man was a reporter for some American newspaper and that the preacher, Reverend Jones, had been talking to him about the young American missionary woman who had been kidnapped in Afghanistan.

"I've done what I could through certain channels. It wasn't much, I am very much afraid," the Turk had told her.

Emma understood very little of what had happened. A party of Americans had gone out to distribute food and clothing near Kabul, in good Christian loving defiance of the events of 11th September. Several Americans had been captured by the Taliban and imprisoned for the crime of spreading Christianity. That much she knew from several media reports. What happened next was a little more mysterious. The big blonde American preacher suddenly fell to his knees. With his phone to the side of his head, he arched his back until he faced upwards to the ceiling. "God be praised!" he shouted. "They have found her!"

This made so little sense that almost everyone ignored it. Reverend Jones was an embarrassing acrobat of faith to the reserved English members of the thinning crowd. They averted their gazes, turned their backs. The Professor from Istanbul, however, had suddenly gripped Emma's elbow and smiled, wide-eyed, at the loud American kneeling on the floor. He shook his head in amazement—though just what amazed him was not clear.

As for Uncle Richard, he was talking to an American academic, Professor Friedman and man's student, Helen Willis. Emma remembered shaking hands with Miss Willis and feeling that the young girl's fingers were like the bones of some frightened bird. The girl was staring about the lobby, her face bright red, obviously doubting her own safety. She was quite absurdly clutching a bright pink handbag to her side—almost as if it was her infant child. Emma found herself irritated with this young American woman.

The guests were departing with elaborate bows, vigorous handshakes, a respectful touching of the chest, a placing of the palms and fingers together before the face—all the international gestures of respect, goodwill, farewell. The Archbishop scrupulously apologized to each guest as he left: the fellow in the turban, the man in the saffron-colored robe, the Greek Patriarch in the long black gown, various grey-bearded distinctions of a dozen ancient cultures paraded out into the drizzly evening.

A few stragglers remained waiting for taxis whilst the lights in the lobby ceiling started to go off, row by row. A loud thudding sound, followed by a shuffle and a grunt of pain came from behind the closed popcorn counter, and Jack staggered out, bleeding about the face. He stumbled into the Reverend Jones, who staggered backwards, his white shirt slightly stained with Jack's blood. Rev. Jones dabbed at himself with a handkerchief, then he turned to a pair of Imams and said loudly, "Well suh, there is a mile-wide, nasty streak of violence in Islam. Ya'll have to admit that much." Emma heard his angry, deep voice proclaiming, "Y'all are behavin' evil. Y'all goin' aroun' beaten people up. An' even if they deserve it, y'all *ain't* the one's tuh puhfoam that function. *No suh.* Vengeance is mine, sayeth the Lord."

The Turkish Professor sighed and said to Emma, "The saddest thing is that this American fanatic of yours is probably right about the thugs who have beaten this young man: they could well be Islamists."

Rev Jones collapsed to his knees beneath the one remaining lit spotlight in the ceiling and roared:

"Brothers and sisters, please join me in prayer for our children lost in the wilderness of Afghannystan. Loahd, let us not merely pray but positively plead with y'all," he bellowed. He clasped his hands and raised a great begging, shaking two-handed fist up toward the ceiling. "Loahd"—he cried in poly-syllabic vowels,—"heah oah prayer for Miss Betsey Barndale, who has been cruelly kidnapped in the desert."

Acutely embarrassed by the public spectacle of prayer, Emma turned to Uncle Richard. He merely raised his eye brows and spoke wordlessly through his twinkling eyes.

A group of four Islamic clergy didn't seem embarrassed so much as horrified, glancing over their shoulders fleeing as if the loud prayer were some great obscenity. The large American shuffled after the four Imams on his knees and cried out to the closed glass doors behind departed Islamists: "Pray with me, mah fellow Christians 'n' other monotheists. Ah ask ya'll tuh pray with me for the safe release of mah disciple Miss Betsey Barndale." His voice fell a few decibels and became somewhat conversational. "Loahd? Yuh listenin'? Ouah Miss Betsey has been kidnapped? By Taliban barbarians? In Afgannystan? 'N' we haven't seen or heard of her—hide noah hair—for months now. Loahd, we ask that you delivah Miss Betsey from evil. Grant huh freedom. Re-unite huh with huh family."

Emma remembered how the Turkish Professor had taken her arm, put it on his arm, and escorted her past the praying Reverend, through the exit into the wet evening air. She'd had the distinct impression that he was flirting with her. But before she had a chance to worry about his intentions, she felt all the muscles in his arm seize. His elbow clamped her hand to his side, and she remembered the sound of air being sucked in and out through clenched teeth. The Turkish professor was staring into the stream of traffic. She looked in the direction of his gaze, and saw a white Cadillac limousine. It looked, like a giant albino dachshund on wheels. All of its black tinted windows were closed, except one, through which a strange face appeared: under a turban a pair of reflecting sunglasses peered into the road like the eyes of some monstrous night bug. A long beard flowed down below the face. Behind the sunglassed face three—or was it even four—young men's heads appeared—all staring out at the scene. Then the window closed and the car pulled away. Professor Ersan's head tracked its movement.

"Today's jihadi must be greater than yesterday's," Professor Ersan sighed.

"What?" she queried.

"The power of the jihadi must exceed the power of haram," he added.

She remained puzzled. He seemed to be quoting something.

"Between animal passion and religious faith falls the shadow that is mass murder."

"Who said that?" she asked.

"I did," he replied, smugly. Then he raised a commanding arm and hailed a taxi. In the fashion of the good gentleman, he put her in it, and then—halted in traffic—she watched as he returned to help Jack out through the cinema doors and into the waiting police car, which would take him to the hospital. Emma felt a pang of guilt. She should have been helping Jack herself. She should have gone with him to the hospital. But Uncle Richard waved at her, indicating that she should wait for him. So spoke to the driver, waited, and watched the scene. Miss Willis and her American Professor were standing in front of the cinema, trying to hail a cab. Suddenly Miss Willis stood up on her toes and called out. Professor Friedman clutched her arm. The girl was calling something into the night. At first it seemed that she was saying "I'm, I'm." But that made no sense. It was only later that Emma realized what she'd heard. Not "I'm, I'm," but "Chaim! Chaim!"

In a Darkroom

Enter the Client, visible in the spot, bandaged.

"Been in a bit of a scrap, have we?" asks a sarcastic voice.

"My poor, poor boy." The older woman touches his face. He brushes her hand aside, violently. A pen she had been holding arcs through the shaft of light and clatters into the shadows. He slumps into the director's chair set for him in the spotlight. His face is bruised. His upper lip is fat. Someone has stitched up a slit in his skull. His hair stands up on edge from some chemical treatment around the wound. One eye has been bandaged over. A short line of stitches serrate his forehead.

"Who did this to you?" she asks.

"Thought you folks might find out."

"Possibly," she says cautiously.

"Where'd it happen?"

"On the roof of the Swiss Cottage cinema," he says.

"No CCTV there."

"But get images on cameras from a perimeter around the area?"

"Try concentrics. Start with closest, move out to half a mile," Instructs the woman. The young people go to work.

"Hold it. We've caught a break. One CCTV tap's got balaclavas."

Five men in a shadowed alley, appear on the largest screen. The camera zooms, refocuses, over adjusts contrast, under-adjusts, settles down. Murky images of men with masks emerge.

"Location?" asks the woman.

"Finchley Road tube station—access alleyway west."

"Tracking possible?"

"Dunno."

"Hold it. Here's a third image. And . . . yesssss! . . . . There's the film DVD in his hand."

"Where?"

"Avenue Road. Just north of the park. There. DVD in pocket! See?"

"See it. How'd they get there?"

"Unknown. Taxi?"

"London mosque is nearby."

"More Islamophobia from you?"

"Maybe."

"Check storage for mosque camera after . . . time?"

"Time. Eight-fifty-one-fifty."

"Checking."

A minute's silence punctuated by keyboards clicks, machine beeps, the static buzz and hum of the cosmic background radiation of the internet.

"Got 'em," says a boyish voice. "Just going into the big mosque."

"Sooooo . . . " breathes a boyish voice, "the Islamic fringe terrorizes the atheist cinema-terrorist."

"That's me," says the Client, ruefully. You folks are pretty good at finding stuff out. You're almost omniscient."

"We workers in the global brain come closer to full knowledge than most members of old Homo Sap."

Now comes a big interruption.

"Hey wait just a second. Get this," says a boy's voice. "Some military geezer in the States has agreed to a blackmail demand for the release of some hostage or other from someplace. The demand was for a tactical nuclear device. I think the hostage might just be that girl from Kansas who went to in Afghanistan and got herself kidnapped."

"How do you know this?"

"We have taps into Mossad and MI5, my friend."

"OOoops!"

"What's wrong? What have you done?" asks the older woman.

"I'm afraid . . ."

"Of what, now?"

"I'm afraid I pushed the wrong button and sent the demand for a Nuke to that reporter for the Wichita Falcon.

"Oh no."

"Oh well."

"Why not let Wichita know."

"Why not indeed."

VIII

POOR UNCLE RICHARD

The Archbishop's Interfaith Conference, in its extended planning phase, was just one big media black hole from which no news escaped until the altercations at the movie house converted it into a near catastrophe that was mildly interesting. A few tabloid papers had their usual high times with headlines: "Religious Bust-Up," "Burn this Movie," and "Punching Peaceniks." One featured a photo of Jack's bashed-up face, captioned "The Director's Cut!"

A serious editorial in *The Guardian* called the Conference an "idealistic but naïve attempt by the retiring Archbishop to address the urgent problem of Religious Fanaticism in the modern world." However, the writer criticized the Archbishop for allowing his conference to be "hijacked" by *Deus Ex Machina*—that "ridiculous protest group with no clear agenda and no known base of operations, who have disrupted various IMF, World Bank, Group of Seven, and European Union Conferences." *Deus Ex Machina* was dismissed as a "witless bunch of anarchists—puerile and incompetent, sowing chaos but taking no responsibility for their actions." The *Daily Mail* called the proposed conference a "fool's paradise." Jack Foote had produced a film that "was an insult to all the world's religions." The paper then went on to wax scathing about the presumed Islamic fanatics who had disrupted the screening: the journalists punched all the right Islamophobic buttons with words like 'Jihad', 'faith-schools', 'Immigrants', 'Shari'ah.'

A few Twittering Birdbrains condemned Israel for not trusting the Palestinians—though neither had had anything to do with organizing the conference. A terrorist expert on the Today program criticized Christians like the Archbishop for being naïve about the violent, unforgiving tendencies of Islam and Judaism. "We must fight fire with fire not with meetings and words," he concluded. Hinduism was mentioned only in one London Asian paper, whose editorial recalled the "Miraculous Boy" in an ambiguously condescending way, while they also noted that the child's great and good idea lived on in the purpose of the Interfaith Conference. In the global game of who's-got-God-on-their-side, the only major players whom the media did not criticize were themselves. (They didn't recognize their own pseudo-divinity.) Nonetheless, it was another blessing in disguise for the Archbishop. He was headline news once again, thanks to that atheist Jack and especially his terrorizing detractors.

Many years later Emma wrote a memoir "Deus Ex Machina," in which she recalls, how, despite it all,

> My dear Uncle Richard, undefeated, decided to continue with the Planning Plenary Conference. As he pointed out to me and Mrs Brumley, several hundred delegates representing more than a dozen world religions had agreed to attend and many had already come to England; it was too late to cancel the proceedings. Mrs B grumbled her assent. Worse yet, in a fit of what I distinctly remember Mrs B's calling "sheer perversity," Uncle Richard decided to hold the Planning Plenary in the main hall of Canterbury Cathedral. Of course an Arch Deacon, a Precentor, six Sextons, two Vestrymen, three Vergers and a Dean, led from the rear by Mrs Brumley, all objected to such abuse of the sacred precincts. But Uncle Richard ignored them. After all, he would officially retire ten days later. He wouldn't have to put up with these people—or they with him—for very much longer. I think, too, that he wanted to score a final winning goal on home ground as Archbishop of Canterbury. He wanted to deliver a swan song that would be remembered for all time, that would have the vast cathedral resounding like a football stadium with joyous whoops of new communion amongst peoples of the world. Perhaps he had one eye on the Nobel Peace Prize? Perhaps he really believed he could bring peace to the nations. I remember Uncle Richard saying to me, "I

haven't come this far for nothing, Em." *The Guardian* was wrong about him. Yes, my uncle was idealistic, but he was certainly not naïve.[7]

In her memoir, Emma remembers how, in Canterbury, she watched groups of the faithful come wandering into the great hall—mere mortals lost in the cathedral's 12th-century Gothic immensity. She remembers one image in particular:

> Mr Jack Foote, bandaged, bruised, slumped sideways on a wooden chair, propping himself against a great stone pillar, exhausted—but milking his injuries for all their worth. And now, as 'Atheist-Martyr' he apparently considered himself the star of the show!
>
> I loved it when Mrs Brumley popped out from behind Jack's pillar and whispered loudly "For goodness sake, Mr Foote, sit up straight for once in your life." I could tell that she believed Jack knew exactly who had assaulted him but wouldn't tell the police."[8]

Emma found herself in one of her sympathetic-to-Jack phases, and for a brief time hovered over her wounded on-off lover. Sympathy was all Emma could offer. "Sometimes I wanted to punch Jack myself," she admits in her memoir. "His egoism was truly monstrous." Jack had never mentioned his mother, but Emma assumes "he must have been spoilt rotten as a child." For the moment, she was tempted to play mother. After all her lover had taken a severe beating. She don't know if it was Divine Retribution or not, but she did see that Jack was in pain. He had several stitches above his left eye. Both eyes were plum black and the bridge of his nose had turned a spectacular green, yellowing at the edges. "My poor little Atheist!" Emma whispered kissing him on the head. As they waited for events to begin, people gravitated to Jack, who slumped theatrically against his pillar while Mrs Brumley turned her attention elsewhere.

"Do we ever get to see the rest of the cinema?" asked the Turkish Professor. "Call me Ersan," he said, shaking Jack's hand.

---

[7] Williamson, Emma, *op cit, p* 15.
[8] Williamson, op cit, pp 44-46, 105.

"It was very good in parts," remarked Professor Friedman, looking at the huge mauve egg on Jack's forehead.

Edward, the founder of the Arab-Israeli Friendship Foundation, bent above Jack and whispered something; and one of the rabbis touched him consolingly on the shoulder. Then an Imam passed and performed some little ritual of greeting and respect with his hand on his chest, after which he nodded respectfully at Uncle Richard, who stopped by to quip, "I trust your acrobatic Ropeman has mastered the art of entering through doors by now? It would be such a shame if our Theological Windows were shattered today." Throughout it all, Jack said nothing. He just sat there, 'The Victim' star of the show for now. However, Emma's memory of the scene soon faded into something stranger than Jack.

> The next thing I recall is that awful Reverend Jones barnstorming into the cathedral bellowing like a bull. "Very dangerous, suh. Those folks are the same ones that have kidnapped mah precious Miss Betsey," he was saying to someone just as he entered the great hall. "Those folks may . . .," then suddenly he fell silent, just as he stepped through the portal. With his head back, he stared up into the glorious heights of the cathedral and fell to his knees "Alleluia!" he breathed. For a moment, he was simply a man humbled by the noble creation of his own species, overawed by this god-inspired cathedral. With no deity to inspire us, there would be no Canterbury Cathedral, no St. Paul's, no Sistine Chapel, no churches, no mosques, no shrines anywhere—the world would be devoid of human wonders. No Handel's Messiah, no Verdi's Requiem, no Bach Mass, half the music, half the art would vanish. How barren life would be. I remember suddenly thinking all this, and then looking at Jack. How small and pathetic he seemed.[9]

Then Emma remembers Mrs Brumley's whispering: "Those two petrifying Islamic gentlemen have arrived."

---

[9] Williamson, *op cit,* pp. 40-1.

For years afterwards, I retained the feel of her breath on my cheek and ear. I watched those two long-robed figures entering the Cathedral very slowly, one leading the other. It had been like a moment in a dream, when something was happening—or trying to happen—and wouldn't. It was as if the forward chronology of the cosmos had faltered. I recalled my new Turkish friend, Professor Ersan, making that sucking sound through his teeth from behind me—the same sound he had made outside the cinema. I remember how, upon the entrance of the two Islamic gentlemen, the buzzing of conversations ceased. [10]

"It's Sheikh Abu," whispered Ersan. "He's accepted the invitation! Hamdilillah!"

Sheikh Abu, like the man who led him, was dressed in flowing robes. Both wore full beards that Emma calls "grizzly." Each wore an immense turban. To her eye they were figures out of some Arabian Nights fantasy, except for Sheikh Abu's remarkable glasses: mirrored surfaces that reflected back to the people in the room only images of themselves. His glasses were like a movie screen projecting a movie the Sheikh could never see. He was stuck behind the screen, staring inward, into his own blind imaginings. Patiently, his guide, a man called Imam Kureishi, led him through the great doorway, shuffling so slowly that sometimes they hardly appeared to move at all.

"Sheikh Abu! You are most welcome here!" Uncle Richard proclaimed, gliding up the aisle, arms spread outward as if to offer a welcoming hug. But the Sheikh said nothing, gave no response, moved no further into the great hall. It was as if someone had pressed 'Pause' on a remote control. Nothing moved in his glasses. The actors waited—waited for the Sheikh to say something, do something, give them a cue so that they could press the 'Play' button again. A hundred eyes were riveted on him. Could he feel the force of their focus? Did he have a sixth sense alive to atmospheric fibrillations from an audience? Could he sense the invisible crisscrossing energy waves? Did his left index finger just twitch? It must have done, for suddenly action resumed. Slowly, Imam Kureishi put his lips to the blind man's ear and whispered a long, long whisper, longer than a simple

---

[10] Williamson, *op cit*, p. 42.

translation of the Archbishop's welcome. He must have been describing the scene for his master, speaking the movie that reflected in the blind man's glasses.

Emma remembers Uncle Richard balanced on one foot—indecisive about how to communicate with this alien human who could neither see, nor understand any language except Koranic Arabic. He reached out to take the Sheikh's hand from under his robe. The attending Imam whispered lengthily into his colleague's ear and the cathedral held its breath until a collective gasp resounded like the swish of a giant scythe. Instead of a right hand, a hook appeared. Emma remembers how her Uncle Richard slowly dropped his hand back into its folds of cloth, unsure how it might be possible to shake hands with a giant metal question mark.

Nevertheless, the Archbishop recovered his composure and guided the Islamic gentlemen to convenient seats, before the great baptismal font. Beside it stood a tall brass candlestick that had been placed there the previous year to honour the reign of the 103rd Archbishop of Canterbury. Emma's memoir recalls her Uncle Richard stooping down to the Sheikh, trying to establish contact, speaking softly now to Abu himself and now to the Imam, who was standing beside him, translating.

"I keep meeting this man!" Ersan hissed to Emma, watching the Archbishop's chivalrous grovelling. "I never really thought that he'd accept the invitation. What is this terrorist doing here?"

"Trying to help bring about world peace?" proposed Emma. "Isn't that why we're all here?" she added, a little surprised by the elegant Turk's anger. As Emma's book explains, she did not yet understand what her Turkish friend knew. Nobody could take their eyes off the Sheik in sunglasses. Was it rude to stare at the blind, Emma wondered? If so, Jack was being unforgivably rude, again. He was mesmerized by the Sheikh, staring at him with his one good green eye.

> I had the sense that I was witnessing the wounded fanatic of the unborn future contemplating his maimed doppelganger, a surviving militant from an unvanished past.[11]

A few pages later, Emma reports,

---

[11] Williamson, *op cit,* p. 50.

> Uncle Richard must have judged that all the important delegates had by this time assembled. I did not know what he had planned, but I remember watching how purposefully he paced down the central aisle and climbed to the nave pulpit. He obviously intended to deliver his last sermon, the crowning glory of his reign as Archbishop. Beside him stood those two life-sized statues of saints. He was at home in the pulpit at last. He turned the microphone on, rested both hands on the lectern and his first words were—I remember them vividly—
> "Excuse me."
> At first no one paid any attention. But he waited patiently until his motionless silence eventually commanded people's attention. Indeed, he had waited many years. But now the stage was his. It was time to leave his mark on history.[12]

Then a pew cushion thudded in the aisle and the Reverend Jones was suddenly on his knees again, his hands clasped before his face, his blonde head lifted heavenward, as he roared:

"WE PRAY FOR OUR DEAR IMPRISIONED SISTER. LORD, RELEASE HER FROM HER CAPTIVITY. SAVE HER BODY AND SOUL FOR HER DEAR FAMILY. IN JESUS CHRIST'S NAME WE PRAY. AH BEG OF Y'ALL TO JOIN MAH FERVENT PRAYER."

The Reverend Jones needed no microphone to broadcast his overblown personality into the vast spaces about him. He bounced his message off the walls, up into the organ loft, the Bell Harry Tower, into the apse, the cloisters, the Trinity Chapel, through Christ Church Gate. Everywhere the Cathedral buzzed and hummed with his show-stopping oration. He clasped his hands together with such fervor that his muscular arms trembled and the veins in his neck bulged like fat worms beneath his sweat-glistening skin. Emma thought he might burst. In fact, her book suggests that she half wished he would explode.

People shaded their eyes, massaged their foreheads, straightened their ties and fiddled with their hair. Someone blew his nose. Everyone felt embarrassed. Everyone felt guilty about feeling embarrassed. The Reverend

---

[12] Williamson, *op cit*, p. 50.

was only being emotional after all. Emotions were human. Somewhere a human was being held hostage and they were all responsible. They were guilty of being human. That's why their gods existed, to make them feel guilty—especially if innocent. The only person who didn't seem to be in some variety of exquisite existential guilty embarrassment was Sheikh Abu, who sat completely at ease while Imam Kureishi whispered in his ear. When Reverend Jones's loud oratorio had ended with an unfortunate sneeze from a distant pew, Sheikh Abu slowly raised his hooked arm, pointed toward the doorway and, for the first time, he smiled.

> Two rows of perfect pearly white teeth flashed from the midst of his grizzly beard. I just assumed the teeth were false and must have cost a fortune. It was a cold smile, a shark's smile. The smile of Mac the Knife! [13]

Imam Kureishi nodded toward the doorway, as if inviting someone to enter. Turbans, yashmaks, hoods, wimples, tonsures, white, grey, brown, black, ginger, mouse, fair, bald—all heads turned.

> And in walked a young woman of extraordinary yet utterly vulgar beauty. She was majestic—tall, buxom, brunette, smiling, magnetic–a starlet to outshine all the wannabe stars in that hall. She was the pagan Female incarnate, the embodiment of divine sexuality, fully aware of her god-given assets and quite used to being gawped at. She just took it all in her sensuous stride. She was dressed with just the right balance of revealed and unrevealed flesh. Her red silky dress hugged in all the right places and rippled and rustled as if partnering her body in a dance. And I thank the Lord that Sheikh Abu was blind! That the devout old Muslim should never know what unholy Hollywood carnality he had unleashed again upon the world!
> The young woman approached Reverend Jones from behind and touched his shoulder. When he opened his eyes and turned about, he blinked. And blinked . . . and blinked.

---

[13] Williamson, *op cit,* p. 60.

O JERUSALEM

He rubbed his eyes. He inhaled. He held his breath. He stared at the young woman. He almost fell over backward.

She threw her arms around him—giggling, weeping. He knelt with the girl in his arms, his face buried in her bosom, sobbing dramatically. He rose to his feet still hugging her, —his blonde bouffant nuzzling into the great cascade of her brown hair—and his face, when it surfaced, expressed the utter shock of beatitude.

"Loahd be praised. Mah prayah is ansahed!"

"Rev Jones! Rev Jones!" the girl exclaimed repeatedly—as he lifted her off the floor and twirled her about. I half expected the credits to roll![14]

"Sheikh Abu is happy to announce the release of the American missionary, despite her offensive proselytizing," intoned Imam Kureishi, who was not far away from the theatrically embracing couple. "As you will see, she is unharmed, in perfect health, until now untouched by male hands."

"Betsey mah Betsey mah beautiful Betsey," the Reverend whooped.

"Arrahman . . . " came a sound that meant nothing to Emma's ears. "Arrahman."

"Allah is merciful!" proclaimed Imam Kureishi.

"Allahuakbar!" intoned Sheikh Abu.

Emma writes in her memoir how, despite herself, her spirits rose:

> It was pure schmaltz, a real life cinema weepy. I had a lump in my throat. I wanted to cry. I thought that we should hear the bells of the cathedral chiming out in celebration. There should have been choruses of angels singing hallelujah. It was embarrassing, yet at last, despite the frustrations of the last few days, something good had come out of the Interfaith International Conference at last. I looked at Uncle Richard in his pulpit. He was smiling. He might even have been crying. My heart rose up![15]

---

[14] Williamson, *op cit*, p. 60.
[15] Williamson, *op cit*, p 65.

Only a few moments later, however, a young man came charging into the Cathedral, shouting, waving his arms. Emma had seen him before but couldn't remember where. He cried out in loud American, "The Islamic terrorists have acquired a nuclear bomb. They are going to nuke the Israelis! They will plant their bomb in Jerusalem!" His hysteria was contagious. "The war has begun!" he shouted in his loud, slightly nasal American. "The war has begun." Emma didn't understand what he meant. "We'll be invading Islamistan! God Bless America!" he cried.

Reverend Jones responded right on this cue, in hallelulah basso: "As the Good Book says, 'O daughter of Babylon, who art to be destroyed . . . happy shall he be that taketh and dasheth thy little ones against the stones.' It has begun and vengeance will be ours! Praise the lord 'n' pass the ammunition." He bellowed out his cliche.

People rushed out of the cathedral. Others rushed in. The Sheikh rose, then sat down hearing the confusion, perhaps he was somehow sensing the vibrations of distress. Imam Kureishi was whispering into his ear. Uncle Richard descended from his pulpit back into earthly chaos. One of the elderly Rabbis walked unsteadily up to him, bumped and jostled by other delegates.

"I am sorry . . . absurd. . . we have no time . . . ." Emma heard the rabbi say to the Archbishop.

A Greek Orthodox priest with a long beard was lurking in one corner. His fist was entangled in long facial hair, which he seemed to be trying to pull out by the roots. A Franciscan Monk in brown robes hovered beneath the stained glass clerestory windows, studying Christ in action. A Buddhist priest in yellow robes steadied himself beside a stone column, as if he felt the earth shifting under his feet. The great front door slammed and slammed again. All plans for the Interfaith Conference dissolved.

In a Darkroom

Very dark.

"Encrypted message decrypted," reports a bored voice that sounds like it knows everything there is to know.

"What's going on?"

"Someone trade a bomb for a pretty girl."

"A real bomb?"

"I doubt it. I mean what sort of US General gives a nuclear bomb to a Taliban crazy like Sheikh Abu? Must be some kind of dummy device; but maybe he's hoping the Arabs don't realize it until he gets his daughter back."

"So where's the dummy bomb?"

"In a cave. That's the drop-off point."

"Won't they check the bomb's real before handing over the girl?"

"Who knows? How would you tell a real bomb from a dud? Geiger counter? False readings are always possible."

"A fake bomb's almost as good as a real one. Better in some ways."

Then Jack cried out; "I've got it! Eureka! We'll teach the delusional idiots a lesson about delusions by means of a delusion. I've got it! You guys make another movie. Now. Tonight. Immediately. It'll be a nothing more than a quick film clip. One scene. We'll send all three religions into imaginary oblivion. That's almost as good as real oblivion. Imaginary death to the imaginary gods. All of 'em. Let's blow up belief itself! What a great idea! Let's have mushroom clouds erupting out of the Temples, the Mosques, the Churches. Let's make faith radioactive!" He is entirely self-congratulatory, and leans back in satisfaction—his bandage and bruised face now lit vividly by the pin-spot above the central stool where he has taken his accustomed place.

His production team is silent. Perhaps they are thinking how to make his mad plan come true; perhaps they are so appalled by his idea that they are momentarily speechless.   The older woman observes cautiously, "Wouldn't an imaginary nuclear event be just as dangerous as a real one? Might the nightmare cause real-world retaliation?"

"It just might," says Jack the Client, hesitant and thoughtful for once. "We'll have to make pretty clear that it's just a—what can I call it?—a pedagogical hoax. We'll be teaching the lesson of the Sacred Child: make peace or die."

IX

THINGS BLOW APART

Ersan walked out of the London hotel to which many disappointed attendees at the Planning Plenary Session had retired. He breathed deeply, comparing the London air to Istanbul air. London air was good! Polluted, damp, torpid. But it was London air, the air of capitalism, thes air of risk and also reward, of energy and action, not indolence and acceptance. He would take dinner in Kensington, in one of those wonderful little restaurants. The collapse of the grand conference in Canterbury would—he thought it probable—only increase sales of his book. He had delivered *The Cognitive Structure of the Terrorist Mind* just this afternoon to his prospective editor. All intelligent readers should be interested to learn how Islamic extremist thought.

The only disappointment at the moment was his solitude. He felt very much—albeit heroically—alone. Bu lo! His mobile vibrated in his breast pocket: Professor Friedman was proposing dinner, back at the hotel dining room.

"See you in twenty minutes," said Ersan. His spirits soared. His heart beat so triumphantly he stopped to take his pulse, which was only a little elevated. It began to rain, but Allah be praised. He pressed the button on his umbrella handle, and a large black canopy opened above him. He listened to the rain applauding him. He thought of his book, he thought of dinner, stimulating conversation. He felt like singing, dancing in the rain. Yes, tonight he was prepared for anything!

"Professor Ersan!" a woman's voice called. It was Emma, that utterly charming niece of the Archbishop. She ran laughing up to him, her face wet with the rain, her blue English eyes sparkling in the street lamps.

"Emma-hanım!" he exclaimed.

She looked at him archly—questioning—and he realized that he had used the Turkish for "lady." He explained.

"So I've become a Turkish lady?" she proposed—quite provocatively. He invited her to join them for dinner.

"Actually," said Emma, "Professor Friedman's invited me to join him and Helen, his doctoral student, for dinner too! It's a Godsend I've met you! You've saved me from turning up like a drowned rat!"

As if this English rose could ever look like a drowned rat! Emma slipped her arm through his. It was a gesture as spontaneous as her laughter. That he was a man and she was a delightful young woman was apparently quite irrelevant to her. They were just two people linked in friendship, sharing an umbrella and memories of recent events.

At the hotel restaurant, they found Professor Friedman already seated at a comfortable corner table. Smells of garlic, seafood, Parmesan, black pepper and bubbling pizza filled the air. Wine glasses tinkled, conversation buzzed. Then the American professor's student Helen appeared with her oversized pink handbag. She came fluttering through the door to elaborate gestures by the head waiter. "Yoo-hoo!" she called waving across to them. *Charming! Hamdillilah!* Ersan smoothed the brilliant white tablecloth, and accepted his colleague's suggestion of a bottle of red wine. He virtually never drank alcohol, but it seemed rude to decline the offer—and with one sip he was in heaven! Perhaps these westerners knew something with their little superstition that a glass or two of red wine was good for the heart. Ersan sighed. After the tension of the meetings with religious people, it was—what was the phrase Emma had used?—a *Godsend*—to sit with a man who held no dogmatic beliefs. From previous conversations, Ersan soon saw that everything in Professor Friedman's academic soul was hypothetical, reasonable, intellectual. Everything he said was accompanied by a silent "But of course, that's only my opinion. What do you think? Tell me. I'm interested." Professor Friedman was utterly unlike Reverend Jones, Sheikh Abu, the Rabbis, the Priests. Talking to them was like talking to a man high up on the parapet of some impenetrable fortress. You were the outsider, looked down upon, and they were the keepers of The Castle of Truth, built with ancient bricks of inviolable text. It didn't matter that they were all keepers of *different* Castles of Truth. Contradiction never troubles fundamentalists, thought Ersan. They just ignore the bits of the Bible or the Qur'an that don't fit their ideas. Perhaps was impossible to break down great walls of faith. But Professor Friedman was different. He was all open doors that let you come in and have a look around. He was Jewish in the same way that Ersan was a Muslim. It was in his background; it was where he came from; it was the stuff to which he might perhaps return on his deathbed, and to which he paid lip service at marriages, or when confronted with fanatics like Sheikh Abu. Otherwise, he lived his life. This life.

"What will happen now?" asked Helen, breathless either from the enterprise of her entry, or with naïve expectation of coming events.

"You mean with the collapse of the Conference?" asked Ersan.

"Yes. And the report of the danger of nuclear bombs!" Helen's manner was almost enthusiastic. Was she enjoying the apparent apocalyptic danger? Ersan hoped that not too many Americans were carried away in this enthusiasm.

"Let's us eat," intoned Professor Friedman, in the same way that—Ersan imagined—a Christian might say, "Let us pray." They ordered dinner.

In the silence that followed the waiter's departure, Ersan could feel that his new friends were all thinking—considering, wondering, a bit fearful.

Emma Williamson confirmed his inference, "What do you think could happen in the next days and weeks? Isn't Miss Willis right to be worried?"

"Of course she is," said the American Professor.

"Evet. Certainly she is," said the Turkish Professor.

It was not reassuring in any way that Mr Jack Foote—bandaged and bruised—now suddenly appeared beside the table. "May I join you?" he seemed to address the question to Emma. She gestured to an empty chair, which Jack picked up and placed beside the Archbishop's niece. He slumped down and said nothing further. Ersan concluded that the young man was certainly not English: no gentleman from this country would slouch low in his chair, spread his legs wide, and glower so at his dinner companions.

"We were just asking ourselves what will be happening with the threat of nuclear explosions." Emma informed the late comer.

Jack looked around the table, saying nothing, as if measuring the character and intelligence of the various people at the table. Ersan watched him—watched him evaluating each of them. When in the long silence his own turn came to be scrutinized, the Turk stared right back at the wounded atheist. Jack—it struck Ersan then, though perhaps he thought that he'd thought this only in hindsight—that the young man knew something the others did not, or thought that he knew some such thing, some such hidden truth.

The silence needed breaking. So Ersan exercised his pedagogical habit of interrogating the student. "Helen, why don't you tell us about your dissertation. Professor Friedman mentioned to me that you were studying Jewish extremism. He said you have one particular subject."

"Ah yes, Chaim," chimed in Professor Friedman. "The self-appointed New Messiah. I'd thankfully forgotten about him for a little while now. But *you* tell us about him, Helen. He's *your* 'baby'," said the teacher smiling at his student. Helen blushed.

"He's your baby *too*, Professor. You're as much involved with this poor lunatic as I am," said Helen. She let out a long sigh whilst the Professor topped up her wine glass. She looked at Ersan and Emma, and rolled her eyes to heaven. "Chaim is my project. I'm making a study of him, for my thesis about Jewish Extreme Fundamentalism? He's turned into a classic case of hubris. Chaim thinks he is Einstein's grandson and believes that he has the scientific power to catalyze the arrival of the Messiah...yes?"

"An excellent opening," said Professor Friedman. "Go on my dear, go on!"

So, after a few quick sips of wine, Helen continued to recite her facts. "Well, Chaim was raised as a Hasidic Jew? Yes? You know, those men with the long black curls at their ears and the big black hats? Well, Chaim's father died when he was very young? Yes?" She had a way of turning every sentence into a question, which at first confused Ersan. "After that he fell under the influence of an extremist called Meyer Kahane, who started something called the Jewish Defence League? OK? I'm sure you've heard of them?" Ersan had not, but he nodded *yes, of course*. Helen went on: "These JDL people decided that Jews would no longer be victims; instead, they would be the victimizers. The oppressed becomes the oppressor? Got it? But no! Even the JDL didn't go far enough for Chaim. Mere "defence" was not enough. And anyway, Meyer Kahane died. Or was murdered? Yes? So Chaim dropped out of Hasidism and the Jewish Defence League and started his own one-man movement. Ready for this? Chaim is such a traditional Jewish name, isn't it? It means 'Life?' And now Chaim thinks he's invented ways to *destroy* life? He thinks he can *actualize* Biblical prophecies?" Helen looked around at her audience.

"Chaim thinks that his Chosen People finally evolved and produced a

Jewish Superman? A couple of key figures in modern history were Jews. Yes? Einstein? Freud? Chaim generalizes: he's a Jew; he's the heir to Jewish genius. He thinks he's Einstein's grandson and ergo, ipso facto, he's a subatomic genius and knows the secrets of the universe. *"I will bring on the end of the material world with material knowledge. I have chemistry and physics in my soul and I shall mix them with the oxygen of my faith."* She recited the quote from Chaim. Paranoid grandeur or what!? Yes?"

Professor Friedman nodded approval and patted Helen's hand. Ersan guessed that she was expressing Friedman's ideas. The student quoting the master. Professor Friedman wasn't adverse to a bit of idolatry, especially from a pretty girl.

"Well, he sounds like a complete nutter to me," said Emma.

"Oh yes, he is! He's a fundamentalist. He's insane!" cried Helen, just a little too loudly. Ersan looked around to see if they were being overheard. "Chaim is so strange that he gave us a sample of his own flesh so that we could prove by his DNA that he is a descendent of Einstein. Yes? Can you believe it?"

Professor Friedman explained that Einstein's brain had been preserved in a jar in some laboratory. "Only in our good old USA," lamented the American. "The brain of Einstein in formaldehyde. But it really happened. And after much trouble I did manage to have the DNA compared. And of course, he's not remotely related to Einstein! Still, it makes an interesting chapter in Helen's book. She's thinking of calling it 'The Chosen Gene.'"

"Of course the question is who chose the gene. Was it God or man?" Helen laughed, seemingly embarrassed.

Ersan realized that this brightly colored girl, with her unlined face and great around eyes was making a study much like his own. She was writing her thesis about this man Chaim's ideas and his position in the evolution of ideas. Even if it was under the close supervision of her Professor, it was still quite a feat for somebody so young. Ersan had only come to such a wide historical perspective late in his life. And now his next book, his great work, would probably be his last. He was reaching his end. But this affluent, pretty girl had been handed the elaborate gift of the long historical view *already*. Her Professor pre-packaged the historical synthesis for her and handed it out like baklava! Western secular education was indeed remarkable! He'd had to lose half his hair before coming to these broader understandings. Ah! But that was the key word, *understanding*. Western secular education may dish out knowledge on a platter. But how could Helen *really* acquire 'wisdom' at her age? She was too young, too inexperienced. She hadn't suffered enough.

The naïve scholar was coming to the end of her doctoral précis. "Anyway, we've decided Chaim is dangerous? Probably a murderer? And we hope that if we give him the results of his DNA tests we might be able to disillusion him? I'd written to him at his mother's—he still lives with his *mother*, can you believe it!—saying we had the results? I said the Professor and I were attending this Interfaith Conference and on our return to New York we should meet? But he's in London already! I saw him outside the cinema, after that awful movie? Ooops!" She stared apologetically at Jack, who was unflinching. She turned bright red. Her presentation collapsed. But her professor steadied her with his hand on her arm. She took a deep breath and proceeded despite her *faux pas*. "I *knew* it was him! And that evening he texted me to say '*I'm here. Where? When?*' I mean, desperate, or what?!" Helen sipped her wine. "Actually, I was a bit naughty," she whispered, glancing coquettishly at her Professor.

"Yes?" he prompted, pouring more wine into her glass.

"Well, in my text back to him, I suggested that he come to our hotel to receive the results of his DNA comparison to Einstein." said Helen "in addition to saying that we had the DNA report, I suggested, just a little, that I would like to see him personally? I mean I really can't stand him. Yes? He makes me shudder. You know? Ugh!" She grimaced as if she'd just nosed a carton of mouldy milk. "Yuk!" She gave Emma a sisterly roll of her eyes. "But the thing is," she continued, "Professor Friedman and I feel that we must try to help him . . . he needs psychiatric treatment? . . . And, well . . . we must try all tactics possible. Yes?" Friedman nodded, in confirmation.

"Anyway, he's coming here, tonight," said Helen, brightly. "He's not Einstein's grandchild and that's that." She sat up, pert and proud, quite certain of herself.

"Where are those results, Helen?" asked her teacher.

"They're up in my room."

"Go get them?"

Helen hurried out of the dining room and through the lobby. As they watched her go, Ersan saw a vaguely familiar form cross the open archway between the several rooms. He looked at the others and saw in Professor Friedman's face a look of puzzlement, rising into real consternation. She looked again at the archway, but the figure did not reappear. The Professor's face was frozen as if in thought.

"What's wrong, Dr Freidman," Emma asked

"I'm afraid that Chaim is following Helen up to her room."   E m m a was quick to act. As a sister female she had understood the sexual content of Helen's revulsion for Chaim. She had an intuition and she acted upon it. "Jack?" He looked at her. "Go follow Helen and make sure she's safe." Jack stared at her, not understanding. "Jack? Go! Professor? What's her room number? Do you know?"

"I do. Let's see. It's 3113."

"Jack?"

But somehow Jack had understood and was already through the archway between the rooms.

Helen assumed that the knock on the door was her teacher. She quickly straightened her skirt and checked her face in the mirror. She always liked to look her best for the Professor. She didn't *fancy* him—of course not! But she wanted him . . . well, *everyman* . . . to find her attractive . . . as long as they didn't act upon it. Not the ugly ones, anyway.

"So you've managed to get away from that Turkish man!" she joked—opening the door. "Oh! . . . "

It was Chaim. He pushed past her into the room.

Helen left the door behind herself ajar. She wanted to run away. "Well," She tried out her voice. "You're a bit early," she said. "Professor Friedman's downtairs." Her voice seemed to be under control.

"I wish to have the results of the tests," said Chaim.

Helen stayed with her back to the door and took a deep breath.

"Chaim," she began. "Chaim . . . Chaim . . ."

"Yes! Chaim is my name. I am Chaim," he said sarcastically, standing before her, legs astride, arms crossed, guarding himself. He didn't look anything like Einstein, thought Helen. His head was still shaved, and his tight grey t-shirt stretched like a second skin over his gym-worked body. His combat trousers had a tear in the knee. Otherwise he looked . . . almost normal. But he wasn't. He was insane, and Helen suddenly wanted to get the whole thing over with as quickly as possible.

"Chaim," she began again. "Chaim, you are not Albert Einstein's grandchild." There! She'd said it!

But Chaim didn't seem to have heard her. He was listening to someone or something else. He cocked his head and turned his eyes upwards to a point just above her, over the door. Then slowly, slowly he lowered his gaze and scanned her body from collar bone to ankle—leaving out her face. Helen felt her heart thumping in her chest. Blood rushed into her face and pounded her temples as if trying to escape. *Let me out! Let me out!* It pulsed. Chaim's animal gaze returned to Helen's face, hovered over her mouth then looked into her eyes.

"Show me the evidence," said Chaim

Helen gave a little cough, pushed past him and went to the desk for the envelope containing the results.

He snatched it from her and pulled out three sheets of paper. He dropped one page to the floor—the accompanying letter—and held the other two pages, one in each hand. His gaze shifted back and forth between the two complex bar charts that compared Einstein's DNA to Chaim's. Helen watched his gaze flickering over the papers. But his face remained motionless. Dead. Only his eyes, feral and furious revealed his confusion.

"It is still possible," he said, abruptly.

"What is?" asked Helen.

"That I am Einstein's grandchild. These papers do not rule that out. If they are genuine, that is. They could be fakes."

"They're not fakes," she said.

She wished he would go away—or that Professor Friedman would come. She moved to the phone on her bedside table.

"Professor Friedman will explain everything," she said. "He's in the dining room? Why don't we go and join him downstairs? I could do with a coffee."

"Even better," said Chaim walking towards her, "will be that we stay . . . right . . . here."

Helen tried to dodge him, but he grabbed her by the and threw her onto the bed.

"You leave me alone!" Helen shouted. The voice came out of her; but it wasn't her own voice. It was a stand-in, an automaton covering for her whilst she fled. She felt herself vanishing inside, fleeing her skin, her body, shrinking inward, shrinking into some hard impenetrable nucleus severed from sense. She watched, she heard, but *she* wasn't there.

"Professor Friedman! Help!" that strange, very loud voice screamed as Chaim clamped one hand over her mouth, and gripped both her wrists in the other.

"Shut up Shiksa whore," he breathed.

She bit his hand, but he held it pressed against her mouth.

"Whores don't kiss," he said dropping his muscled weight upon her. Helen felt the air go out of her. She couldn't breathe. She couldn't move. She felt him tearing at her clothing. The lights got very bright, then very dim. Something had happened. Nothing had happened. She couldn't remember. She didn't want to. She wasn't there. She smelled an awful odor of Chaim's breath. She heard the door bang hard against the wall.

"May I come in?" a male voice called.

Chaim leapt to his feet. Helen felt her body decompressing as she filled herself with oxygen. She saw herself lying on the bed, her legs dangling off the edge.

In the doorway stood a man with a bandaged head and two bruised eyes asked: "You okay?" he asked her.

"Oh yes, yes. I'm fine . . ." the voice wobbled, but Helen didn't cry. She was still in that nucleus of selfhood—the numbness of shock protecting her until it was safe to emerge.

"I'm a friend of Emma's," the man said. "My name is Jack Foote. I'm a bit early, but I couldn't wait. I've come to meet the new Messiah who looked to me suspiciously like a rapist. May I take a seat?"

"Yes! Yes! Do sit down!" said Helen, absurdly cheerful.

She watched Jack calmly lower himself slowly into a chair. Helen moved near the half-open door. Yes! Yes! Jack Foote. Emma's boyfriend. The one who'd made that film, whom she had just insulted! She wanted to . . . she wanted someone . . . she didn't know what she wanted. She just stood there, dazed. Then she looked at Chaim. She stared right through him till he was just a blur of unfocused light, standing by the window, gripping his DNA reports. *Chaim! It means 'Life'.* Helen felt hate like she'd never felt before. Every cell of her vibrated with hate. Hot, absolute, skin tingling *hate*.

Jack turned his chair to face Chaim.

"So," he said. "What's this I understand about Einstein, Mr Prophet?" Chaim turned to face Jack, his gaze fixed on the bandaged man. Chaim very deliberately ripped the two DNA print-outs to shreds, then dropped the fragments. He lowered his hands to his sides and stood squarely facing Jack. He said nothing; his body was a force field of anger.

"So you're another Einstein, are you?" said Jack casually.

Chaim raised one arm and pointed his forefinger at his antagonist.

"You've inherited the great scientific mantle, have you?"

Chaim turned his body sideways, while the forefinger still steadily pointed, as if aiming an imaginary gun.

"You're a genius who can understand big secrets, are you?" Jack went on.

Chaim's knees bent slightly, as if he were fixing his target, preparing to shoot.

"Don't tell me. Your secret is that the world is going to end very soon. Oh yeah. Hallelujah! You think you're going to be the one to end it. Right? I know about you."

Chaim's posture became more and more a crouch. But Jack went right on taunting him. "So you're going to find some way to pull the nuclear trigger, are you? You're going to tell the rest of us—if we get a chance even to hear your ravings—that you acted on Yahweh's instruction. You got some hotline to the Big Guy in the Sky? You think you're some special 'Chosen Person?' Some nuclear Messiah! " he sneered.

Chaim was shaking his head very slowly from side to side.

"You're pathetic," Jack continued. "You religious Jews are like one of three pathetic children, each clamoring that Daddy loves me most. This monotheistic crap is absurd sibling rivalry. Naah nah, I got Jersusalem. You can't have it. Nah naah! Just try and take it away! I'm king of the hill. Nah nah-na naaah naaaaahh! And what is Jerusalem? Nothing but the omphalos of illusion! And if I can't have it, I'll blow up something big just to teach you. Naaah nah nah. I'll have a real temper tantrum! Just watch me."

Chaim went into a deep crouch. He spoke like a robot: "I protect my people. I kill our enemies before they kill us."

Jack exploded: "So this girl was going to *kill* you, was she? This girl was threatening the Jewish race, was she? What you have been doing to her, it was just an act of tribal defence, was it? I pushed the door open. I saw. I saw you on top of her! I *witnessed*. And you say you did it to protect your people!!?"

"I have done nothing that was not demanded of me," said Chaim mechanically. "The Shiksa wanted it. But unfortunately, you arrived too late Mr Foote! You missed her begging act."

"And you say you're one of the 'Chosen People'!" roared Jack. "*People!* You're not even human! You're not even animal. You're pond life, mere scum! You feel entitled, *entitled*, to rape and murder fellow humans because you just happen to come from a Jewish womb! What's so special about a Jewish womb? Your faith is an accident of birth! A bad accident! Like all damn religions! You're a piece of chance, that's all you are! But for some reason you're alive! Isn't that enough for you? *Life!* Do you know how *extraordinary* Life is? Even Einstein couldn't comprehend it! And every life-form is *unique*! Every rock, every petal, every eye, ear, brain, finger print... *unique!* But no! You God-crazies have no idea what extraordinary means! What wonder feels like! All you know is hate. And being a unique human isn't special enough for you! You want to be more special! Extra-unique! Super-human! Chosen! And you're prepared to blow up the whole miracle of existence defending your little patch! You make me sick!" Jack dropped his bruised face into his hands. "Fucking religious thugs!"

Chaim said nothing. He wiped his chest with his hands, flicking off invisible specks of rain. He stared at Jack. His dead face seemed to say: "*Your words mean nothing to me. I am impenetrable.*"

Then suddenly, the door opened wide and Professor Friedman and Emma appeared. "Helen, my dear!" he said cheerily. "So sorry I'm late. Well, only a few minutes! Everything all right, my dear?"

He looked at Helen. He looked at Jack. He looked at Chaim. No. Everything was not all right.

Chaim stared impassively at Professor Friedman then walked slowly up to him, fixing him with his gaze. The Professor stood his ground.

"*I whet my glittering sword, and mine hand takes hold on judgment; I will render vengeance to mine enemies,*" Chaim breathed into the Professor's face. "Whatever the Shiksa says, it's her word against mine. Her word against The Prophet's." He smiled. "She hasn't got a hope in any court. Case dismissed." And he left. So quickly that the air seemed to whirl behind his departure.

Professor Friedman walked up to Helen. He knew something very unpleasant had happened, but he couldn't bring himself to ask what. Not yet. He put his arms round her and she burst into tears.

"Helen, my girl! My dear, dear girl!"

Outside the hotel, Emma helped her wounded Jack into a cab. He was exhausted, hurting, furious. His body had had enough but his mind was in overdrive. Impotent rage was eating him up.

"If I ever see that bastard again, I'll ... Ow! Ow! .. Careful Em! Everything hurts...Everything... Ow!"

"You must sleep Jack," said Emma. "We'll talk tomorrow."

Her phone rang.

"Uncle Richard! Uncle Richard! I'm so glad you called!"

"Are you alright?" he asked.

"Yes, yes, I'm fine. Where are you? Can I come and . . .Hello? Uncle Richard?"

The connection failed. She redialed and was put through to voicemail. "Uncle Richard, it's Em. Where are you? Please call me when you get this message. Speak to you soon I hope."

Perhaps his battery had run out? Oh well, he'd call again. Emma walked on, heading home to her flat in South Kensington; the night air was restoring her to some sense of sanity. Or maybe it was hearing Uncle Richard's voice that had suddenly earthed her back in reality. She wanted to talk to him more than anyone right now. The last few days had been such a blur. She hadn't seen him since they'd parted at Victoria Station after the Canterbury debacle—Uncle Richard had been too busy to meet her. He'd been entertaining the few remaining delegates, trying to salvage something from the great flop. Dear Uncle Richard! He had tried to bring about something extraordinary, but it simply hadn't worked. Human beings just weren't ready for inter-faith conferences, thought Emma. Not even Uncle Richard could accomplish that miracle.

She tried calling him again. Still no reply. Did I sound too happy on the phone? thought Emma. Perhaps he thinks I don't care! Is he angry with me and *deliberately* not answering? It was she, after all, who had got him into this mess . . . because of Jack. Jack! Jack! Jack! Why did everything bad in her life seem to come back to Jack? She remembered his skin, his touch, that night in Canterbury. But perhaps another man could have made me feel the same, she thought. Damn! Her weakness was responsible for this whole fiasco. For Uncle Richard's humiliation. His pain. He must be hurting inwardly far more than Jack—and she hadn't even apologized!

"Taxi! Taxi!" Emma yelled, frantically waving her hand at a passing cab. "Lambeth Palace"

She had to see Uncle Richard. Now. Tonight. And if he wasn't 'home' she would wait for him to return. All night if she had to. *But I must see him. I must,* she thought.

The driver deposited Emma outside Lambeth Palace, observing the "Funny old building that! Don't know what it is! Thanks luv. Have a good evening." Emma hurried round to the private side entrance of the residence-proper. She rang a secret bell and a voice came through a hidden speaker in the gloomy archway above her head.

O JERUSALEM

"Yes?" said the peremptory voice.

She asked for her Uncle, without identifying herself.

"The Archbishop is not here. Please come again during daylight hours, and please make an appointment first," said the guard mechanically. There's no arguing with *that* voice, thought Emma.

She looked at her watch. Eight fifteen. Where could Uncle Richard be? She tried calling again. He still wasn't answering. Then suddenly she remembered a church in Deptford. She and Uncle Richard had stopped by there once.

Her phone rang suddenly, startling her.

"Uncle Richard, at last!" she said, not looking at the caller's number.

"No, it's me, Em," said Jack. "Can't sleep. Where are you?"

"Nowhere you'll understand!" she said tetchily.

"What? Are you at home?"

"No."

She told him where she was going "... because I've got to find Uncle Richard. I've got to apologize. And you're not invited."

"But I want to apologize too, Em. To both of you ... That's why I can't sleep ... I've been thinking ... please let me meet you, Em ... Please ..."

She relented. As always! Why did she *always* give in? But it's the last time, she thought. He can apologize to Uncle Richard and then get the hell out of our lives. She gave Jack the name of the Church where she hoped Uncle Richard might be praying. Yes. That's what Uncle Richard would be doing—praying. And perhaps she would too. 'God give me strength,' she muttered, and meant it.

The harmonies of an organ were filtering through the tombstones when she arrived outside the church. Weak electric light fell in shafts across the grass and stones. She half anticipated some horrible urban monster—an alcoholic vagrant with long tangled hair and a filthy beard rising up from the graves, whiskey bottle in one hand and a toothless leer on his face; but the graveyard was deserted as she passed along the walkway up to porch.

A shadow fell on the porch floor. The shadow moved its arm, and she stopped two steps from the top. Emma's breath caught in her throat. The organ sounded louder as she stepped backward down the stairs. The figure emerged from behind the pillar. She screamed a very small scream that she stifled . It was Jack, looking like a movie monster with his bandaged head. His taxi and got him here before her.

The church itself was locked, but that didn't matter. Leaving Jack behind, Emma hurried into an ancient burial crypt below the main hall. Gravestone shaped panels still paved the floor, but their memorial messages had been worn smooth by centuries of foot-traffic, so that they were now no more than large flag-stones. Today people were no longer buried here. The crypt had been transformed into a 'life-support machine' operated by the Church of England. Here drug addicts, bums, schizophrenics, alcoholics—a motley crew from the leprous underworld—sought sanctuary and warmth. Here, Christian volunteers served food to the Borough's lost souls—hot tea, coffee, steaming soup. Here desperate humanity clung to life. And here, too—at last!—was Uncle Richard, sitting, anonymous, in a corner—a sovereign surveying his realm.

Emma felt overjoyed to see him, and usually the feeling was mutual. Usually, Uncle Richard would grin mad with delight whenever he saw his niece. But tonight, he just shook his head when she came to him. He looked tired, older. She sat beside him, not knowing what to say. She was thankful that Jack was lingering, hidden in the shadows of the crypt, letting her have Uncle Richard to herself for the moment.

After a time the Archbishop murmured, "This is what I—we, the Church—can do, really do, Em." They stared at the scene before them. One man had his head in his hands, another stood in a corner rocking on spindly legs muttering at the stone ceiling. A toothless woman zipped about cackling, talking to everyone and no one and nearby a man hacked violently, gobbing his rotten lungs into a paper cup. Some of the humans just sat politely eating, chatting, looking quite normal, except for little give away signs—stains on jumpers, huge holes in trousers, unlaced shoes, odd shoes, and, if you walked too close, the unmistakable stench of poverty—stale urine, sweat, dirt—civilization's great unwashed and diseased discontents.

"I can't save the world. Apparently I don't have it in me for that." said Uncle Richard. "Not even the Church has that power. Not these days, Em. I fear the world has outgrown our reach. Technology has taken over, connecting humans to virtual truths too disparate for our One Truth." He sighed, spilling his musings into the bustling crypt. "How on earth does the Church reach a humanity so disconnected from reality, Em? How can we reconnect with the human heart? Do humans even have hearts these days?" He stared at the fragments of men shuffling in the dim, broken rays of light shed from unshaded bulbs above. Human scraps fallen through the holes in the World Wide Web. *Windows? You mean what you look through? Glass and panes and all that?* These men were offline, not 'connected'; but they were all the more real for that. "Forget the global, Em." Uncle Richard said. "Concentrate on the local. I can come here and know that we are making some difference, that the Church is still alive if not vigorous."

Through the thick stonework ceiling came the faint sound of an organ, sacred music offering relief at higher altitudes. Perhaps. She squeezed her uncle's hand and he returned a long squeeze of his own—an indomitable something was connecting them.

"This is what it's all about, Em." he said.

"I know," she replied, feeling more certain, more at peace than she had for a long, long time.

"Where is your friend Jack?" he asked, after a time.

Emma puffed out an irritated sigh. Uncle Richard raised his bushy eyebrows: "Oh dear! Have I put my foot in it?" he joked mischievously. "Do I sense all is not well between the two of you?"

"Oh Uncle Richard!" said Emma, her face contorting with confusion. "There's so *much* I want to talk to you about! I've been all over London trying to find you. I didn't know where you were. Your mobile cut off and then I kept getting your voice mail . . . and then I started worrying and I thought you were angry with me . . . and now I've found you and Jack is here too—across the room. It's all coming out wrong. Oh Uncle Richard! I'm so sorry. That's all I wanted to say, really. I'm sorry for all the pain I've caused you. For getting you involved with Jack! And all this conference stuff that's been such a catastrophe . . ."

"Hmm." said Uncle Richard. "We'll let time and your personal Archbishop be the judge of that, shall we, Em? God works in mysterious ways, you know." He brushed a wisp of her black hair off her cheek. "In fact, the reason I called you, before the wretched battery went dead, was to ask if you'd care to join me here tonight. I thought it would help put a sense of perspective on the last few days." He smiled. "But there was really no need to reach out for technology, was there. Providence has guided you! Or you've guided yourself."

"And you're not angry with me, Uncle Richard?"

"Good heavens, no! I'm grateful. To you and Jack for recharging my faith, as it were. Do you know, Em, if I'm honest, right now I can't wait to be done with this whole Archbishop business and get back to simple faith again. My head's been buried in administration, ecumenicalism and theology for so long, I'd quite lost touch with what it's all about. *Knowledge puffeth up, but charity edifieth.* Too much knowledge at the expense of understanding, if you know what I mean, my Em."

They sat in silence and watched the living damned find salvation in their bowls of soup. Life didn't have to be a hell for so many, thought Emma, if only religion was *practiced* more often than preached.

Then Jack appeared across the room. With two his two black eyes, a bandaged head and a broken nose, he fit right in with the bums—only his jumper was cashmere; his shoes were expensive trainers. He navigated around the intimidating urban pond life, finally collapsing onto a safe chair next to the Archbishop.

"Coffee?" asked Uncle Richard, diplomatically.

"I'll go," said Emma, leaving Jack to make his peace with the Uncle Richard. And then maybe he would vanish from her life, Emma hoped. When she returned, Uncle Richard was saying, "that's all right. All right. Apologies accepted. We understand. We all did what we could. We can ask no more of ourselves now."

Jack's hand trembled when he picked up the coffee. "But, sir, I make no apologies for my defence of atheism. I still believe 'Religion' with a capital 'R'—is a force for evil—not good—in the modern world."

"For God's sake, Jack, let it drop!" Emma blurted out in exasperation. Her memoir comes to this scene and reads:

> I wanted to pour the cup of scalding coffee on Jack's head. It was impossible to understand how he could be so completely oblivious to where we were sitting—in this heart of Christian charity, in this active force field of religious good, caring for the least among the many, these lowest amongst the fallen. Had he no charity in his own heart? Was he not moved by this spectacle of suffering? Perhaps compassion was becoming an endangered emotion. [16]

"Maybe we should get some credit in heaven for running soup kitchens?" suggested Uncle Richard.

"Yeah. You're all right at this kind of thing—at least when it operates strictly in your own little community. But without these bums you wouldn't

---

[16] Williamson, *op cit* p 140.

have community! The actual labor of volunteers like the genteel lady ladling out the soup over there behind the counter is quite real. But bystanders who so observantly appreciate her active charity and use it as an excuse for continued existence of the church are mere sentimentalists with no virtue of their own."

Her uncle Richard shook his head. Emma put her hand on the Archbishop's shoulder. But Jack wasn't done, even then.

"I've come to apologize for my role in the collapse of the international conference. But there's something more important now happening. This evening I have heard the most alarming news, my Christian friends. I bear terrible tidings! Apparently several religious madmen are planning to bring in the New Millenium with a bang. Someone's going to set off a nuclear explosion in your Holy City of Jerusalem."

"Oh dear," said Uncle Richard.

"Oh please! Get a life!" said Emma blurted out. "I'm sick to death of you! Leave us alone, please! Go! Go!"

"Yes, you're right Em. I have to go save the world and teach it a lesson." Jack stood up abruptly and turned to face them. Looking straight at Emma like a rebellious teenager performing a forbidden act in front of his parents, he took out his mobile, dialed a number, and then spoke as Emma reports:

> "That Holy City Project that we agreed upon? Tomorrow. Do it."
>
> Those were Jack's words. I could recall them precisely when the police asked me, two days later. I can recall them now. I remember all too vividly how Jack's face looked-- beaten up with fury, inside and out.
>
> Then one of Uncle Richard's poor souls, carrying his food tray, accidentally bumped into Jack as he shuffled past. Jack put his mobile on the table and glowered at the man who had bumped him. When he saw that it was an accident, he shrugged and turned back to speak to us.
>
> "You two make me feel completely alone now—a party of one," he proclaimed, petulantly. Then he left, without saying goodbye—leaving his mobile on the table.
>
> I put his mobile into my handbag. I had no intention of giving it back. I had cut his life line.

O JERUSALEM

Quite which way Jack went when he left Deptford I never knew. I sipped the last of my tea while the Archbishop thanked the volunteers, letting them know they were doing vital work. And their payment was equally vital, I thought: not money, but spiritual satisfaction. Yes, the scales of my moral mind were starting to tilt. Uncle Richard was right. Providence really had guided me here. [17]

Skilled hands have manufactured a clever device. Chaim is functioning at the peak of his powers. A pair of delicate wire-cutters clinks softly onto the marble counter-top in the hotel bathroom, which is lit only by the nightlight. The lead of copper wire shivers in the fingers. His hands are steady at their work. It is a delicate arrangement of springs and levers, of wires and a battery. There is a white package that the wires run into. The whole is flat, and could fit easily into a small space, such as an envelope or a file folder.

No light switch is thrown. Virtually no sound is made. The bed-clothes are lifted in the gloom, and something is placed under the mattress. Chaim is nothing more than a shadow who does this work, then stands for a moment in the opened door before he vanishes.

A few hours later, under the weight of a human body, the pressure-sensitive device collapses onto the metal plate; electrons from the battery beneath the bed sheet flow into the coil, leap across the gap and make a tiny spark that hangs for the merest instant in the bomb's dark interior. Then the device lifts up its burden into the air, pushes the human rib-cage upwards and outwards, propels the skull backwards, and impresses the torso of its victim upon the ceiling of the room, which in turn spreads, in a shock-wave of lathe-and-plaster, slate roof-tile and miscellaneous debris that spreads upwards from the roof of the hotel, up toward the sky and stars.

Emma and Uncle Richard were just emerging from Green Park tube when they heard the boom. At first Emma thought it might be another airplane crashing into a building. It even occurred to her—quite irrationally—that somehow it might have been a meteor fallen at random on some London rooftop. They stopped on the pavement for a time, listening and looking around. Emma remembered:

---

[17] Williamson, op cit, p 150.

The evening traffic continued. It seemed as if the people in their cars had heard nothing. But other pedestrians had also stopped, and were standing, heads back, looking up at the clear night sky. Then it suddenly started to rain hard. But it wasn't rain—it was dry. Fragments of something were falling from the sky, bits of tar, or sand, the debris of something. Hard lumps were hitting the pavement, thumping down on the roofs of the cars. Then the 'rain' stopped. My hair was full of sand and tiny bits of gravel. I saw the same fine detritus on Uncle Richard's broad shoulders. We said nothing to each other at first, and then a siren sounded, and then another, and another . . . [18]

"Terrorists?" Uncle Richard asked.

They had continued to walk toward the hotel where many of the delegates to the conference had been staying—the same hotel Emma had left in shock four hours earlier. When they turned the corner they could see flames feeding the sky from the roof of the hotel. Several top-floor windows were ablaze, angry square eyes of fire.

"Oh my God," was of course what Uncle Richard said.

Emma echoed him. "Oh my God." Then heard herself praying, "Have mercy on us. Jesus Christ." These phrases, so deeply fossilized in the bedrock language of her world, she now uttered with conviction. She brought words back to life for herself. She spoke to some greater power, though she still didn't know what to call it. But the name didn't matter. Her words were sincere. "Oh my God, save the poor people in the building," she prayed beside the Archbishop.

---

[18] Williamson, *op cit,* pp 130-150, *passim.*

In a Darkroom

"Client didn't show this morning."

"Nope. No word from him."

TV heads talk silently. A picture of a building appears, smoke pouring from its roof. Sound returns and says, "So, Michael, to recapitulate the evening's main headline. A small but powerful explosion gutted the upper floor rooms in the Connaught hotel. The blast mainly exerted its force upwards, and very little damage has been done below the roof. We still do not have any word about casualties, although anyone in the room where the bomb was planted has obviously . . . ."

"So where's our client?"

"Don't know."

"Anyone tried his mobile? That's what our leader might do. And where is she?"

"She didn't show this morning either."

"Well, let's call him!"

The ring of a tuneless phone fills the room.

Then Emma's voice says, fearfully, "Yes?"

Silence.

"This is Jack Foote's phone," says Emma more strongly.

Silence.

"Are you Emma?"

"Are you . . . are you Deus Ex Machina?" she replies.

"Hang up! Hang up! Hang up!"

Connection is severed.

"Back to work, now. Watch this live feed."

A shuddering image seems transmitted from a night bird flying above a desert. The moon is bright. The land is colorless. Now and again a shadow flits across empty cliffs—the shadow of the drone itself. Distant lights flicker on the desert plain, its smooth sand-ripples giving it the appearance of a vast lake. Then the image swings away from the sand lake towards cliffs, and—briefly—what looks like two helicopters fly across the moonlit rocks.

"Two choppers?"

"One and its moon-shadow."

The shadow and then the helicopter itself disappear around a promontory. The drone picture dives down. In the Darkroom, several young people suck in breath, anxious about the machine. The drone re-orients itself and moves toward the gully where the helicopter disappeared. We sense great emptiness in the small screen: nothing living, changing, knowing—mere rock, moonlight, shadow, silence.

Then one screen shows a black insect ascending the cliff-face on a cable, holding something heavy. The camera tilts away, awkwardly, then looks back to the cliff. Now the figure repels down and vanishes. The helicopter reappears, rising out of the dark.

"Drone footage stolen from which agency?" asks a voice.

"US," says another.

"Who's in the chopper?"

"Unknown."

"What's in the package?"

"A bomb."

"Where's the bomb going?"

"Jerusalem."

"Where's the bomb come from?"

"Who knows?"

"It got promised to Sheikh Abu. Maybe a ransom demand."

A great shin and knee of rock glow in the moonlight. The camera wavers, then focuses on a second tiny figure in the distance abseiling down the stone shin from above in the brilliant night, disappearing into the dark opening of a cave.

"Where the hell is this place?"

"Khirbat Qumran. Dead Sea. West bank of the River Jordan."

"Why here?"

"'Cause it's famous."

"Famous? For what?"

"It's where they found the Dead Sea Scrolls."

"What're they?"

"Fragments of the Old Testament. Book of Isaiah, I think."

"Why was the drop just there?"

"There used to be two camps of archeologists: one at the top and one at the foot of the cliff. The camps are empty now, deserted. Perfect for silly spy games."

"Who gets the bomb? Sheik Abu? Is it real? Fake? What's going on?"

"Who knows? Even we don't."

"Anyhow, we've got this video to make, don't we? Let's get it finished up now. Right?"

"Client wants nuclear images imposed on Jersusalem."

"I've got the bomb-blasts ready."

"I've got the Holy City on screen."

"So let's put 'em all together and make some imaginary plasma!"

"Holy plasma. The world ends with a big bang."

One screen shows Jerusalem from above. Other screens develop bright flashes and mushroom-shaped clouds from side views.

"Get the video mass distribution file addressed to all major media networks: BBC, NBC, ABC, CBS, CNN, FOX, Al Jazeera, and all the rest."

"And a couple more pranks, compliments of Deus ex Machina. Listen up! The Sheikh and the Minister are both programming their minions to plant bombs. We know from our phone and email taps. We've sent them both suggestions that they use the Jerusalem sewer system to plant their little nukes. We found half a dozen ways to whisper I their ears. And they took the hints! It's an atheist's miracle! They *both* have ordered up HAZMAT equipment to use in the sewers of Jerusalem. They are each going to give their two human tool, an impermeable protection suit, breathing apparatus, and a GPS. So it's all idiot systems go. But wait—wait still longer. Before they even plant their bombs, we'll make absolutely certain that there will be no explosions at all. We have already rendered the trigger signals inoperative. How's that for humanitarian cleverness. And—wait still longer for it, non-believing brothers and sisters—after the bombs are planted and the terrorist stooges are trying to return to base, we will cross the GPS signals. So the Jewish terrorist will return to the Sheikh, and the Islamic guy will return to the Israeli minister. How's that for true mischief? Good stuff?"

"Big Momma will be proud of us!"

"Client's gonna love this!"

"Anyone heard from either of them?"

Silence. Black out.

X

JERUSALEM IN THE NEW MILLENIUM

L ess than a week after the collapse of the Interfaith Conference in Canterbury, Chaim is back in Jerusalem. Two men know of his presence. One is Edward; the other is the Lollypop Minister.

Edward knows because Chaim has come to see him. The young madman wants to communicate with Professor Friedman, whom he requires should tell his mother where he is and that he is doing well. Edward obliges Chaim and calls the professor.

The Lollypop Minister has been having Edward's phone tapped, so he knows that Chaim is in Jerusalem. The Minister is in the process of responding to reports that Sheikh Abu has acquired a nuclear weapon. He is devising counter-measures. He will let the Islamic madmen know that he has his own mad scheme, his own bomb. He wishes to speak to Chaim. He contacts Edward, who very reluctantly arranges for Chaim to visit the minister in a secret office.

B lack shoes belonging to the Minister appear beneath the small table. That is all Chaim can see of the man, who sits behind a screen.

The voice of the invisible man states by way of asking, "You have killed people?"

Chaim is silent.

"My information is that you planted the bomb two days ago in the rooftop of the hotel in London."

"Yes, sir! That was my work."

"You are a murderer?" comes the statement-question again.

"I am a soldier."

"Ah. In which army?"

"The army without name, the army that is no longer the Jewish Defence League, but is instead a league of active, aggressive Judaism."

"I see."

"Do you?"

"I really do. Would you be willing to kill again?"

"For what purpose?"

"To eliminate an enemy of Judaism."

"Ah. Perhaps."

"Do you recall that the Lord said to Moses, *I will send an Angel before thee; and I will drive out the Canaanite, the Amorite, and the Hittite, and the Perizite, the Hivite and the Jebusite.* Do you recall this?"

"I do."

After a pause, Chaim's invisible friend continued: "I have a theory. A theory of mass extinction. I will tell you. We have faced a campaign of terror for many years now. Yes?"

"Yes."

"Young Islamic madmen blow themselves up to try to frighten everybody and especially the Jewish nation into abandoning Eretz Israel. Or retreating to some new Masada and committing mass suicide. That is their purpose. Correct? However, they cannot succeed. Why? Because terror in the modern world has lost its effect. We are beyond terror. We are numb. Mass murder leaves us indifferent. And there is another reason why terror no longer works. This reason has to do with economies of scale. Consider. There are perhaps six million Jews here in Israel now, and no matter how often the suicide bombers come, the odds of your being killed, or my being killed, or any one person we know being killed, are very small. Correct?"

"Correct, Sir."

"So. QED: Traditional terror fails in the modern world—it has no real effect on the community of its victims, even if it gratifies the primitive feelings of the families and friends of the terrorists. Old style terrorists will now fail. You agree with my conclusion." It is a statement, not a question. It is an order. Chaim is being told what to think. He thinks it.

"Correct, Sir. I agree."

A large lollypop wrapped in cellophane appears just under the screen. Chaim's blank eyes fall upon it.

The voice continues: "This line of thought allows us to dismiss the notion of fighting fire with fire, of visiting terror back on the heads of the terrorists. That has proved futile. The military eliminations of Palestinian terrorists have not reduced the number of Palestinian bombers. Correct?" He now mimics Chaim's single word. "So my theory is not a theory of mere terror. For mere terror can only at best cause incremental, gradual change. I believe we should take control of history. It is not a theory of the great man. The great man—Moses, Alexander, Christ, Muhammad, Napoleon, Hitler, Einstein—must wait for centuries for the full effect of his acts and ideas to be felt. My theory is better than the great man theory. My theory is a theory of the great moment, the cataclysm. What have been the great moments? The asteroid struck and wiped out the dinosaurs. That was a great moment. What have been the great moments since then? There have been only a few. The holocaust was a great moment. Hiroshima and Nagasaki were great moments too. Or they might have been, if the men who dropped the bomb had really known what to do with their opportunity. Perhaps the moment when the madmen flew their planes into the World Trade Center was a great moment. Or perhaps not. We are still awaiting the final judgment on that—awaiting the eventual winner's version of history. You see, my friend, a great moment occurs when the direction, the vector, the momentum of events is changed forever, so that the world goes spinning away on some new axis. You understand?"

"Correct, Sir."

The stubby fingers pick up the lollypop. There is the sound of cellophane being ripped. A slurp. A tongue tastes its candy.

"So," says the voice, "so, we make a great moment. You and I. We change everything. We can cut the heart out of the enemy, demoralize him for all eternity. We win the battle with Islam."

Chaim waits.

"We end the Muslim misadventure. Forever." He pauses.

Chaim does not chime "correct." Instead, he inclines his head to one side listening to the whisper behind the screen.

"We set off a nuclear device below the Dome of the Rock. The world will be outraged. The Islamic snake will writhe without its head for a year or two, but then it will die. History will prove the false prophet false. Of course the deluded fanatics from Indonesia to Britain will rise up and slaughter Jews and Christians. This will happen for months, years, decades. There will be a price to pay. But even the moronic Madrassa teachers will get the message: Islam has been decapitated. It is in its death agonies. The prize will be well worth the price. No more Islam in the end . . . of a new beginning.

Chaim does not move.

"So the great image, the thing to keep in your mind, is the picture of a mushroom cloud above the Dome of the Rock. The Dome is vaporized. Islam is vaporized."

"Correct, Sir. But Sir? The Second Temple? Sir? When will it be built again?"

"After a few years the radiation will dissipate. Then we will build again."

Chaim nods.

"So, my son, into the sewer."

Chaim cocks his head, listening.

"The sewers under the Rock give us our opening."

"Sir?"

"A GPS will guide you to the proper location for the device."

"Sir."

"We have protective gear for you."

"Sir?"

"You will come up through the plumbing just below the Dome."

"Sir."

"And plant the device."

"Sir."

"Then you come back to the entry point and throw your switch."

Meantime, in the basement of a Jerusalem mosque, Sheik Abu is instructing one of his minions in his own craft of eliminating Judaism. He may not express his reasoning to his acolyte, but his motives are similar to the Israeli Minister's. The tiny room is crowded with young men who anticipate every wish their Sheikh expresses. He whispers to his handlers, who in turn explain his plan to a youngster named Muhammad, whose dead-eyed face stares submissively into the mirror image or himself that his master's glasses provide. The hook that has replaced the hand peeks out from under the man's gown.

"You will plant the bomb just beneath the Jews' Knesset."

"How will I get there, Sheikh Abu?"

"Easily, through the sewer system. He points to an open hatch in the floor of the room. Allah will provide you with appropriate clothing to protect you from all the foul excrement of the Jews."

"But I must breathe until I arrive at my destination."

"Allah will provide breathing apparatus."

"How will I know the path?"

"Allah will provide GPS."

"How will make explosion?"

"Allah provides button."

"And Allah will take me to paradise."

"Perhaps he will, in the end. But your time to enter paradise has not yet come. You will survive this mission. You and all your family will be greatly loved throughout the Umma. Your martyrdom will come another day. Allah be praised. For now you are just his messenger."

Sheik Abu's handlers dress their messenger tenderly in what looks almost exactly like the spacesuit worn by astronauts. While they are working intensely to equip this latest Muhammad of Sheikh Abu's, they turn their back on their master. The old man sits on a wooden bench and cannot watch but can only hear the proceedings. What he know is, as usual, a mystery.

That hidden life, however, ends suddenly, just after the last Muhammad departs through the hatch in the floor. Allah works in mysterious ways, hidden even from his most passionate servants. Sheikh Abu tilts sideways, rolls onto the bench, and then off the bench onto the floor. His acolytes rush to him; but he is already dead, lying peacefully behind his mirrored spectacles. The elimination of the Knesset will be his last act, his ultimate intention realized. The young men kneel around his corpse, slowly realizing that their beloved leader's heart has ceased to beat. Now they are leaderless. Now they must decide for themselves.

In still another room in Jerusalem, a mobile phone rings: "Damn it! Damn it! Marx was wrong! Religion isn't the opiate of the people! It's the fissile material of the fanatic!" Jack Foote's voice sounds in Edward's ear from the other side of the world. Edward waves his free hand in dismissive irritation at this Atheist-Prophet's preaching out of the blue. He recognizes the voice of the young man who made such a show of himself in the Cathedral. But, being a civil, sensitive man, he politely replies: "Well, my friend, I understand how you feel; but you must appreciate things from the Jewish point of view. This is our homeland, after two thousand years of exile. We are still engaged in pioneering, building a country. We're under threat and some of us Jews are still primitive folks who respond in primitive ways. An eye for an eye. Some small few of us would exterminate the enemy who would exterminate us. Yes?"

He waits for a response. Silence. Then Jack's voice says: "Damn it! Damn! Marx was wrong! Religion isn't the opiate of the people! It's the fissile material of the fanatic!"

"Jack? Jack Foote?" asks Edward. He takes the phone away from his ear and stares at it, incredulous. Someone is playing him a recording.

Chaim creeps through the sewers to a point beneath the Dome of the Rock. He leaves his package; he retreats to a safe distance. His moment comes. He throws his switch. His signal travels up in waves—invisible and potent. It finds its satellite and electrons swirl through circuits. It beams back down to one unique numeric sequence—the special code that contacts a mobile inside a leather case that activates what Chaim thought was the bomb he placed under the golden dome.

There is no bomb. Nothing happens.

Mudhammad, as instructed by Sheikh Abu, has found his way to a location just under the Knesset. He leaves his package. He retreats to safety. His moment comes. Half expecting to become a happy Islamic plasma himself, but now as instructed having withdrawn to a distance from the drains of the Knesset, he breathes deeply of the highly oxygenated air supplied him, and throws his switch.

There is no bomb. Nothing happens.

Puzzled by the failure of the bomb to explode, Chaim followed his GPS and found himself in a barren room. It was not the room he expected, the room where he had left the Minister. Instead of the plastic, glass, and steel table and screen, he found only a primitive wooden bench upon which sat a pair of silver-lensed sun glasses, and a metal hook. He removed his space-traveller's helmet and stared at the objects, not understanding what they were or where he was. Into the room burst four burly Jihadis, who stared at him just as uncomprehendingly as he at them. No one knew what has just happened. They pushed him roughly out the door and telephoned for a car. He was blindfolded. Edward, Professor Friedman, and Chaim's mother never hear from him again. He vanishes.

Utterly baffled both by the absence of any explosion and by his own continued existence in this world, into a room where he has never been before, up from the trap door that leads to the sewers, comes young Muhammad. The Jihadi stares about himself in confusion. There is a great commotion just through an open door. He removes space-suit helmet and gazes into the tussle in the next room. One man is dressed in a business suit; he is wrestling with men dressed in police uniforms.

"I am innocent. You are making a terrible mistake. You will regret this for the rest of your careers, for the rest of your lives." But out the further door the police drag the protesting Minister.

There is a bright-red candy lying on a steel-edge plastic countertop, just below an opaque glass screen. None of this makes any sense to him at all. Muhammad decides to return to the sewers. He replaces his helmet, rotating it around his head until the catch clicks and he knows he will be safe from terrible odors. But before he can step back onto the ladder leading down into the filthy depths, four burly policeman suddenly surround him, remove his helmet, and study his face. They know he is not Chaim. Not only has no bomb exploded; several other things have gone very wrong. The Lollypop minister has been arrested for corruption. The plot to vaporise a competing faith has been revealed and thwarted. There was no law against blowing up the Dome of the Rock; but his political adversaries have used the excuse of the Minister's alleged financial wheeler-dealings to have him arrested. The timing has just failed to prevent the nuclear explosion that never happened.

The police manhandle the young Muhammad out the door, down the stairs, and—blindfolding him—hustle him into a waiting car. None of his family—not his Sheikh, nor anyone he ever knew—ever sees or hears of him again. He vanishes into the limbo of eternal detention.

XI

END OF DAYS IN THE DARKROOM

In the Darkroom the proficient youngsters have catalysed the great non-event. They have discovered how to reverse their feeds—how not just to watch and witness but also how to kidnap and terrorize the dream-worlds of the communication media.

"Here's to the Client! We've made his outrage safe." Three figures from Jack's abortive Trial of the Gods appear together on the screen: Yahweh, God, and Allah. Each wears a large, glowing name-tag like a participant in some cosmic conference. A high wind is blowing through their beards; it rushes their long gowns off to one side and over their heads. Yet they float, unperturbed above us; they hang their arms over each others' shoulders—like sportsmen celebrating victory. The voice of the Sacred Child intones, "Make peace or die." The three gods intone together: "Make peace or perish." The screens burst into fireballs. Millions of sparks of orange light, which become incandescently white starbursts, emblazon all the televised worlds. Red, orange, yellow, green, blue, indigo, violet luminous chemical projectiles shoot through day and night skies of every continent and country. Pillars of flame reach to the photographically false heavens. Viewers of televisions all over the world hear the warning in every language, followed by an image of ninety seconds of utter destruction: a vast explosion erupting out of the Golden Dome with concentric shock-waves burgeoning outward from the vaporized center of Jerusalem. Following fast after the brilliant sunlight of glowing plasma, a nascent mushroom cloud is what everyone sees on all screens everywhere in the world—in a kind of global tsunami of a fake apocalypse lasting only two minutes.

The soul of the world goes numb—but this time only very briefly. The shock was fleeting—and yet permanent in memory.

XII
AFTER NOTHING HAPPENED

Emma was invited into the Darkroom by the Deus Ex Machina, who honoured her role as Jack's girl-friend. An excerpt from her report of her experience follows:

> I spent much of those last few days of this tumultuous period in the Darkroom watching multiple realities being conceived, created, transmitted, disseminated. The Machine God's minions recorded, watched, and waited for events catalysed by their fantastic delusional powers all over the world. They heard phone conversations between London and Jerusalem about the non-events that they had caused. They played themselves chatter in Arabic and Turkish that I could not understand, but which they thought important.
>
> "Something evil this way comes," cackled that weird voice whose face I never saw.
>
> "Watch out! We've stolen reality!"
>
> The collective voices shrieked with laughter. It was utterly spellbinding. Utterly false. Utterly real. For two minutes millions imagined the world's end.
>
> I somehow felt safe in that Darkroom—safe and hot at the heart of the mad conspiracy of false truth. For me events were mere dreams. After many hours of dark snooping on the world, when I returned to street level reality, I felt threatened, exposed, watched. Something had happened to my conceptual apparatus, to my perceptual

processes, to my soul. All London felt like a movie set. I was being framed for photographic purposes by invisible eyes behind imaginary lenses of directors of cosmic photography. I couldn't wait to get off camera again, back to the safe Darkroom. Delusions of grandeur were profoundly unpleasant.

Back I went to the Darkroom of Deus Ex Machina. I returned to the underground tunnel in the abandoned dead end of the re-routed Jubilee Line. I pressed the proper combination of old tiles in the wall. The door opened as before.

But *Deus Ex Machina* had vanished. The Darkroom was empty of people. One video screen played an endless loop. A headshot of Jack Foote was making a speech: "Now, above the Holy City, rise! Rise up, you clouds of ash and dust. We humans—and all the myriad things we make and mar—must now return to our dusty origins. O dull deposits long ago rained down from brilliant stars, henceforth contain our dying spirit, returning to its own dull, first and final home. Then shall we be at peace at last—inanimate, beyond all harm and harming. What can we know when we are simple stardust? What deluded dreams may ashes have? The hatred felt by rocks, the anger known in the soil itself, the fury felt by rivers streaming to the sea can come to nothing whatsoever—unlike our savage human animus, so full of its own consequence. We will be safe from every one of our false faiths when we become inanimate, when we are only atoms that buzz and hum, and never bear the slightest witness to anything at all. Now comes the peace that passeth understanding: the peace of nothingness, the peace of no more minds that delude themselves with knowledge."

My first thought was that just when I'd heard the last of Jack he spoke again. He never did know when to stop. But the video and its sound track had a sudden, jerky quality that made me finally understand this wasn't really Jack's voice, but merely what the dark-room denizens thought he would have sounded like and therefore synthesized for him. I don't know whether or not these were his actual words. But Deus ex Machina certainly breathed their false, electronic life into his ideas. And that, I have come to think, is as much immortality as an atheist deserves. Only his barbaric, nihilistic warning survives him.[19]

---

[19] Williamson, *Deus Ex Machina*: 'Jerusalem: Countdown to Nothing,' Ch. 33.

Ingram Content Group UK Ltd.
Milton Keynes UK
UKHW040617250723
425738UK00001B/69